An Arrangement of Sorts

Also from
Phase Publishing

by
Lady Jane Davis
The Original Pink Collar Workers

by
Christopher Bailey
Without Chance

Coming Soon
by Rebecca Connolly:

Married to the Marquess

An Arrangement of Sorts

Rebecca Connolly

Phase Publishing, LLC
Seattle

Cover art by Tugboat Design
http://www.tugboatdesign.net

Phase Publishing, LLC first paperback edition
June 2015

ISBN 978-1-943048-01-4
Library of Congress Control Number: 2015942610
Cataloging-in-Publication Data on file.

Acknowledgements

To Baga for being the most influential reason I became a bookworm years and years ago, teaching me all about Jane Austen and starting me on my love for all things British (and introducing me to the magic of Colin Firth), fostering my creativity from day one, and encouraging me every step of the way. I love you!

And to Stephen's Gourmet Hot Cocoa. You are a magnificent gift to the world and I am a devoted admirer for the rest of my days.

There are so many people to acknowledge for bringing this book to life. Christopher Bailey and his team at Phase Publishing for seeing something worth pursuing in my work and giving my dreams a chance. Deborah Bradseth of Tugboat Design for bringing my vision to life in the cover art. Sarah Connolly for the fantastic pictures (and the fantastic price!) and for working on them while gallivanting across Europe. Caity, Whitney, Lori, Lisa, and Jenny for their support, reading, input, and not thinking I'm crazy… or at least not telling me so.

To my family, you are the best. You're all crazy. I love you. Don't change. I like being this lucky.

And my personal Three Musketeers. Steph, Alicia, and Whitney, you gals have been with me every step of the way. Thank you forever for reading and re-reading (and re-reading again…), editing, brainstorming, enduring my rambling ideas, talking me out of my freak-outs, and seeing this insanity through to the very end. Thanks for the playlists, the pins, the inspirational pics, letting me know it's okay to have cupcakes for breakfast because they're really just muffins… I'd be lost without each of you. Seriously. Let's be friends, 'kay?

Chapter One
Hampshire, 1818

"I must confess, my lord, it was quite a shock to see you dressed like this today."

Nathaniel Hammond smiled and glanced over at the older man working beside him. "Really, Jameson? And how should I have come dressed to work? In my eveningwear?"

The old man returned his grin and shrugged. "Well, yes, I expected your finery, my lord. It is the usual apparel of a gentleman."

A snort escaped Nathan and he shook his head. "Nothing usual about hard labor in such things. Didn't I say I would help you with your repairs?"

"Yes, my lord, but I hardly expected you to come dressed in plain clothes, or that you would bring your own supplies, or that you would bring volunteers."

Nathan chuckled and went back to his work. "My friends are good men, Mr. Jameson, and they came of their own accord, ready to work as any man. Fortune and title have no place up here."

"Hear, hear," softly called the oldest of the Jameson sons, working steadily behind him.

His father threw him a cheerful smile, then looked at Nathan again with steady eyes. "You are a hard worker, my lord."

There could be no question but the man was impressed, and Nathan was humbled by it. "Thank you."

Jameson suddenly laughed. "If someone had ever told me that I would have the Earl of Beverton on my roof making repairs, I would have carted them off to asylum!"

The three men laughed and Nathan clamped a hand on his tenant's shoulder. "This particular Earl of Beverton will always be at hand to help those he can, whether it be on a roof, in a field, or a crowded London ballroom."

"Bet you prefer the roof to that ballroom, eh, my lord?" suggested the son with a knowing laugh.

Nathan had to laugh again and nodded. "Absolutely, Elliot. Absolutely."

As he helped the Jamesons place the final patches on the roof of their too-small cottage, he wiped the sweat from his brow and sighed, looking out on the land that had only recently become his. The area was poor and had suffered much, and would require much rebuilding, both of homes and of trust. The late earl, his uncle, had been a decent man, but had long since lost interest in his tenants and his estate in favor of an ignorant solitude.

Now, Nathan hoped, things would be different. He had spent as much of his time as he could among his tenants, learning about them and from them, discovering their expectations and their needs. He wanted to know everything he could about them, for them to see him as the new earl, and trust him with their care. He could do no less.

"Nate!"

He shook himself from his reflections and looked down where his friends, as dirty and sweaty as he was, stood looking up at him.

"Thorn says he insists we all take some refreshment at the Horse and Rider, just up the road. If you've finished with the Jamesons' roof, he is up there waiting for us." Colin Gerrard spoke for the assembled group, as usual, and was the only one who didn't look the least bit winded.

Nathan looked over at Mr. Jameson and Elliot. The elder man smiled and nodded at him. "We're finished for the day, my lord.

Thank you for your help."

He inclined his head and reached a hand out. "Any time, Jameson. I am at your service. Please give my regards to your wife."

"I will, my lord, thank you."

Nathan shook his hand, then made his way down to his friends. It was a short walk to The Horse and Rider, and before long they were all seated around a sturdy table with tankards in front of them. Thorn, another tenant, was the proprietor of the establishment, and from all appearances, it was a fine, well-kept pub and the drinks were as good as any to be found in London.

"Ah," the man to Nathan's left sighed as he drank deeply. "That is good stuff. Remind me to visit you often, Nate."

He snorted and quirked a brow. "I don't recall inviting you back, Duncan."

Duncan shrugged his broad shoulders easily, as was his nature. "I am rarely invited anywhere. Doesn't mean I don't go."

"Now, isn't that the truth?" Colin crowed with a laugh from Nathan's right. "I remember distinctly the time when Lady Sutherton very publicly forbade any man by the name of Duncan Bray to ever set foot in her gardens again, and not ten minutes later, there he was! And in her fountain no less!"

"Oh, please!" Duncan protested over the good-natured chuckles from the table. "I was fourteen!"

"And more than slightly rebellious, as I recall," came the amused voice of Geoffrey Harris, directly across from Nathan.

Duncan leveled a glare at him. "You are the one who pushed me in that fountain, Geoff, and don't bother to deny it."

He held up his hands and shook his head. "No one ever proved that. Mary Hamilton swore that she saw me in town with my mother at exactly the moment you were found dripping wet in Lady Sutherton's fountain."

"Only because you paid her, Geoff, and rather exorbitantly, at that," the last companion, Derek Chambers, Marquess of Whitlock, chimed in, leaning back in his chair for another long drink.

Geoffrey's jaw dropped, and his blue eyes widened. "How did you know that? Nobody knows that!"

"Everybody knows that," Nathan assured him with a consoling

smile.

Geoffrey buried his face in his hands. "All this time I thought Mary kept that a secret."

Derek eyed his tankard and spoke easily, as if his words meant nothing. "She did…" he began, his lips curving into a grin and successfully gaining the attention of everyone at the table. He paused for effect, and then continued, "…until my sister managed to extract that particular bit of information from her one night about ten years ago. And you all know that Diana cannot keep anything from me, so, needless to say, I have known ever since."

"Your sister should work for the Bow Street Runners, Derek," Duncan crowed with a laugh, saluting him.

"She married one, which seems close enough," Derek pointed out, receiving nods all around.

"So, your mighty Earlship," Colin broke in, giving Nathan a wry grin. "How do you like your new home and when should we start calling you Lord Beverton?"

He shuddered. "Never, if you please. But the lands and people show great promise, and I think we have made some fine advances towards healing injuries my uncle might have caused."

"I would agree with you there," Duncan said with a nod. "Especially with the manual labor you have had us all employed in, and dressed in such plain clothing!" He sniffed at himself and winced. "I think that my aunt would be ashamed of us all, could she see us as we are now. 'Fine gentlemen in the shoddy clothing of commoners, what will the kingdom come to?' Cannot say I would disagree entirely with her on that point. I look like a farmer."

"You can work in your finery if you want, Duncan, but I prefer to wear it as little as possible. Saves me the cost of a tailor," Colin retorted with a laugh. "Besides, I think we all know some very fine farmers. And if no one else noticed, there is a quite charming looking maiden a few houses down who was mending some shirts quite remarkably like the ones we wear now. I'm of a mind to pay her a visit before the week is out."

"Don't start trouble in my earldom, Colin," Nathan warned, smiling. "I have just gotten people to start liking me, I don't need you proving their fears aright."

Colin laughed again, grinning cheekily. "Very well, but she may mend my clothing yet, you know. I have no need of a wealthy wife."

"Nor I, but modesty and decorum would be appreciated all the same."

"Well, Nate, your new and appallingly large fortune should prove quite useful to you now, I should think," Geoff suggested, bringing them back to topic. "Your *own* estate, for one, needs some attention."

He shook his head, recalling his first impression of the ancient Beverton House in all its decline. "Years' worth, I should think. It might be better just to pull the whole thing down and build a new one."

Four voices cried out with varying opinions on what to do with the place, but none of their words reached his ears as his eyes caught sight of something far more interesting. A young woman with hair the color of copper, which was fast unraveling from its no doubt once-intricate style, had entered the pub. She seemed to be searching for someone, though he had no idea whom a woman such as she would hope to find in a place like this. As she scanned her surroundings, he glimpsed a pair of bright sapphire eyes that intrigued him almost as much as the determined set of her very fine jaw.

He was just about to begin his not-so-subtle examination of her person when those blue eyes landed on him, freezing him on the spot. And then, as if she knew his simultaneous fears and desires, she marched over towards him. In the same instant, all conversation surrounding him ceased.

"I am looking for Nathaniel Hammond," she announced in a crisp voice that he instantly liked, along with all else he could see of her from his seat.

She quirked a brow at the lack of response, and he realized with a jolt of embarrassment that he had not managed to answer.

"He's the attractive, silent bloke staring at you," Colin chimed in with a grin.

She flicked her piercing eyes to him. "So everyone but you then? Marvelous."

Colin's eyebrows shot up and his mouth clamped shut, a

glower forming, but smiles grew on every other face.

Nathan stood and inclined his head. "I am Nathaniel Hammond, Miss…?"

"Dennison. Moira Dennison. You can sit back down," she told him, her eyes raking over him with apparent distaste. "I have a proposition for you, Mr. Hammond, and I would appreciate being heard out before you make a decision."

Slowly, Nathan sank back into his seat, not entirely certain if he ought to be offended or amused, but he was leaning more towards the latter, against his own will and better judgment.

"I am looking for my intended, Mr. Hammond. Charles Allenford. He has not been heard from in over a year and I refuse to wait for someone else to find him and bring me word. I was given your name by an only moderately reliable source I happened across as I left my home in Gillam, and he assured me that if someone needed to be found, you were the man to do it. Therefore, I have sought you out to ask if you would accompany me and assist in finding Charles and seeing us back home to Gillam in safety." Her words came out in a rush, as if she couldn't wait to finish them, but one look at her proved she was set on her course, regardless of what anyone said or thought.

Nathan sat back in his seat, considering this woman and her outrageous offer. Accompany a young, single woman without any life experience outside of a dance hall across who knew how many miles to search out her so-called intended, reunite the lovers, and then see them safely returned to their presumably happy existence? It was madness.

"I would pay you handsomely, Mr. Hammond," she said with a firm nod, all business despite the ridiculous nature of her venture. "Of that you can be assured. It would be enough to allow you a comfortable life for the rest of your days."

He highly doubted that. Obviously, Miss Dennison had no idea who he was. All the better for him.

"It may take us some time to locate Charles, and though I know little of you, I have every confidence in your abilities. I have heard rumors of your bravery in the army, so I know that you are not one to shrink in the face of danger, which is encouraging, as I have no idea what we shall be up against." She paused only to take a breath, and then went on. "As you can see, I am quite determined and will not allow the slightest obstacle to deter me. I will not be condescended to, dictated to, pitied, persuaded, brought down, set aside, or left out. I do hope I have made myself clear."

Yes, rather clear, indeed. Nathan could not have spoken should he have wished to. This was truly the most bizarre situation he had ever been in, and that was saying a great deal.

"I shall give you ten minutes to decide, Mr. Hammond, and then I shall go elsewhere." She swept from the room with a slight toss of her hair, leaving the entire table of men stunned in her wake.

"Holy..." Colin breathed, unable to complete the sentence.

"Mister?" Derek offered with a snort. "Impertinent thing. If I had a coherent thought in my head, I'd have set her straight, believe you me."

"Nate," Geoff broke in, leaning forward, "are you mad?"

He shrugged and heaved a deep sigh. "I know. I cannot leave, not when I just took over the earldom. There is far too much work to be done."

The entire table was silent, staring at him. "He *is* mad," Duncan insisted, looking at the others.

"Absolutely mental," Colin agreed.

"Daft as a duck," Derek said, nodding sagely.

"What? Why?" Nathan asked looking back and forth between his friends.

"Because you are thinking about *not* going," Geoff retorted, leaning back. "That breathtaking woman is everything you've ever wanted, and you're letting her believe you need time to think? Please."

"Seriously, Nathan, if it were me, I would have said yes long before she started her rant." Colin shook his head, looking appalled.

His friends were, yet again, making no sense. He looked around at them. "But she wants me to help her find her intended! It wouldn't matter if she were Aphrodite, I still would balk."

"That's no object. No ring means fair game," Geoff said, waving it off.

"Sometimes even then it is still fair game, depending on the woman," Derek chimed in quietly. The table stilled, and he looked up to find them all staring at him with varying levels of disgust. He hastily brought his hands up in surrender. "I don't condone it! I am only stating the fact that marriage, to some, is not as morally binding as it is to others."

"Says the only man here already with a wife," Duncan pointed out.

Derek glared at him darkly. "Katherine is not a wife. She is a tyrant. A cold, heartless tyrant who exists merely to make my life more of a miserable hell than it already is."

"Charming, Romeo. Please save your happy thoughts for a more appropriate time. Like a hanging," Colin replied, putting his hand over Derek's face, and turning to Nathan. "Go, Nate. Go now."

"I have nothing ready," he protested lamely.

All of his friends laughed. "Please, Nathan," Geoff said, clapping him on the back. "We all know you've yet to unpack a thing and that you have had a bag ready to go since you got here in case you changed your mind. We'll look after things here until you return. Go!"

He looked at them all for a moment, then pushed back from the table and strode out of the door at a rather fast clip, bringing more laughter and some applause from his friends behind him.

Moira Dennison took a deep breath of the fresh air once she exited the building, hoping that somehow it would calm her slightly trembling body and addled brain. Her aunt Miriam would have been ashamed and sent her to the cellar for a week with nothing to eat but bread crusts had she known of this. Luckily for Moira, Aunt Miriam was six feet under the ground and nobody was left to care if she were to sell her soul to the devil or elope with a cobbler or join the circus or any other equally disastrous and ill-conceived action.

But even this was one deed that she never imagined herself undertaking.

Inviting a man she knew very little about, almost nothing,

really, to accompany her alone, quite alone, across Lord knew how many miles so that she could find Charles and bring him back to Gillam so they could finally be married and put all the rumors and gossip to rest, was madness.

She shook her head and started to walk a bit. Pacing was hardly ladylike, but considering the show she had just put on for that table of rather ordinary looking men, she doubted anybody would consider her ladylike anymore anyway. Not that she cared all that much, she didn't know them enough to care, but she did want to be respected.

The crazed woman that had just marched into a pub and told an entire table of men what she was going to do, what Mr. Hammond would be expected to do, and then marched back out again without breaking composure was surely deserving of a little respect. But as for little Moira Dennison… she just wanted to curl up under some wagon and cry until her body no longer shook with fear.

Three days. It had been three days since she had left Gillam, and she was no closer to figuring out what she was going to do than she had been weeks ago. Being from a small village had its advantages she was sure, but at the moment she knew of none. The pitying looks she received when people thought she wasn't looking, the way a room would quiet when she entered, the soft snickers of other girls when she went for a letter and returned empty handed… She had had quite enough.

What drove her to bits was that if these people had known just who she was, not who they thought she was, but who the rest of the world would see her as, they would not have pitied, gossiped, or snickered. She was wealthy enough to buy up the whole village, force them all out, and fill all of their homes with sheep, should she have had the desire. Or goats. Goats were notoriously meaner and would be better than sheep at keeping unwanted people from her property.

But sadly, she had no goats or sheep. All she had was money, and she had no idea what to do with it. It had not been a part of her life since she was very young, and she had not been informed of it until much later in her life, under sworn secrecy. Not even her aunt had been aware of the magnitude of Moira's inheritance, only that there was one.

Her biggest regret had been that Charles hadn't known. Perhaps if he had known what would have been theirs, he wouldn't have…

"Miss Dennison?"

Moira shook herself out of her melancholy reverie as soon as she heard her named called. That would be Mr. Hammond, no doubt coming to his senses and telling her to shove off and find someone else to bother about her love. Even so, she fixed her most determined, unflinching expression on her face, brushed the stray hairs away from her face, and turned to face the approaching footsteps with her hands on her hips.

He was much taller than she expected him to be, and rather imposing when headed in someone's direction. She could see now what her source had been going on about. No one seeing this man would have doubted his authority or his power. Any man who wished to stand against him would be a fool three ways from Sunday, and would lose unquestionably.

It was a pity he would turn her down.

She swallowed and looked up at him. "Mr. Hammond?"

His dark eyes were unreadable as he stopped before her. "I apologize for not answering you promptly in there just now. I'm afraid you took me by surprise."

She smiled without humor. "Yes, well, I fear I have that effect on people. At least, that is what I have been told. It's a terrible flaw."

Now he returned her smile, but his was one of genuine warmth, and suddenly her chest did not feel quite so tight. "Not necessarily, Miss Dennison. I am not one to mind surprises, as a general rule. But I daresay we shall find real flaws in each other soon enough."

"I should hope not," she said before she could stop herself. "I would rather keep my flaws to mys…" She stopped short as she realized what he said, and she tilted her head as her eyes widened. "We? So you are coming, then?"

He nodded, his eyes still on her and still mysterious. "Yes, Miss

Dennison. I accept your offer." His smile turned wry. "And now I anticipate your next command."

Moira couldn't decide how to respond to this reception. How could he be so casual about what they were about to undertake? Had he no care for her reputation, or his own? What sort of man had she just decided to trust her future with? She opted for confusion and frowned. "A command, sir? How could I command you in anything?"

His smile faded slightly at her tone, but not completely. "I spent nearly eight years in the army, Miss Dennison. I have grown quite accustomed to the sound of commands. And your behavior in The Horse and Rider just now mirrored some of the most terrifying commanding officers I have ever faced."

She frowned slightly. "I don't know if I should be flattered or offended by that comment, Mr. Hammond."

"Nor do I, Miss Dennison," he replied without missing a beat, "but you have commanded, I have seen fit to obey, and now await further orders."

Moira had to force herself not to gape openly at him. She had not thought beyond getting him to come with her, and had fully planned on him being insistent on taking the lead in their expedition, expecting her to ride passively along with him. She had even been practicing her grumbling complaints about men and their expectations of women. Now she was supposed to believe that he was willing to bow to her unseemly demands, without question or concern and without pride, and go along with whatever she wanted, however she wanted?

How unnatural.

How disturbing.

How was that possible?

Once again, she had to swallow hard and fought to keep the fear from her face. "Very well, Mr. Hammond. I have secured a horse for myself, but was under the assumption that it would not be necessary to do so for you. Am I wrong?"

He shook his head, those dark eyes still fixed on her, as if assessing her. "No, I have a mount. I can be ready to leave immediately."

Immediately. That was rather soon. She chewed on the inside of her cheek indecisively.

"If I may offer my opinion, Miss Dennison?" he said quietly, as if he could sense her turmoil.

"You may," she allowed, waving her hand impatiently.

"The day is more than half gone. If we were to depart at this time, we would have to stop for the night before covering much ground. Perhaps if we left at first light? Then we would have a full day in which to begin." He shrugged lightly, as if it made no difference to him. "Just a thought."

It took all of Moira's considerable self-control to avoid releasing a heaving sigh of relief. She could certainly put something together by first light tomorrow without a problem.

She nodded after appearing to give his suggestion some thought. "Very well, I believe that would be wise. Tomorrow at first light it is." She allowed herself to smile up at him. "You see, Mr. Hammond? I knew you were the right man for this." She turned and went to take her horse's reins. "I shall meet you back here at first light tomorrow. Good day, Mr. Hammond."

Proudly, with her head held higher than normal, she walked towards the boarding house she had passed a few buildings before, hoping for a vacancy. If there wasn't one, she would make do with sleeping out in the stables behind. She had slept very well in less, and at this moment, all she cared about was that Mr. Hammond had said yes, and they would finally be on their way tomorrow. Everything was working out perfectly.

Chapter Two

As the first rays of morning light began to filter through the hills, Nathan rode atop his second best mount, Mercury, towards The Horse and Rider, where a lone figure stood beside her horse waiting for him. He smiled tightly to himself.

This Miss Dennison was an interesting woman. She was well-equipped for a long journey, if the state of her pack was any indication, and she was bundled up against the morning chill rather smartly. He found himself wondering how long she had been waiting for him, what sort of person she was in the morning, and, oddly enough, if she would be riding side-saddle or not.

Mercury shuffled anxiously beneath him, no doubt wanting to break off into a hair-raising gallop across the countryside. Nathan leaned down and patted him, soothing him softly. He had briefly considered taking his prized stallion Galahad, but bearing in mind that he was assumed to be a working man in need of funds and he had no intention of altering that opinion, he had settled on Mercury.

"We will be able to ride soon, my boy," he soothed, rubbing his side gently. "Now behave for the lady, you hear me?"

The horse responded with a toss of his head and a snort, which he took to be an agreement.

"You have a fine ride there, Mr. Hammond," Moira called as he approached.

He inclined his head. "You as well, Miss Dennison." A mischievous impulse took over and he offered a smile. "Are you certain riding on horseback is what you would like? Perhaps a carriage? It is generally preferable for a lady."

She bristled slightly, which made him smile to himself. Not a morning person, then. He suddenly had the urge to ruffle as many feathers as he could, just to see what lay beneath. "I am perfectly capable of riding on horseback," she snapped, "and it is generally preferable for one's hired help to keep his opinions to himself."

Oh, but she was feisty. He liked feisty. He tipped his head in acknowledgement. "Of course, Miss Dennison."

She scowled and muttered an insincere, "I trust you slept well? I hope you are fit to ride."

He tried not to smile. "I slept very well, thank you."

"How fortunate," she said in a voice that indicated she couldn't have cared less. "And your dreams? Were they as pleasant as you anticipated? I should hate for you to have been disappointed."

He bit back a grin. "Alas, I cannot say that I was. I never dream, Miss Dennison."

That actually seemed to surprise her a little, but she quickly recovered. "What, never?"

He shook his head. "Never."

"What a pity that your sleep is as tepid as the tedium you call your life."

His smile vanished and he now found himself stiffening. Tedium? Tepid? She had no idea what his life was like, what he had to contend with. All she knew about him was that he had been in the army and he was currently residing in Hampshire. Everything else she thought about him was a lie and he was of half a mind to tell her so when she waved a hand.

"Enough, I apologize. I fear my attempts to be accommodating this morning have left me quite shrewish. If you wish to ride away and leave me to the birds, I quite understand." Her voice had almost no emotion in it, yet she would not meet his eyes.

He cocked his head, watching her with continued interest. Did she truly think their little bickering was enough to end this? He had quite a bit more stamina than that, he was proud to say. If he had to deal with temper and quick retorts and what had to be the furthest thing from demure he had ever encountered, so be it. It would make for an exciting journey and excellent tales, if nothing else.

"I am afraid that, tempting as it sounds, I cannot abandon you to the birds, Miss Dennison," he said with a sigh. "Hampshire birds are notoriously picky as to their food, and as inviting a picture as you might present, you would find their disinterest disappointing, I am sure."

He was finally graced with the sight of her eyes as they clashed with his, an odd mixture of confusion, relief, and amusement swirling about in them. "That is a relief, Mr. Hammond. I should not like to find someone else to take me. I spent quite enough time looking for you."

He grunted as she turned to mount her horse. "Apologies that I was not more unavailable. If I had known someone was looking for me, I'd have hid myself better." He watched her struggle, wondering if he should offer to help her. He highly doubted she would appreciate his gesture.

"That makes absolutely no sense, Mr. Hammond," she said as she set her foot in the stirrups. "If someone was looking for you, shouldn't you wish to be found quickly and have done with it?"

He considered her actions with interest. She was clearly struggling against the height of the horse and maintaining her maidenly modesty, yet she did not ask for help and nor, apparently, did she expect it. "If you knew some of the people that have looked for me in the past, you wouldn't ask," he said.

He heard her huff in irritation and smiled as she shoved some of her stray hairs out of her face. "Fair enough, I concede your point. I have no doubt you've spent quite some time avoiding being found. I can hardly blame you for that. I should like to avoid being found myself at times," she added very quietly, as if to herself.

Nathan, who happened to possess a rather unnatural sense of hearing, picked up her soft words and wondered at them, but said nothing.

He exhaled and prepared to dismount and offer her assistance regardless when he heard her sigh and mutter, "Oh, to hell with it."

Then she hiked up her skirt slightly, flashing more than a touch of leg, and mounted her horse in one swift movement. Once seated, she readjusted her skirt and turned her horse to face the road.

He stared at her in complete shock, unable to respond.

"Is something amiss?" she asked superciliously.

Nathan was not entirely certain which "amiss" thing he should discuss first. All had stunned him out of thought and now he was trying to avoid the embarrassment of being found without a snappy retort, though he quite honestly would rather have complimented her on the lot.

Hastily, he chose. "Did you just say what I think I heard you say?"

She sniffed and her nose rose even higher, if it were possible. "I don't believe you heard me say anything at all, Mr. Hammond." She nudged her horse on, and he turned Mercury around quickly, riding up beside her.

"No, I am quite certain I heard you say something, Miss Dennison, and not something a well-bred lady would say." He was ruffling more feathers, he knew, and soon enough she would snap at him and he could volley thinly veiled insults with her until his brain was clear again.

She glared at him, which was quite a thing to behold. "A gentleman would never accuse a lady of something of the sort, Mr. Hammond." She turned to face forward again, her voice full of disdain. "But I forget that I am not with a gentleman, so I suppose I cannot expect gentlemanly behavior."

He ground his teeth together and forced himself to speak with restraint. "Perhaps I could manage something resembling gentlemanly behavior if I were dealing with an actual lady."

The moment he said it, he wished the words unsaid. Her head snapped around and the flash of hurt and vulnerability in her eyes surprised him. She rode on ahead before any other words passed his lips, and he was left cursing himself behind her.

With a groan, he urged Mercury on again until he was nearly beside her. She saw him from the corner of her eye and immediately began riding faster, but he matched her.

"I have nothing to say to you, Mr. Hammond," she said airily, seemingly in control once more.

"Well, I have something to say to you, and I will say it. And when I have finished, I will fall back and let you have your precious solitude until you wish for me to speak again." Well, *that* was certainly a well-spoken thing. So much for soothing wounded pride.

Her pale eyes flicked to him only briefly. "Very well. Say what you wish."

He let out a breath and cleared his throat. "My words just now were spoken in anger, and were entirely inappropriate and rude, Miss Dennison. I apologize."

She faced him now, her brow furrowed in confusion. "You do?"

"You doubt me?" he asked stiffly, more insulted that she doubted his sincerity than that she thought he was ungentlemanly.

"No, no, I believe you. I just didn't think you would." She tilted her head slightly. "I thought I needed to apologize to you for my words, yet again, and hardly expected you to apologize first." She offered a very small smile. "I did not mean to slight you, nor to say you were not a gentleman… I mean, obviously you are not, but…" She winced and clamped her lips together.

Nathan chuckled softly. "It's all right, Miss Dennison. I aim to act like a gentleman regardless of my station in life, as my mother raised me to be. Good manners should be universal, don't you think?"

She nodded and sighed heavily. "It has been quite a morning for me, I find."

Now that was true. "For me as well. I'm not the most accomplished conversationalist, nor particularly gifted when it comes to a new acquaintance. But I can promise you this, I will never intentionally say anything to wound or offend you. I may do a bit of insulting all on my own by sheer stupidity, but it will never be intentional. I'm afraid I have been teasing you this morning, I thought it might make the day easier." He shrugged in another silent apology, hoping she would take his meaning.

She looked up at him, one brow raised, which was oddly charming on her. "Teasing? Already?"

He nodded and shrugged one shoulder again.

She bit her lip. "Teasing," she mused, her eyes clouding in thought. She wrinkled her nose a little as she looked back up at him. "I'm afraid that I am unused to teasing, Mr. Hammond."

"Now that is a shame," he said with a sigh. Unused to teasing. That just would not do. "Well, you shall have to get used to it, Miss Dennison. You will have much of your share before our journey's end."

One corner of her mouth curved up ever so slightly. "And how shall I respond to such teasing?"

"Oh, return them, by all means, if you can. I can appreciate a fine show of wit and a sharp tongue."

"Be warned, Mr. Hammond," she urged, her eyes dancing, "I sharpen my tongue nightly."

He fought the urge to laugh. She was warming to this already. "Consider me warned. And do let me know if you wish to borrow my whetstone."

"I've brought my own."

Now he did laugh, and turned to applaud her. "Bravo, Miss Dennison. You're already in fine form."

She laughed once. "I highly doubt my form has anything to do with it, but thank you." She seemed a bit impish at the moment, smiling as if she were rather pleased with herself.

Actually, he was rather pleased with her too, and her form was fine indeed. Her short coat and gown were shades of green and seemed to accentuate her figure quite well, giving her a rather slim waist and trim hips, but were thick and sturdy, perfect for travel. Though it was the middle of April, the mornings still held quite a chill in the air, and he silently praised her wise choices in apparel.

What Nathan also noticed was that her clothing looked rather well worn. And not just from recent wear, but from a history of use. As if they had been mended many times. And the boots he had been so fortunate as to glimpse earlier also showed very obvious signs of use. Yet she had told him she had enough money to pay him handsomely. Where was that money going to come from and, if she had it, why was she wearing things so well used?

She also chose not to wear a bonnet, oddly enough. He thought he saw one tied somewhere on her horse, but she was not wearing it. Her hair, which truly was a remarkable color, seemed determined to not be tied up as long tendrils hung down her back where they had slipped from their knot. He had the oddest desire to twirl one of those locks around his finger, just to see if it would curl.

He shook himself out of his examination and paid attention to where he was riding, which was no doubt a safer course. But of all the things he had just noticed, one of them kept burning in his mind until his curiosity could no longer stand it. "If you'll forgive my impertinence, Miss Dennison," he began.

She arched a brow at him, but said nothing.

He tried not to smile at her expression, which he understood all too well. He'd been nothing but impertinent since they'd met.

"Why don't you wear a bonnet? I can see that you have one, but you do not wear it. I don't mean to pry, nor to imply that you ought to, I'm only curious."

"Oh, is that all? It's quite simple, really," she said with a shrug. "I don't like bonnets."

He had to chuckle, mostly out of disbelief. "You don't… like them? That is all?"

"That is all. I didn't start wearing bonnets until recently, and I find that I don't like them. I hardly like having my hair up at all. I would much rather leave it all down and let the wind carry it as it will, but that is hardly sensible."

"No, of course, hardly sensible," he murmured in absent agreement, forcing himself not to look as amused as he felt.

"If I must wear my hair up, then I would much prefer to leave the rest of my face exposed to the light, rather than shield it," she continued, completely unaware of Nathan's struggle. "I do so love the feeling of warm sunshine on my face."

He made a non-committal sound, but kept mostly silent. This was far more inane than he ever imagined a discussion of bonnets could be, should he ever have imagined a discussion of bonnets at all. He couldn't say he had.

"I know, I know, it simply isn't done, and all ladies must wear bonnets," she said with a slight roll of her eyes, as if he had protested her shocking lack of bonnet-loving. "But honestly, wearing a bonnet is almost akin to putting blinders on a horse! I would have to turn my head all the way around to have a proper look at someone who is directly beside me. I just don't think it is necessary to restrict myself in that manner just for the sake of my complexion."

"You seem to have quite a lovely complexion without worrying about a bonnet, Miss Dennison." Somehow, the compliment slipped out without Nathan actually thinking about it. It was a true statement; her complexion was one of the loveliest he had ever seen. But to just blurt that sort of thing out was not something Nathan was accustomed to doing. At one time in his life, not so far gone, he'd had quite a way with words.

She smiled shyly. "Thank you, Mr. Hammond. You are too kind. My aunt was forever bemoaning my paleness and declared it was not healthy, and sent me out of doors so as to darken up. I am afraid it only helped a little. I seem to be doomed to paleness."

"So have you never burned, then?" He could have slapped himself for such an inane question.

She grinned a rather impish grin. "Just once. My aunt had sent me out and forbade me to come in again until she called for me."

He returned her smile, no longer scolding himself. "And she forgot?"

"And she went out. I was out in the garden for the entire day. My poor nose has never been the same again." She rubbed her nose tenderly as if the memory still burned.

He leaned forward and peered intently at her pert little nose, as if examining it. "Well, it certainly looks healed well enough to me. But then, I know nothing of noses."

She shook her head, still smiling, which delighted him. "You certainly don't. My aunt assured me it was ruined." She sighed dramatically. "Quite ruined. She was convinced it destroyed any chance I ever had at being beautiful."

"She was mistaken."

Moira was more than a touch confused by the sudden change in him. One minute they were throwing insults at each other, the next they were teasing, and the next he was complimenting her? How on earth was she supposed to react?

She looked away and tucked an errant strand of hair behind her ear, knowing full well she was blushing now. What had come over her? She had been so confident, so sure only moments ago, and now she was shy and retreating and awkward.

She suspected it had little to do with her and everything to do with the man riding beside her.

He rode rather well, and even if he had been a real gentleman, he would have been skilled. The time he had spent with the army must have really improved him. He spoke well, he rode well, he obeyed well… she found herself wondering what other skills he had that were not common for a… well, for a common man.

And she was not too proud to admit that, out of the entire group of men she had seen at that pub, he was the most attractive, for whatever that was worth. He had dark hair that he kept cropped short, though there was slight curl to it, especially where it met his neck. His eyes were darker, and she already felt the power in them. He was tall and broad and muscled, she expected, given the way his rather plain clothing fit him. His skin was tanned, but not especially dark, which was most likely due to working outside. She had seen some men working on a cottage, and wondered if he had helped them. His boots were clean, but rather well used. She suspected they were his best, and she would not say anything about it. How could she, considering what she herself was wearing?

She only had three dresses and this was her sturdiest, not to mention her most comfortable. She had brought the others along, but she did not know what sort of washing she would be able to do along the way, if any at all. She could certainly mend them, if it came down to it.

Some day she would have to find a town with a proper dressmaker, now that she had the funds.

"Well, now that we have begun, Miss Dennison, perhaps you would care to inform me as to our destination and anything else you may find relevant for me to know?"

His low voice, apparently unaffected, cut into her thoughts and she was grateful for the distraction. "Yes, you are quite right, Mr.

Hammond." She held her breath, knowing she could not keep it from him any longer, and that this could change everything. "The last information I had was that Charles was heading for Preston."

"Preston?" he cried.

"I know," she said morosely, knowing just how impossible it sounded. "And I don't even know that he is still there."

Nathan bit back an entire string of curses and struggled for calm. He rubbed his brow with one hand and forced himself to exhale slowly. "Well, what *do* you know, if I might be so bold?"

She looked over at him, and her expression slightly mollified him. She was exhausted, even though they had just started. This had been weighing on her for some time and she knew exactly what she had just asked of him. "Should I tell you the whole story, Mr. Hammond? Or would you prefer to have no personal information, merely a destination?"

It was said without malice, but that did not make her words any less stinging. He had been wishing only for an endpoint, and that was all that had mattered. He had not even considered what this would mean for her. "You may tell me whatever you wish to, Miss Dennison," he said softly.

She nodded and looked away. For a long moment, she said nothing. But he was in no hurry. If they were going to Preston, there would be quite enough time for everything, and they would no doubt run out of things to talk about before they were even halfway there.

"I was fifteen when Charles Allenford came to live with his cousins in Gillam," she began in a voice that hardly sounded like her own. "He was a little older than I was, but we quickly became friends. Both of us had lost our parents and were living with relatives. We were lonely. But suddenly, we had each other."

Nathan watched her carefully, but her expression was surprisingly devoid of emotion.

"We became betrothed when I was nineteen," she continued, thankfully skipping extraneous details. "We decided not to be married until we could properly afford to do so. Charles was determined to provide for me." Here she broke off with a small snort of derision, which he did not understand, but made no comment. "Around my twentieth birthday, Charles decided that he could not make any sort of living in Gillam. He was going to try for Preston, but would seek work of any kind along the way. He wrote to me faithfully for three months, and then nothing. I have not heard from him since."

A multitude of thoughts flooded Nathan's mind. The first was the oddity of the choice of Preston as a destination for one living in the southern part of the country. The second was the sudden stop of letters to Moira. Two questions sprang to mind: Why would a man be willing to go so far from the woman he supposedly loved if all he wanted was to provide for her, and why would he stop writing to his betrothed if he loved her so much to go to the opposite end of the country?

Nothing Moira was telling him made sense, but he could not ask the questions he wanted to. He doubted she had answers herself.

"How long since the last letter?" he asked as gently as he could.

"Eighteen months, perhaps a week besides."

"And his family is not looking for him?" That was another point that bothered him.

"His uncle died shortly after he left and the cousins decided not to remain, and moved their mother to the coast. I have not heard from them." She sighed and looked up at him with a wry smile. "I know it is a great deal to ask of you, Mr. Hammond, but are you still willing to help me find him?"

It was, as he always knew, a foolish trip by a young romantic with no notion of how the world worked. The likelihood of any of this working out in her favor was far less than probable. Frankly, it would end badly. It would hardly be worth his time to continue on with this excursion. It was certainly not something he should be doing.

And yet…

"Of course, Miss Dennison. I am at your disposal."

Chapter Three

"We should be married."

Nathan jerked, startling Mercury so badly he sprang ahead suddenly. Once Nathan had his horse under control again, he turned back to Moira, who still sat primly on her mount, watching him. "I beg your pardon?" he managed to ask in a voice that was quite a bit higher in pitch than it had been in his mind.

Moira seemed confused by his behavior, as if her words had been perfectly sound. Then she stopped short, her eyes widening perceptibly and her hands shot to her mouth.

"I meant as our story!" she cried, her cheeks flaming. "When we meet people. To protect our reputations. Oh, it made perfect sense in my head!" She covered her face with both of her hands.

Now that Nathan's heart had stopped racing so frantically and he'd caught his breath, he had the oddest desire to laugh. "I take it your thoughts went ahead of your mouth?"

She nodded, still keeping her hands over her face.

He allowed himself a chuckle. "It happens to the best of us. Now, if you would please remove your hands from your face. I would feel much better about your riding abilities if you could see where you were going."

She slowly dropped her hands and looked up at him, her

cheeks still delightfully pink. "I am so sorry."

He smiled at her kindly. "Think nothing of it. I actually had that thought as well, but it was hardly decent to bring up."

"Wonderful," she muttered, her eyes turning colder. "You are accusing me of being indecent again. I have had quite the day, it seems."

He groaned and pointed at her. "Stop putting words into my mouth, Miss Dennison. I did not say you were being indecent. I said it would hardly be decent for *me*, as a man, to bring up the idea of a marriage between us. There is a quite distinct difference."

"Yes, I suppose there is, you are right," she grumbled. "Again, my apologies."

"I think you should stop apologizing for everything you do, Miss Dennison. Not everything you *think* offends me actually offends me."

She nodded with a grateful smile.

"It's also quite irritating," he added under his breath.

Her suddenly narrowed eyes told him that she heard him, and he quickly changed the subject. "As I mentioned, I had that thought as well."

"We could just as easily be brother and sister," she interrupted quickly, her cheeks flushing again.

He silenced her with a look. "Who would look at us and allow for that story, Miss Dennison? We look nothing alike."

She frowned, but said nothing.

"The only logical choice to save our reputations and allow us to keep looking would be if we pretend marriage between us."

She nodded at his words, but still said nothing.

"Miss Dennison," he said quietly, more than slightly unnerved by her sudden silence. "You are the one who brought this up. Are you having second thoughts?"

"I think I am up to about fourth thoughts at the moment," she answered in a very small voice, avoiding his eyes.

He was startled, he had to admit. This was not the sort of reaction he had expected Moira to have. She didn't think twice about marching into a pub in a town she did not know to find a man she had never met to tell him, not ask him, what he was going to do, but she became shy and retreating upon reconsidering the prospect of a pretend marriage?

"I can understand your reluctance," he began slowly, praying he was going about this in the correct manner. "If we proceed with this, it will certainly place us in situations that neither of us have faced before, and would probably be very uncomfortable due to the level of familiarity that people will assume of us."

Moira nodded silently, swallowing with difficulty.

"But I think that you see as well as I that it is the safest course."

"Yes," she whispered, still not looking at him. "It's the only way we can accomplish what we must and maintain our reputations."

"I don't wish to add to your discomfort, Miss Dennison," he started, wondering how to approach the idea he had formulating. "I know that we had a bit of a rough beginning..."

Her eyes finally met his and she managed a weak smile. "I hope you understand that this is not about you, Mr. Hammond. I would feel reluctant pretending marriage with any man."

He returned her smile. "Well, thank you for that, but yes, I did gather as much. I have an idea that may help the situation, if it is agreeable to you."

"At this moment, I am willing to try almost anything to make this more comfortable," she offered, sounding relieved.

He was not entirely sure she would be willing to try his suggestion, but it was all he could think up. "I think that it would help matters a great deal if we were more familiar with each other in private. For example, no more of being Miss Dennison and Mr. Hammond. We could just be Nathan and Moira. It might allow us to be more comfortable with each other, so that when we are expected to appear close, it would not be so awkward." He held his breath and waited for the tirade to begin, afraid to look at her.

To his astonishment, he saw that she was nodding to herself. "I think that would be a very sensible thing to do."

"You do?"

She grinned. "Taken you by surprise, have I? Now, that is refreshing, Nathan."

The fact that she tossed out his name so easily, and that it sounded so good to his ears, was something else he was entirely unprepared for. "I suppose you could say that," he managed, barely remembering that he could say her name, and hastily added, "…Moira."

It felt good to call her by her given name. He liked her name. It suited her. But he couldn't tell her that. He had his own reputation to uphold. Giving her as severe a look as he could manage, he said, "Though I can hardly call it refreshing. If you keep taking me by surprise in such a way, I cannot be held responsible for my actions."

She smirked. "So I have your permission to call you Nathan, then?"

He snorted and gave her a look. "It was my idea, if you recall. I would have hardly brought it up if I had a problem with you using my given name. I assume that I have your permission to do the same, Moira?"

"Yes, I suppose..." She wrinkled her nose a bit. "This is going to take some getting used to, isn't it?"

He chuckled. "Probably. Breaking habits usually does. But my friends have all called me Nathan for years, so if we just consider each other as friends, perhaps it will be easier."

She tilted her head and her smile grew. "I would like that very much. Nathan."

"As would I." Unable to help himself, he grinned. He really would like to consider her a friend. He would like to know what was really going on in that head of hers, and what drove her to march in demanding to see him the way she did. But more than that, he wanted to know her, the woman she was on the inside. Ironically enough, he thought he could quite genuinely like Moira Dennison, if she would let him.

Or parts of her, at any rate.

"I think we are in for a very interesting experience," Moira said, musing aloud.

"I fail to see how it could be anything but," he agreed. "If we view it as an exercise in creativity, it could be very interesting indeed. Imagine the sorts of scrapes we could get ourselves into."

"Then let's do it," she piped up with an impish light in her eyes. "I can spin quite a tale, if called upon to do so."

"Can you now?" he queried, not sure he believed her. "Well then, when we first have to pose as man and wife, I will let you do the talking."

She narrowed her eyes. "You don't think I can do it."

He held up his hands in surrender. "On the contrary, I think you will have no trouble convincing people that we are married."

"Hmm," she murmured, still eying him warily. "I don't trust you."

"Then we are better friends than I thought."

Her face broke into a smile once more, and it was as if the sun had suddenly broken through a dark blanket of clouds. It transformed her face from merely attractive into something so stunning it was all he could do to blink.

He hastily swallowed the unexpected choking sensation that was now in his throat and somehow managed to speak. "I have a ring."

Well, now *that* was certainly coherent of him.

He cleared his throat and tried again. "If we are to be traveling as husband and wife, we should try to do so from all outward appearances. I have procured a ring for that reason." There, that was much more sensible.

She nodded thoughtfully. "Excellent idea. I will, of course, compensate you for it."

He shook his head. "No, it is not worth very much. Besides, it has been in my family for some time. I will just collect it when we are through."

"If you wish. I am impressed by your forethought, Nathan." She smiled at him, and he found himself returning it, despite his twinge of guilt.

She might not smile so fondly if she knew where the ring had come from.

He pulled out the ring from his pocket and handed it to her. She took it and slid it onto her finger. "Perfect fit, how fortunate."

He took a silent breath in.

Enough of that. He cleared his throat and was about to ask her something when she spoke.

"I have a thought," she said, straightening slightly in her saddle.

"I think we ought to get more acquainted with each other. For one, going about all day only commenting on the weather or the state of the roads is not going to engender any sort of warmth between us. And for another, I happen to be intensely curious about a great many things."

Her blunt admission of that small detail caught him, and his defenses were suddenly more alert. He would have to be very, very cautious, or this could all go wrong rather quickly. But the opportunity to learn more about her was tempting.

"Therefore," she continued, as if he hadn't just had another wave of his own curiosity thrust upon him, "I think that, since we are friends now…" she paused, looking at him.

"We are," he confirmed quickly.

She nodded, and continued, "… Then I think we ought to be able to ask each other any question we wish."

Any? Oh, that was not going to go well. He had so many questions for her, some he knew she would not like, and he dreaded the ones she might come up with for him.

"Any, you say?" he offered, stroking his chin thoughtfully.

"Yes, any," she said, shaking her head at him. "And whoever is being asked is allowed to pass on the question, if they truly do not wish to share the answer. And since we are friends, we will trust that they have a good reason for not sharing."

Ah, now *that* was an interesting clarification if he had ever heard one. Not that he disagreed, but what sort of things did she want to hide from him? As seems to be the case in all situations, the restrictions made the unknown so much more tempting.

But, above all else, Nathan was a gentleman, and he would prove it to her. "Agreed, then."

Moira sighed to herself in relief. She knew that she would have gone mad on this long journey without having any sort of real conversation, and the only way she knew to do that was to ask questions. She was surprised that he was going to allow her the liberty of asking any question she wanted. True, she had added the option of passing on a question if one did not want to answer it, but that was mostly because she had seen how he had stiffened when she had mentioned the "any question" part. He had secrets, it seemed, but then, so did she.

All things considered, she really did want to be friends with him. He seemed a very good sort of person, and they'd been thrown together in this strange arrangement of her making. Perhaps with this little question idea of hers, they would eventually get to be friends in truth.

As if he could sense her thoughts, he asked, "Might I start off this 'any question' game?"

She nodded and smiled in encouragement. "Of course, please do."

He almost looked uncertain at first, but then he asked, "Why me?"

The question startled her, which must have shown on her face as Nathan smiled at her and continued, "You could have had any number of people help you with finding your betrothed. Why did you choose me?"

She had hoped they would not reach this question until much further down the line, but she knew she owed him an answer. With a sigh, she shrugged a little. "I started off from Gillam four days ago without any help at all. I did not think that I would need any, which, as I soon came to find out, was quite ridiculous. And it was not long before I realized the dangers of a single woman traveling alone on unfamiliar paths. Oh, don't look so murderous, nothing happened," she scolded, waving a hand at him as he opened his mouth in outrage.

"At any rate," she continued quickly, ignoring his glower, "I was already beyond the boundaries of propriety and all else I knew, so I merely started asking any who would listen to me. It seemed better to refer to Charles as a brother instead of telling people I was looking for my betrothed. A desperate sister is more respected than a desperate lover, don't you think?"

He did not look as though he would like to answer that, and she did not wait for him to.

"So I began asking if anyone knew my brother. I quickly

learned that was not helping; he had been gone far too long anyway. I switched my pleas to asking if anybody knew someone who could help me find my brother. As you can probably imagine, most people were not receptive to my addresses."

He nodded, clenching his jaw, but saying nothing.

"But one man took pity on me," Moira continued, "and listened to me, to the whole story. He immediately told me to find Nathaniel Hammond. He told me all about serving in the army and how when someone needed to be found, they called for you. He and his companions provided detailed accounts, but I'm not entirely certain how much of their tales I put credence to." She smiled at him, wishing he would not look so irritated. "You made quite an impression on them, Nathan."

"I doubt half of the stories were true," he said gruffly. "Did you get the man's name?"

She thought back, wondering if he had told her. "The others called him Carpenter, but I couldn't say if that was his real name."

"I would assume it was Daniel Carpenter. Yes, you were right to only think him moderately reliable." His eyes took on a far-off look that Moira was desperate to ask about, but something held her back.

He shook himself from his stupor and looked back to her, his expression still cloudy. "Apologies, Moira. Please go on."

Ignoring the compulsion to ask him anyway, she continued, "Well, since the information this Carpenter fellow gave me was all I had to go on, and I was ready to try almost anything, I paid him and went out in search of you."

"And you found me," he finished softly, as if he wasn't sure he liked that she had.

"Well, Carpenter did tell me that the last he heard, you were somewhere in Hampshire, and once I knew that, things were much easier."

He gave her a look. "Easier how? Hampshire is a rather large and general area in which to find one man."

She shrugged. "I had a general idea of location and a description of you from my sources. Not that it was very good, but you would be surprised what a less than decent description, a name, and some money will get you. I am very grateful that you were not further into the country than you were."

"Convenient," he murmured, still looking at her oddly. "So you took the word of one source of questionable reliability and started on your own manhunt for me, knowing that much of the information had probably been fabricated."

"Yes," she said shifting uncomfortably in her saddle. "As I said, I had nothing other than that, and it seemed my best option at the time. I did tell you this when I first met you, and you still agreed to come."

He made some non-committal noise, still staring at her.

Moira was not sure what that was all about; everything she had told him was true. She had not left out anything that was pertinent, and had been completely candid about her lack of information. There was no cause for him to stare at her as though she had committed some sort of crime, or gross error in judgment.

Well, perhaps the error in judgment was well-founded, but even so...

Finally, she couldn't stand it. "Now what, Nathan? I have answered your question and you look as though I have fed you stockings for soup."

He managed a thin smile at her phrase, but then he was serious again. "Moira, how many pubs did you go into before you found me in The Horse and Rider?"

She ducked her head, her cheeks flaming. "Five."

"Uh huh. And how many of those were places you should have gone into?"

Her eyes flashed. There was no way that he was going to be permitted to criticize her for her choices and actions when he did not know her. "Oh, what does that have to do with anything?" she snapped. "I was looking for you and I found you. I don't see how any of this makes any difference at all."

"Were you trying to get yourself killed or worse? For pity's sake, woman!" He ran a hand through his hair and glared at her. "Did you think at all before you...?"

"Oh no, you don't, Nathaniel Hammond," she overrode loudly, her face flaming in indignation. "We have been friends all of twenty minutes, which is not nearly long enough for you to disapprove of my past behavior. You are not my father, brother, husband, or anything else that would give you the right to even have an opinion on what I have already done. I did what I had to do, and I would do it again. Now what have you to say? I know you have something to say. You always *must* say something, you simply cannot help yourself, so come on and spit it out, then."

Nathan stared at her for what felt like ages. Then he grunted a sigh and said, "Have you ever been informed that you are the most infuriating woman on the planet?"

She exhaled through her nose sharply and tried not to smile. "As a matter of fact, no, I have not."

He grunted. "You are."

She fought it, but she had to smile now. As aggravating as Nathan was, she actually found herself enjoying their banter. They might kill each other before the trip was complete, but at least it would be good fun while it lasted.

She snuck a peek back over at Nathan, who was still fuming, but seemed calmer.

She appreciated his concern, she really did. But she would do whatever she needed to in order to find Charles, regardless of what he or anyone else thought. She had come too far, had hurt too much to let anything stop her.

But that did not mean that she had to dwell on it now. What she wanted at the moment was to know more about this man she would be pretending to be married to.

"Well, if you don't mind humoring the most infuriating woman on the planet," she began, throwing a measure of playfulness into her tone.

"Oh, lord," he groaned, but with a smile. "What now?"

She ignored him and looked as superior as she could. "What are some things that I need to know about my husband before we meet the public?"

He gave her a quizzical look. "Excuse me?"

"It cannot be that complicated. Tell me some things I need to know about you."

"What kind of things?" he asked slowly.

Moira rolled her eyes. "Oh, for heaven's sake, you can't help yourself from spewing forth unwanted speeches, but getting personal details out of you is worse than drawing teeth! Very well, I will go first."

She looked away in thought for a moment, then heaved a sigh and looked at him once more. "I hate cats, and they hate me. I don't eat tripe, I can whistle like a man, and I enjoy taking long walks. I like hearing rain on the roof, I take rather large bites when eating an apple, and it takes me ages to fall asleep at night. My middle name is Patience, and I hate it, so you may never speak of it again."

Nathan stared at her, as if he had no idea what she had just said. But then, she had said it all rather fast and in one breath. It was no wonder his brain took a little time to process and catch up.

"Interesting," he said, musing aloud to himself. "I feel oddly enlightened now."

"So you should," she quipped rather smartly. "Now you know what is expected of you, so it is your turn."

"Very well, give me a moment." He appeared to give it some thought, just enough to make her roll her eyes and huff in frustration again, and then he snapped his fingers. "I've got it. Are you ready?"

"Quite," she retorted dryly.

"Hush, I am humoring you," he growled, giving her a severe look, to which she responded by making a face. He sighed a long-suffering sigh, then began his own response: "I can sneak up on a bird without startling it, I would rather eat breakfast every meal instead of only once, and I do not enjoy dancing. I can speak French fluently, I hate cravats, and I do not gamble. I like dogs, but not in my bed, and I have a brother who cannot stand me, and I don't want to talk about it, so don't ask."

Moira was staring at him now, trying to remember to breathe. She knew immediately that he wished back the part about his brother. She could see it in his face that he did not mean to share that with her. Her mind scrambled to come up with something clever to say, but all she could manage thinking was that she should apologize, which he had already told her to stop doing.

"Well," she started off, completely at a loss as to how she was going to end this, "that *was* enlightening, you are quite right."

He didn't look at her, but his jaw tensed.

She gave him an odd look. "You don't like dancing?"

The relief that coursed through him was so evident that she almost cheered. He returned her look, and she could see the gratitude in his eyes, but decided to focus on the amusement he was trying to show.

"I don't," he said with a shrug. "I simply cannot stand it. I avoid it at all costs."

She shook her head and gave a rather un-ladylike snort. "Were you by chance raised by wolves? Everybody enjoys dancing!"

"Obviously not. And I will let you in on a little secret, Miss Moira Dennison," he said with a smile, crooking a finger at her.

She nudged her horse closer and made a show of leaning in.

"Most men do not like dancing," he told her in a conspiratorial whisper.

She reared back in mock outrage. "Impossible!"

He shook his head somberly. "No, it's true."

"Why do it, then?"

He shrugged slightly. "That is where the women are, and the women like to dance, so the men must endure."

"Oh, the sacrifices that you noble men make for we poor, demanding females," she said with a heavy measure of sarcasm. "However do you manage it?"

"Very carefully," he replied in sober tones, which had them both laughing at once.

Chapter Four

"Now you promised to let me do the talking."

Nathan closed his eyes and groaned. "No doubt, that was the thickest decision I ever made," he lamented, as they approached the inn where they would stay for the night.

Moira glared at him fiercely. "Well, I can hardly convince anyone if you look so pained about it."

He arched a brow at her. "Would you like me to be overtly affectionate, then? That would certainly convince the good patrons of something, but given the long day we have just had, I doubt they would be thinking marriage…"

She swallowed hastily and slid off of Flora. "Stop being impertinent, Nathan. Just be quiet and look… husbandly."

He stifled a laugh as he dismounted and took Mercury and Flora's reigns, then handed them to the stable hand that approached. "Yes, dear."

She gave him one more severe look for good measure, then allowed him to escort her into the inn.

It was relatively well lit, for an inn, and the patrons within looked to be of decent stock. That eased Moira's nerves, which, she had to admit, had been less than steady as they had approached. But Nathan thought she was a strong woman, so she had to be. Or at least, make a good show of it.

She looked over to the desk, where a less than pleasant looking man with a dreadful mustache sat, pouring over a ledger, his spectacles perched precariously upon his unusually shaped nose. The innkeeper, no doubt. She marched over and waited for him to look up. When he did, his eyes flicked from her to Nathan and then back to her. He drew the spectacles from his face and sighed. "Can I help you?"

"Yes, you may," she responded in her best superior voice. "My husband and I would like a room for the night. Together, you understand, as we are married."

The innkeeper's brows rose slightly, and Moira could almost feel Nathan groaning behind her. She resisted the urge to shove her elbow into his stomach, but only just.

"I see," the innkeeper said, looking back down at his ledger. "Well, you are in luck, Mrs....?"

"Lancaster," she said rather quickly, panicking in spite of her attempts not to. "Margaret Lancaster, and this is Rupert. He is my husband." She indicated Nathan behind her and smiled in what she hoped was a pleasant manner.

"I should hope so," the innkeeper muttered, shaking his head. "You are in luck, Mrs. Lancaster. We happen to have a few rooms available that a husband and wife can share, if they wanted. Since you are married, as you say, you may have one. With your husband."

"Thank you, we would be most appreciative." She smiled again, and was slightly mollified to see the mustache twitch in a manner that could have been a smile. She must be better at this than she thought. Emboldened, she decided to keep going. "My husband and I have just come up from Portsmouth. We have been married for three months now."

"Congratulations," the man mumbled in an offhand manner as he searched for their key.

"Yes, thank you," she said with a grateful nod. "It was rather exciting. Being married is wonderful. I have always wanted to be married. Such a pleasant surprise, I recommend having a husband for all women."

Nathan was in anguish, and no longer paying any attention to Moira at all. He had the strongest desire to clamp his hand over her mouth and apologize to the innkeeper for his poor, ridiculous wife, but he didn't know if he could refer to her as his wife without snarling. What was taking him so long to find the stupid key? He was desperate for just a room, any room. The man could have picked up a key to a broom closet and Nathan would have thanked him profusely. Once he had sent Moira up to the room, he could get down to work, but if she were going to continue like this, he would have to do so elsewhere. No one hearing her would believe anything he said.

"We are now searching for my brother, Charles Allenford. Have you ever heard of him?" she asked, even as Nathan began clenching his fists.

"No," the innkeeper told her handing over a key. "Room twelve. Good evening." With what could almost be called a pitying look at Nathan, he trudged away from the counter and through a door that seemed to be headed for the kitchen.

"Do you think he went to see about some food for us?" she asked Nathan, turning around to look at him. He closed his eyes and exhaled rather harshly. "What? Na… uh, Rupert? Husband?"

"Stop," he hissed, taking her arm forcefully. "Let us go to our room, dear. I think you need to rest from our journey." He knew his voice was taut and agitated, but he prayed for control yet again.

"But…" she began.

He opened his eyes and silenced her with a look.

She nodded and allowed him to take, or haul rather, her to their room. The moment the door was shut behind them, he released her arm and sank into a chair, running his hands through his hair.

"I thought I was rather good just then," Moira commented as she made for the bed and sat down on the edge of it, swinging her legs a bit. "Charles used to say that I could be a very clever actress, if I had the desire."

Nathan dropped his hands and looked up at her incredulously. He was beginning to think this Charles fellow was really a git.

Moira caught Nathan's expression. "What?"

"I am trying to figure out if you are serious or not," he said, his brow furrowing.

"About being an actress?"

"No, about you being good just then."

She frowned, evidently not understanding. "I was. I even added extraneous material to make our story more real. The bits about when we were married and where we came from, for example."

Nathan groaned and sat back against the chair. "And that was your best attempt at a convincing story? I think you just ruined the entire excursion, and made us a laughingstock, to boot. They will be talking about us downstairs right now, wondering why in the world I am married to you."

She gasped in indignation. "That was uncalled for! Is this because I named you Rupert? It is a perfectly good name! What was wrong with my story, may I ask?"

He sat forward and gave her a steady, yet disbelieving look. "So much. Where do I even begin?"

She glowered. "What, you can do better?" she scoffed, leaning back on her hands.

"My horse could do better."

She sputtered, but did not formulate any sort of coherent response.

"I will try to mend the damage down there and see if we can still get some useful information out of this place," he said, getting to his feet. "You had better stay up here and play ill. Perhaps I can come off as a man who married a ridiculous woman for her money."

"Mr. Hammond!" she screeched as she shot to her feet, finding her voice at last and letting him hear fury ringing through it.

He glared at her. "That would be Mr. Lancaster to you, my dear Margaret. And keep it down! You wouldn't want all of your hard work going for naught, would you?" He moved for the door, then stopped and turned back. "What does this so-called brother of yours look like anyway?"

She folded her arms and looked out of the window, her jaw clenched.

"Come on, Moira," he said in a quiet, but still harsh tone. "I don't have time to patch up your pride at the moment. If you want to find this idiot and get on with your life, I need to know what he looks like so I can ask about him. I need a good description."

"Fine," she spat, still not facing him. "But only so I can get away from you faster. Charles is shorter than you by a good six inches. He is thin, has brown hair, blue eyes, and is slightly freckled. He also has decent teeth. Is that enough for your precious description?"

"It will do. Set some sheets by the window before you go to bed."

She half turned to look at him, her curiosity obviously piqued. "Why?"

He was tempted to say so he could jump from it, but she was already agitated as it was. Adding more fuel to the fire would not help matters. "Because I do not think we should be sleeping in the same room. Thanks to your insistency, we only have the one. I will climb out of the window and sleep in the stables."

She sniffed and shrugged. "Fine. As you wish." She turned back around and went to the window, arms still folded. Her left leg shook slightly, as if she wanted to tap her toe, but was resisting.

"Thank you. Good night," he said, opening the door and stepping out. He paused a moment, then stuck his head back in. "And I do hate the name Rupert. Terrible choice."

She whirled and the fury in her eyes was enough to make him a little nervous. He shut the door quickly before she could decide to throw something at him.

It was much later when Nathan made his way back up to the room, feeling rather sluggish and having had too much of whatever drink they were serving in the taproom. But it had all worked out well. It seemed that many of the men at the inn tonight also had wives that drove them to distraction. He was in fine company as soon as he had come down from the room. Even the innkeeper was pleasant, or as close to pleasant as he ever achieved. Apparently, Moira had brought to mind his own wife, and he had not enjoyed the reminder.

Once Nathan had sat at the table with the men, more stories began to come out about impossible wives and unhappy marriages, and he heard far more than he ever wanted to. He tried to play his character as not particularly minding the eccentricities of the woman he was married to, merely accepting it as what he must endure. That also resounded with them, and helped him in his purposes to retrieve information. At least three of the men thought the name Charles Allenford sounded familiar, and of those three, two were able to place the description with the name. None of them had a location, but the fact that they had confirmation of identity was encouraging.

It seemed that Moira's attempt at a story had not been such a disaster after all.

He listened at the door to their room, hoping she was a deep sleeper. He could not hear anything from within, so opened the door as quietly as he could manage and tiptoed into the darkness. He reached the window to find that not only had she put the sheets there, but she had already tied them to the bed post and formed a makeshift rope out of them. He tugged on it, and found that it was indeed sturdy.

"How in the world…?" he murmured to himself.

"I used to sneak out of my aunt's house sometimes," came a soft voice from the bed. "I became quite adept at tying sheets together."

He looked up and saw her on her side staring at him as she lay on the bed, her hands under her face.

"Why does that not surprise me?" he whispered, offering a smile.

She tried to return it, but it faltered. A break in the clouds let a sliver of moonlight in, and Nathan could see tear tracks on her cheeks.

"Are you all right?" he asked, unable to resist going to the bed and sitting down.

She sat up and pulled her knees to her chest, covering her flimsy chemise with the blankets. "I know you told me not to apologize for everything," she said, her voice quivering slightly, "but I have to this time."

"No, you don't," he urged, putting a hand on her foot. "I was out of line, I am the one who should apologize."

She shook her head and sniffed. "You were right to be cross. I was dreadful." She groaned and put her face in her knees.

He couldn't help it; he smiled. "You were," he agreed.

She turned her head to glare at him with one eye. "You could pretend and say 'Oh, it wasn't that bad', you know."

"But it was." He shrugged, still smiling. "I cannot help but be honest, Moira."

"Well," she huffed, setting her chin to her knees, "I am sorry that it was so dreadful. Next time you can do the talking and I shall be the meek little mouse of a wife."

"I would be happy to do the talking," he said, tilting his head to look at her more closely. "But I don't want a meek little mouse of a wife."

A small smile played at the corners of her mouth. "You don't or Rupert Lancaster does not?"

He groaned, but grinned at her. "Rupert Lancaster just received more sympathy from the men of this inn than some people receive at funerals."

She snickered. "I bet he did. I hope it fares better for him in the future."

"It had better. He is not returning." His look turned severe. "Ever."

She nodded, wiping at her cheeks. "I understand. No more Rupert Lancaster. And no more Margaret, either."

"Thank heavens."

Her smile turned rueful. "And what about Nathaniel Hammond? What does he want in a wife?"

"Well, he doesn't want Margaret Lancaster, that is certain," he said with a shudder. "But he doesn't want a mouse wife either."

"What, then?"

"A partner," he admitted, no longer looking at anything. "Someone to work with me, beside me, and ease the burden of life. Competent, caring, and companionable."

"And what about love, Nathan?" she asked in gentle tones.

Nathan sat back in thought. "Love. It's an intriguing idea, but I can hardly require or expect that. Love can grow with time, after all, and the heart is not always as sensible as the head."

"Love is not sensible. If it were, the poets would have nothing at all to write about."

He smiled faintly. "Perhaps you're right."

The silence stretched between them for a moment, and it was the most comfortable silence he had ever experienced. Far too comfortable.

"Well," she said lightly, patting her hand on his where it sat on her foot, "I think you will make someone a very fine husband someday, Nathan Hammond, despite Rupert Lancaster."

He chuckled and brought her hand to his lips and kissed it quickly. "Thank you, my dear. Maybe next time we can have more fun with our marriage, eh?" He grinned and got up, letting her hand fall back to the bed.

"Take an extra blanket, Nathan," she hissed as he stepped onto the window sill. "It's freezing out there."

He snatched one up and stuffed it under his arm. "Pull up the sheets when I'm down. I will walk in tomorrow morning."

She nodded. "Watch out for droppings. I would hate to have a smelly husband in the morning."

He rolled his eyes and adjusted his grip on the sheets. "Thank you. Anything else, wife?" he asked, with a grin.

She smiled and shook her head. "No, I think that is all I had to say, husband. Enjoy the hay."

He smirked, then grew serious. "No more tears, Moira. I mean it."

She wiped at her cheeks again and nodded. "No more tears, I promise. Good night, Nathan."

"Good night, Moira."

Nathan walked back to the inn early the next morning, hoping that he would be able to avoid seeing anyone, and thus have to answer some rather awkward questions about why Mr. Lancaster had been sleeping in the stables.

Unfortunately, the innkeeper was already up and about, preparing the room for the morning meal. He eyed Nathan as he entered and frowned. "Everything all right there, Mr. Lancaster?"

Nathan forced a grimace. "I suppose that all depends on what you call 'all right'."

"Was the room not to your liking?"

He shook his head, leaning against a chair. "No, the room was fine. It was the… Well, my wife, you see… She is…" He was not about to say anything against Moira, but he could not see how to finish the thought.

The innkeeper chuckled good-naturedly. "I understand, sir. Haven't slept in the same room as my wife since our son was born, and I have slept like a baby ever since." He grinned up at him, and Nathan tried to return it, but it was very forced.

He would have to tell Moira about this, and what people thought of her. Well, of Margaret, he supposed. They did not know Moira. He hardly did, either, but he liked what he did. Most of the time, anyway.

"But why did you not come to see me, sir?" the man asked, stuffing his rag into the apron he wore. "I would have been glad to set you up in another room."

Nathan shrugged. "The money all comes from her, I am afraid."

The innkeeper and the few other men in the room laughed. "Ah, the nature of marriage, eh? Chin up, sir. You'll survive her."

They all laughed harder, but Nathan failed to see the humor in the statement.

"Well, is there anything I can do to help you before you have to return to your shrew, Mr. Lancaster?" the innkeeper asked with a slap on the back, and smiling at the general chuckles of their companions.

Nathan would really have loved to start a brawl so that he could lay his hands on every one of them without looking like a crazed animal, but it was hardly called for, considering they were to leave soon. It would hinder their efforts to come and go from place to place without leaving much of an impression.

He sighed, more for their benefit than his. "I suppose just a tray of food will do. Maybe I can speed her along, but I doubt it."

Again, laughter filled the room and the innkeeper waved for a maid to bring him a tray. "Alas, Mr. Lancaster, I don't know of any way to speed a woman up. Not ones that is proper, at any rate." He gave a guffaw of a laugh and gave the tray to Nathan. "But try feeding her, sir. That may just do the trick yet."

"Thank you," Nathan muttered, his patience wearing thin. He nodded to the group and headed up the stairs to the room, still fuming.

There could not be a single woman in the world that deserved a husband who thought so badly of her. When all of this was over, he was going to have a serious talk with Derek about it. Surely even Katherine had redeemable qualities, something positive he could talk about instead of how much he despised her. He thought of his own encounters with Katherine and shuddered.

Then again, perhaps there was one exception after all.

He knocked quietly at the door, and heard the soft "Come in" from within.

The sight that met him almost knocked him flat. Moira was by the window, wearing her dress from the day before, but looking remarkably refreshed after their talk in the night. What was startling was her hair. She had not put it up yet, so the long copper locks fell in waves across her shoulders and ended halfway down her back. It shimmered in the morning light as if it were a river of precious metal cascading along her body. He honestly could not have said if he had ever seen anything lovelier, let alone anything like it.

She smiled warmly at him and he felt another wave of shock from it. She was beautiful. He had known that, but perhaps never more so until this moment.

"Good morning, husband," she said cheerfully, eying the still open door meaningfully.

It took Nathan more than a moment to recover from hearing her call him 'husband' when she was looking like that, but he soon did. "Good morning, Mrs. Lancaster. I hope you slept well."

"Very," she responded with a nod, taking her hair in hand and beginning to plait it. "Have you received word of my brother?"

"Later," he mouthed, closing the door behind him. He set the tray down on the small table in the corner, and turned to face her again, wondering what had happened to his foul mood.

"What is it?" Moira asked softly as she continued working with her hair.

"What is what?"

She gave him a look. "Something is troubling you. What is it?"

"How could you possibly know that?" he asked with a laugh that sounded as forced as it felt.

"You don't hide your feelings nearly as well as you think you do, Nathan," she replied with a pitying smile. "Now stop stalling. What?"

He shook his head. "Not here. I will tell you," he promised as she opened her mouth to protest, "but later. Once we are gone."

She eyed him suspiciously for a moment, then nodded. "Very well." She pinned her plait up, then sat down by the tray of food he had brought and helped herself. "What is your plan for the morning?"

He sighed and rubbed his hands together. "Well, first I think I need to tell you just what our fellow patrons think of us, and then we can decide what to do."

Chapter Five

"Well, *that* was a right sight better, don't you think?" Moira asked as she and Nathan rode away from the inn.

"Indeed, it was," he agreed, feeling more relieved to be leaving a place than he had in a long time. "Your performance was much better this morning."

She nodded graciously with a smile. "Why, thank you. I hope they enjoyed my fluttery antics."

He chuckled. "I am sure they did. I received my share of sympathetic glances."

"I reminded myself of my Aunt Miriam," she said with a grimace, shuddering delicately. "It was terrifying, actually."

"I know," he teased. "I was there, remember?"

She gave him a look that he pointedly ignored. "And you played the part of a long-suffering husband with a dreadful wife quite well," she complimented. "I have rarely seen anyone look so convincing while acting."

He snorted and arched a brow at her. "Who said I was acting?"

She rolled her eyes at him, but grinned. "If I were closer, I would smack you for that. I did say I was sorry for ever creating Margaret, but you were the one who decided Rupert was miserable. You could have been hopelessly in love instead."

"I would never have received any sympathy for being in love with Margaret," he protested. "If you could have seen their faces when you were talking last night…"

She sighed, a touch sadly. "It is probably best that I did not. It would have made things worse." She shrugged and then brightened considerably. "Did they believe you when you said you preferred the stables last night?"

"They did. I got the impression that quite a few of them have experience with avoiding sharing a room with their wives. Particularly our host." He frowned at the memory, wondering how much of their behavior was in human nature.

"Oh my, there is a dreadful face. Would you mind sharing what has brought it on?"

He looked over at her, and found her expression full of curiosity, but more of concern. He debated sharing what he was thinking and feeling with her. For some reason he could not identify, he wanted to know her thoughts, and he knew that if he shared this with her, he would get whatever views she had, regardless of if they would be favorable on him or not. She was simply incapable of keeping things to herself.

It was as maddening as it was refreshing.

Finally, he decided that she should know. Why shouldn't she? It had been her behavior that had sparked this, and his reactions to it had helped it along.

"I told you what happened after I left last night, after we… well, after our disagreement."

"Oh, call it a fight, by all means," she interrupted with a wave of her hand. "We were furious. Had we been anywhere else, there would have been a great deal of shouting and throwing of breakable things and perhaps a few tears. It was a fight, it deserves the proper name."

He smiled in spite of himself. She was, without a doubt, the strangest woman he had ever met.

"I was astonished by the number of men that sympathized with me about my supposed wife," he began, his eyes focusing on the horizon, feeling it was the safest place for them to be. "Many of them expressed desires to be rid of their own, and had even thought of how to do it. I heard so many things about marriages and wives, things that I would never dare repeat to you or anyone else." He shook his head with a bit of disgust. "It made me ashamed of men in general."

Moira kept silent as she rode beside him, for which he was supremely grateful.

He frowned and met her eyes. "But it got me thinking, as it did last night, about the sad state of marriage. These men did not know you or me, and based on one brief encounter, they saw their own unhappy marriages in it, and made it seem normal. What in the world is normal about any of it? What man would subject himself to a life of misery with a woman they could not even care for? Not to mention the women involved. Don't they deserve a husband that cares about them?"

Moira did not say anything for a long while, then she began to speak, her voice low, "We are both well aware that people marry for things far less than what you or I desire. It is something we do not like to think about, but we know it happens."

"Oh, I know it does," he said on an exhale. "Money, desperation, family wishes, improvement of station or reputation… But it all seems so ridiculous, doesn't it? Marriage is meant to last and to bring about children and to improve life in general for all parties involved, but that must mean so much more than temporal interest. It troubles me that so many others marry for money alone. If there is a choice, is it really too much to ask that you marry someone you can tolerate? It does not have to be love, I am not so naïve as that, nor do I expect it myself. But friendship, affection, or some other mutual understanding must be considered. And if you do not choose that, and a marriage for temporal reasons is all, then you can have no reason to be unhappy about it, and no room for complaint." He was getting carried away in his feelings, but he had thought about the topic a good deal.

After what he had done to his brother's chances for marriage, he could hardly have ignored it.

"Not all men see the world as you do, Nathan," Moira said quietly.

"They should," he grunted, looking away.

"Yes, they probably should," she agreed, "but they don't." She then tilted her head thoughtfully. "May I ask you something?"

"Of course."

"You seem to have thought a great deal on the subject." She paused, chewing on her lip for a moment. "It seems as if you have had some personal experience with unhappy marriages."

"Still waiting on a question," he prodded, raising a brow.

She smiled. "If it is not too personal, would you share it with me? I don't want to pry, I just want to understand."

Nathan considered that, and finally agreed that it would help her see his point. "It is actually a chief example of what I was saying. It started my thoughts on the subject years ago. I have a close friend, Derek, who has been married to his wife, Katherine, for the past five years or so."

That seemed to take her by surprise. "He must have married rather young for a man."

He nodded. "He did. The marriage was arranged."

"Arranged?" she asked, completely baffled now. "People still arrange marriages?"

"Oh, yes," he told her, shifting a bit awkwardly in his saddle. He did not enjoy talking about Derek's marriage. There really was not a way to go about it without approaching his title, and a common man would have no dealings with a marquess. "It was arranged between them from their childhood, and when Derek became old enough to know what that meant, he also learned that it was as binding as any contract in the world."

"So why marry so young? Surely waiting until they were older and able to get to know each other…"

"They have known each other from the very beginning," Nathan said, stopping her with a shake of his head. "It does not help matters. They cannot stand each other. To be fair, Derek is not exactly easy tempered, and is rather set in his ways and I don't see him changing any time soon. And Katherine is… well, the way Derek describes her is the bringer of all misery, brimstone, and plagues, parading her self-importance in her destructive wake. As attractive as a leech and far less good for the health."

Moira covered her mouth, but it was not enough to hide the

snort of laughter that escaped her. "I'm sorry," she managed when she was composed, dropping her hand, "that is terrible. Humorous, but still terrible."

He grinned. "You have not met her. She is not especially pleasant. But that is neither here nor there. The point is that Derek's perspective on marriage is a little skewed. I rarely take anything he says on the subject into consideration at all."

"I can see why. Poor man. Well, poor Katherine, too," she added as an afterthought.

"Why poor Katherine?" he asked in confusion. "She has everything she wanted, and I'm not being insensitive. I heard her say those very words."

"Oh, no doubt she thinks she does, but to be living with so little expectations of joy in her life, to only view her existence as a series of duties, and to never know real love… It's quite sad." She sighed and shook herself, then looked up at Nathan. "Well, at least neither of us has to worry about that, do we?"

"Lucky us."

Nathan mentally winced. He had been unable to moderate his tone completely, and his cynicism was showing. Truly, he had no reason to be so about the subject of love and marriage, but hearing Derek's tales and knowing his own temperament, he had never quite thought about finding love for himself.

Until she had come along with all her ideas and romantic notions. And now it was all he could think about.

"Well, don't think on those idiot men anymore, Nathan," Moira said firmly. "Just because they don't know how to properly comport a marriage does not mean the rest of us are doomed."

"The rest of us?" he repeated with a hard laugh. "I think most of the world is the same way."

"Stop it," she scolded severely. "You are being very cantankerous, and it does not agree with my preferred form of travelling. So stop it now, or I will find a new escort and leave you here for highway robbery."

Highway robbery? He almost laughed. "Fine," he muttered, pretending he was still upset. "I suppose I will stop."

"That is what I thought you would say," she replied with a regal nod of her chin.

He shook his head. "You are so demanding," he grumbled good-naturedly.

She let out a small sniff of false indignation. "Get used to it."

He gave her a careful look. "Are you always going to try to cheer me up? Or are you just feeling particularly kind today?"

Her cheeks flushed slightly and she ducked her head. "Well, a moody you is not a pleasant thing. It was purely an act of self-preservation, you understand."

He nodded somberly in understanding. "Of course, yes. Self-preservation, that is very wise." But his eyes twinkled all the same.

The silence between them stretched on, nearly to the point of awkwardness.

"So, did you find out anything useful about Charles or was the whole exercise in creativity a loss?" Moira finally asked.

"It was not a loss at all, actually," he told her with a smile, "but it was not for want of trying, thanks to you."

She moaned and shook her head. "When will that cease to be amusing for you?"

"Oh, probably never." He flashed her a devious grin. "The male patrons were very keen to talk to me about whatever they could. I must have been quite the pathetic picture."

"Ah, true to life…"

He chuckled and saluted her. "Touché, my dear." Then he grew serious. "I don't expect to hear too much until we get closer to Preston, unless he really did stop somewhere along the way. But there were three men who recognized the name and two of those could match the description you gave me."

Moira frowned. "But how does that help us? We are not anywhere near Preston, they could be remembering him from when he was in this area."

"Not if they were all from the north."

Her eyes lit up and she grinned. "Really?"

He matched her smile, albeit to a lesser degree. "Really."

"So we are headed on in the right direction, then."

He nodded. "That we are. I think we can just stay along this main road for a while, but we can start asking for the best way to

Preston and see if someone might give us better directions. Did Charles know how he was going to get there? We could follow his route."

She shook her head, her light dimming slightly. "No, he had never been. I am afraid that won't help."

"And there you would be wrong."

She looked up at him, her expression confused. "How would that be?"

"Because if he did not know how he was going to get there, or which way to go, then he would also have had to ask for directions."

"So if we speak with the innkeepers along the way…" she began, her smile starting to form once more.

He nodded. "Then they may remember someone else trying to get to Preston as quickly as possible," he finished for her. "It's not a common destination for someone from this area."

She laughed in victory. "We may actually be able to find him!" she cried, looking over at Nathan with a wild grin.

"Yes, we may," he agreed with a smile. "But with your willpower, Moira Dennison, I would not expect anything less."

Her smile flickered briefly. "I wouldn't be as confident about the strength of willpower, Nathan. It can be quite as easy to be strong-minded about a wrong thing as it is about a right. Just because someone is decided on a course does not mean they are confident about it. "

"You have doubts?" he asked her, his eyes searching her face.

"There are always doubts, even in the most determined. We just don't speak of them." Her voice was soft, and he sensed that he had hit upon a much deeper, more painful topic. He wished she would not retreat so. She was very neatly stripping away his defenses, and while he could understand her desire for privacy, he wished she would allow him to do the same.

He didn't enjoy seeing the vulnerability on her face. It made him feel protective, which was rather impossible to explain, as there was nothing to protect her from save him. And herself. Somehow he would find a way to open her up, but until then, he would have to find ways to distract her.

"I believe it is my turn for a question," he announced,

wondering which of the hoard of questions about her that were floating around in his head he should ask.

She turned with an expectant, and perhaps a touch relieved, smile. "I believe you are correct. What is your question this time? Darkest fears? Secret hopes? Shocking secret that nobody but my dolls knows about?"

"You have dolls?" he asked in surprise.

She smirked. "Is that your question?"

"No!" he hastily said with a laugh. "No, it's not. My question is this; yesterday morning when we set out, how long had you been waiting for me?"

She looked surprised. "That is what you wish to know? Not something more pressing about my past or my personality or my behavior?"

He shrugged. "I have many, many questions, Moira. But there is an order to all things, and I had a few questions yesterday morning, most of which have been answered in their course. Once I know the answer to this one, I can move on to those deeper questions you seem so keen to answer."

"A few questions?" she asked with a grin. "What were the others?"

"It's not your turn," he reprimanded with a finger. "They have been answered and that is all you need to know right now. Are you going to answer or will you choose to pass?"

"Oh, I'll answer," she laughed, batting away his finger, "but you will not like it."

"Why is that?"

"Because I was waiting almost two hours."

"Two hours?" he cried, jerking in his saddle, causing Mercury to stutter in his step and shift restlessly.

Moira laughed again. "I think your horse would appreciate steadier nerves from you, Nathan."

He grunted, patting the horse soothingly. "Mercury can handle it. He just wants to gallop."

"Mercury?" she asked looking at the horse fondly. "He should gallop, if he is named for a god with wings."

"Perhaps he will later, but you need to explain yourself, Moira," he told her with a scolding look. "Why on earth were you there two hours when we agreed on first light?"

"Because I did not sleep well, probably due to my anxiety to be on our way, and so when I gave up on sleeping, I dressed and made my way over."

"Moira!" he protested. "It was cold yesterday morning!"

"I know," she quipped, her eyes dancing. "I was freezing. Believe me, I was cursing your name up and down the entire time."

He bit back the urge to demand why she did not come and find him. She would not have known where, and had she asked, someone might have cast her off as being rude and impertinent and informed her of his identity, and then she certainly would not have allowed him to come. "Two hours," he muttered under his breath. "Fool of a woman."

"You asked, Nathan. I warned you that you would not like it," she reminded him, enjoying his discomfort a bit too much.

"No wonder you were cross."

"I was not cross!" she insisted in mock outrage, trying not to smile and failing.

He gave her a look. "You were very cross. I almost turned around right then."

"You did not. At any rate, anybody would be cross waiting that long in the frigid morning air," she argued, still smiling. "I can only imagine how grumbly you would be if you had to endure that."

"I would not be grumbly!"

"Oh, believe me, you would be," she promised, shaking her head. "You are a very grumbly man. And terribly pensive. You need to let some more light into your life, Nathan."

"I have light aplenty," he assured her, laughing in spite of himself. "I am very pleasant person when I am not in the company of someone who drives me to distraction." Now she let out a bark of laughter, and he grinned. "Besides, there is nothing wrong with being pensive. I find that reflection often brings better insight."

Moira took a bite out of an apple that seemed to appear out of thin air. "Well," she said around her rather large mouthful, "I find that reflection only serves to make me depressed, but perhaps that is only me and my flaws."

"Where did you get that?" he asked, feeling rather hungry himself, in spite of their having had a light breakfast not so long ago.

She grinned, one side of her face puffing out around her bite of apple. "The inn. I took the liberty of packing away some items to tide us over until we stop again. Would you like one?"

He nodded, amused by her minor thievery.

She reached into the satchel that hung on one side of her and tossed the apple to him, which he caught deftly. He took a bite out of it and cocked his head, looking at her. "You were right, you know."

"Of course, I was," she said immediately, which made him laugh. "But about what in particular this time?"

He grinned rather deviously, which he saw made her wary. "You do take rather large bites when eating an apple."

Her eyes widened slightly, but she was soon laughing with him. "I know I do," she moaned. "I can't help it. It seems the best way to eat them. Not very ladylike, to be sure, but…"

"No, not at all, but I agree with you."

She stilled, her eyes wide, her face suddenly devoid of laughter.

"What?" he asked, startled by the change in her. "Moira, what?"

"We… we agree on something?" she asked in a hushed voice, her expression very nearly horror-struck.

Nathan only had to wait a moment before Moira's face broke into a grin and she started to laugh, and, after realizing he had been had, he released the breath he'd been holding and joined her.

"You should have seen your face!" she cried, her cheeks flushing with laughter.

"You are terrible," he told her, shaking his head. "Absolutely dreadful."

"But a much better actress than you give me credit for," she pointed out. "Admit it, I had you convinced."

He shook his head. "Not even for a moment. I knew you had some sort of trick hidden about you, I just was not sure where it lay."

"Oh, please," she scoffed, taking another large bite of apple,

"You were petrified that you had said or done something wrong."

There was no way he was going to let her win this little game of hers. "If we agreed on something," he growled, "then I obviously did."

She threw her head back and laughed, all inhibitions gone. "True enough."

Nathan continued to chuckle, but he knew that he would never get the image of her laughing out of his mind. The way she had simply tossed back that mass of glorious hair and laughed, without restraint or delicacy, had been breathtaking, and not just because she was beautiful. It was simply her, just Moira, her very essence captured in that laugh. It was as though he had suddenly experienced his very first breath of fresh air, and was now wondering what it was he had been breathing all this time. She was so alive, and he wished he could be the same.

He had spent so long hiding from himself, from the world. Only his friends knew him, and even they did not know as much as they thought they did. His own family was in disarray, not knowing if any of the others were alive or dead. He used to be troubled by it all, by everything he saw in the army, by everything he had gone through. He had since learned that the best way to endure life's hardships was to feel nothing.

It was not until he had inherited the earldom that he had realized that in feeling nothing, he had become nothing. He did not want to be nothing. He now had tenants who depended on him, lands that were under his care, and people who genuinely needed him. He could no longer hide himself, and he did not wish to. That was what had brought the earldom down in the first place; his uncle had decided the best course was no course at all, and how many had suffered at that one decision?

Nathan was better than that. He would no longer allow himself to feel nothing but rejuvenating one's dormant heart was not as easily done as he would wish.

Perhaps this infuriating woman could help him find his way back to the living.

If she could not, then he was not certain anyone would be able to.

Chapter Six

"How did you discover that thing with the bird?"

Nathan blinked back the drowsiness that had overcome him and looked over at his companion, who had been surprisingly silent for some time. He had enjoyed the respite from thinking and reacting, and noticed that now the sun was nearing its zenith. They ought to think about stopping for a mid-day meal, if they wanted to have any sort of strength to press on for the night.

"Let's give the horses a rest and walk for a bit," he suggested, reigning in Mercury.

She shrugged and reigned Flora in. "Only if you will tell me the story."

"I will, I swear, but we can walk for a bit. I think my legs need it."

"Oh, well, for the sake of your legs, let's walk, by all means," she commented dryly, shifting in her saddle.

He dismounted and went over to help her, only to find that she had already made her own way down. "I could help you down from the horse, you know."

She gave him a quizzical look. "Why?"

"Because that is generally how things go," he said with infinite patience, or so it seemed to him anyway. "A gentleman assists a lady down from her horse."

"But that is assuming the lady in question requires assistance, which I don't. I fail to see why this matters."

"Of course you do," he muttered. "It's just proper, Moira. I know you can do it, but it would be ladylike to allow me to assist you."

She frowned up at him. "I thought I had made it clear that I care very little for what is ladylike."

He sighed in irritation and threw up his hands. "Forget it, of course, you are right. Get yourself off of the horse, open your own doors, and ride astride, I don't care. Would you like to lead in dancing as well?" He shook his head and moved back to Mercury, taking his reigns in hand, and beginning to walk away.

Moira hesitated only a moment, then she followed. "I have upset you," she commented.

"I am not upset, just frustrated." His voice was more than a touch sharp, but he was trying with all of his might to keep himself in check. If there was one thing he had learned about Moira, it was that, as prickly and feisty as she appeared, she was rather sensitive at heart.

"There's a difference?"

He closed his eyes and fought for control. "Yes, there is. Upset would involve anger. It would be due to something that had been done to offend me or something I had done myself. It would be far more disconcerting. I would be yelling."

"You look as if you would like to be."

He took in a would-be calming breath through his nose and let it out again slowly. "Frustration," he continued, completely ignoring her, "is different. It is agitation due to circumstances that are out of my control. I may become moody or snappish, but as it is not in my control, there would be no cause to be upset."

"So this is you exhibiting frustration."

"Yes."

"Because I wouldn't let you help me off of Flora?" she asked.

He sighed again, this time in resignation. "No, Moira, that is not it."

"What, then? I don't understand what should upset you, excuse me, *frustrate* you, about that."

He could not help the small tick of a smile that threatened. No, she probably did not. It made him wonder again just what sort of life she had led. She had no notion of niceties or decorum, and yet she held herself with such airs. He was unwillingly fascinated.

"That was simply an example. I have been trying to be a gentleman with you, showing the proper respect and honor for a lady, and either you do not understand or you do not wish me to be such a person. It is in my nature to act this way, far beyond habit now." There, that seemed to be clear enough.

"I haven't prevented you from anything. You can act in any manner that you choose, and quite freely at that."

Perhaps not.

"A gentleman helps a lady, whether she needs it or not," he told her, casting an impatient glance at her. "Giving her his arm to lead her across the street, or helping her out of a carriage, or off of a horse, or protecting her when the time arises. It is chivalrous and admirable and what is expected of a gentleman. You are not allowing me to do that."

"But that would put you above me," she protested, still looking confused. "That would imply that I need assistance, that I'm unable to do things for myself. It would make me appear weak."

"No, it wouldn't. It would merely show that you are letting me be a gentleman."

She shook her head. "Nathan, I want us to be equals in this. If I am capable enough to do something, why shouldn't I do it? Why does that have to be unladylike, just so a man can put himself above me?"

"Do I look like I want to set myself above you?" he cried, gesturing to himself. "I have no such designs, I know that we are equals. I accept it and rejoice in it. In fact, I think you are far above me, which is as it should be. But for God's sake, Moira, let me have a little dignity as a man!"

She continued to stare at him and he could see her mind whirling behind those eyes. "If I let you help me, only on occasion..." she stipulated with a warning finger.

He rolled his own and nodded. "Very well, on occasion, then."

She nodded in return. "Then you will be satisfied?"

He grunted. "More satisfied than I am now, but not entirely."

"That is the best I can do, Nathan. I am simply not ladylike and that is all there is to it."

He exhaled slowly, his eyes scanning her face. "It does not bother me if you don't wish to be a fine lady in all things," he said softly. "I know you want to be independent and strong, and I think that a noble thing. All I ask is that you try to let me be who I am, and that is a gentleman. At heart, and to the core. Can you allow me that?"

That troubled her, he could see, but she nodded slowly. "I can try, I suppose."

He continued to watch her for a moment, then cleared his throat. "Now, if I remember correctly, you wished to know how I came to discover that I could sneak up on a bird."

She turned to him with a grin. "Yes, indeed. I have been thinking it over, and I can't see how it can be done."

"Well, it's not easily accomplished, that is for certain," he told her, enjoying the opportunity to share something amusing from his past instead of fighting with her. "And it all started with my friend Colin, who prides himself on being rather mischievous and sly…"

Not much further down the road, they came to a small village with a coaching station, and they opted to stop there for a meal. Moira insisted on paying, which made Nathan grumble, but considering what she thought of his finances, he did not have much of a choice. The meal was rather hearty, but soon enough they decided to depart again. There was not much to be gained from this place, and they would certainly have better luck when they stopped for the evening. Proceeding out of the building, Nathan was shocked to find Moira standing beside Flora and looking at him expectantly.

"What is this?" he asked with a smile.

"I have decided to attempt to be ladylike," she said simply. "If for no other reason than to make you feel useful."

He laughed. "Well, my pride thanks you." He formed a lattice with his fingers and bent down slightly. "Set your foot upon my hands."

She did so, looking rather dubious.

"Oh, come now, Moira, how did you manage getting on a horse without help before?" he chided with a smile.

"There was a stool I stood upon," she said with a shrug. "It was very simple."

"So is this," he replied as he easily helped her onto Flora's back.

"Well," she said, looking a touch surprised, "so it is. That was very easily done, wasn't it?"

"Very," he agreed as he situated himself upon Mercury's back. "And not limiting to your independence?"

She shook her head. "Not a bit. Had I the fortune to be taller than I am, I would not have needed you at all."

He rolled his eyes and turned Mercury away from the station to continue down the road. "You have entirely missed the point, Moira."

"I have not!" she cried as she caught up. "You played the gentleman very well, thank you for helping me onto my horse. I have the ability to do it myself, but it was much faster and more expedient to have you assist. In the future, I will allow you to continue the same. Fair enough?"

He shook his head, chuckling to himself. "Fair enough. Now, I think there is something you can do for me."

"Oh dear. What is that?"

He grinned at her. "I think you need to prove to me that you can whistle like a man."

She blushed slightly, but smiled. "Flora won't like it."

He looked down at the horse, who appeared as though she would not care at all. "I don't think she will mind just once." He peered back to Moira. "Unless, of course, you were not being truthful and you can't whistle at all."

She narrowed her eyes at him, and he grinned mischievously at her. She shook her head and sighed, then placed her fingers in her mouth and let out the loudest, most piercing whistle he had ever heard in his entire life.

He laughed at her embarrassment, but more so at her skill. "Rather impressive, Moira," he said, clapping his hands and still chuckling. "I haven't heard any whistle as loud as that, from man or woman. How did you learn?"

"One of the neighbors taught me when I was a child," she said, smiling faintly. "He raised cattle and it was the only way to get them in at night. I was curious, so asked how he did it. He was more than pleased to teach me. My aunt was mortified."

"I bet she was," he said with a laugh. "She sounds as if a great many things mortified her."

"They did," Moira muttered darkly, not smiling any longer.

Nathan's urge to laugh had faded at her expression. Something had happened to this woman to cause such pain at a simple recollection. There was something deeper, and darker, at work here. He didn't know if she would ever want to open up about it. Not that he blamed her; he had enough horrors in his past to appreciate privacy. But he felt himself wanting to take away the hurt he sensed in her.

Suddenly, Moira turned to him, her face determined to look composed. "So you have told me about some of your friends so far. I know about Derek, who is secretly very amusing and is married to a woman that makes him unhappy, and Colin, who likes to pretend that he is clever and charming and considers himself the leader. There were two other men with you. Who are they?"

Nathan smiled at her attempt to change the subject, but he was more than happy to discuss his friends. "The first is Geoffrey. He is one of the most genuinely nice persons I have ever met, but don't be deceived by it. He has a wicked sense of timing and is actually quite devious, but no one suspects him as he appears to be so very innocent."

"Geoffrey: very nice, but devious and not as innocent as he looks," she repeated as if committing it to memory.

He chuckled, but did not comment. "Then there is Duncan. He is an oaf, but a surprisingly well-dressed one. And the kindest oaf there ever was."

Moira snickered. "Now what in heaven's name does *that*

mean?"

Nathan smirked fondly. "Duncan takes a great deal of pride in his appearance. It makes him a little bit of a dandy, but he would deny that emphatically. He declares it is merely an interest in looking his best at all times. But he is more than willing to help any soul he comes across however he is dressed at the time, whether they be a carriage stuck in the mud or a lost child." As a matter of fact, Nathan had seen him do both of those things, and on both occasions he was quite fashionably dressed.

"So how is he an oaf?" Moira asked, confused.

Nathan gave her a look. "Have you ever seen a raging bull?"

"Of course."

He nodded. "That is what Duncan looks like."

Now she laughed out loud, and Nathan did as well.

"You cannot ever tell them this is how I describe them," he warned her, still chuckling. "They would flay me alive and coat me in honey."

"Oh, I never shall, if ever I meet them," she promised. Then she grinned. "Unless I can see no other way to blackmail you."

"Why would you want to do that?"

She shrugged. "You never know. A girl has got to be prepared for all eventualities."

Nathan shook his head, still smiling. "I shouldn't be surprised, I know, but I am."

"That may be the most concise, yet correct, estimation of my character I have heard yet," Moira quipped, looking mildly impressed and more than a little proud.

"What of your friends?" Nathan asked, feeling rather curious about the adventures of young Moira.

Her smile faded and she shrugged. "I have none."

That took him completely by surprise, and he knew he could not hide it. "Surely you have some friends. You must have some from when you were a child, at the very least."

She shook her head, unwilling to meet his eyes. "Charles was the only person near my own age who would have conversation with me beyond what is polite. I came to live with my aunt when I was eight years old and she was not exactly well liked in the village.

It was rare for us to leave our own garden. And when we did, it was difficult for me to relate with the other children, and none seemed anxious to try. It was… a lonely time for me."

Nathan could not think of anything to say. No wonder she had been so keen to make friends with him when he had offered, and no wonder she had been so drawn to Charles Allenford.

"What happened to you, Moira?" he murmured, half hoping she wouldn't hear him.

She would not meet his eyes. "Pass," she whispered.

Despite his anxieties, Nathan left the matter alone. But he watched Moira carefully until the shadows were gone once more.

"I cannot believe you are making me wear a bonnet."

Nathan tried not to laugh, he really did, but Moira's morose tone, combined with the triviality of the topic and the sudden downpour of rain made for quite the humorous situation. He could not hide the laughter that shook his frame as he tried to keep quiet about it, and received a vicious glare from his riding companion.

"And now you are laughing at me!" she accused in indignation. She huffed and adjusted herself in the saddle. "Some husband you are," she muttered under her breath.

Nathan grinned, unable to help himself. "Come now, Moira, we are almost to the inn and you did say that it would be my turn to speak for us. Mr. and Mrs. Granger have come a very long way, and Mr. Granger is the type of man whose wife wears a bonnet in the rain."

"I do not care for this Mr. Granger at all."

"You had better forget that in the next few minutes," he said with no small amount of warning in his smile, "or we will both be out of a place to sleep tonight."

She made a small noise of protest but said nothing further.

They arrived at the small, but comfortable looking inn and Nathan was quick to dismount and head over to Moira. She glared daggers at him, but at his look, she allowed him to help her down. He set his hands on her tiny waist and lifted her down, still surprised by how light she was. And by the warmth he felt under his fingertips. Quickly, he removed his hands and turned, taking hold of her arm and placing a hand at the small of her back.

"Now be quiet and look ill," he hissed in her ear.

She glared at him, but nodded once.

He patted her on the back. "Good girl."

He could almost hear her bite her tongue. He forced himself not to smile at that. She very grudgingly let him lead her into the inn. The room was maybe half full and the group was rather quiet, in stark contrast to their lodgings from the night before.

"Excuse me," Nathan said pleasantly to the man behind a sturdy looking desk. "Are there rooms available for the night?"

"Why, yes, sir, there are," the man replied with a warm smile. "Would you and your lady like to wait out the rain here?"

"Yes, we were hoping to," Nathan said, pouring as much relief into his tone as he could muster. Then he stepped closer to the man and whispered, "My wife Celia is in delicate health, sir, and the rain does not help matters. Is there any way we can get a quiet room? Perhaps away from the rest?"

Moira was going to throttle him later, he could see it in her face, but for now, she merely coughed weakly into her handkerchief and looked miserable. She played the sickly wife rather well, he thought. The innkeeper looked her over with concern, and nodded swiftly.

"Of course, Mr.…?"

"Granger."

"Yes, Mr. Granger, I will see what we can do. Let me call for my wife, and see if she can see Mrs. Granger situated with a warm bath and some fresh clothing while we have a lad bring in your bags." He waved to a maid. "Lucy, go and get Mrs. Fletcher."

The girl nodded and ran off, and Moira brightened considerably at the mention of a bath.

"Thank you, Mr. Fletcher, that is too generous," Nathan said with a warm smile. He turned to Moira with a raised brow, and suddenly feared she would kick him in his shins. She handed him some coins from her purse and his eyes widened as he looked down at them. It was too much, nearly extravagant for such an establishment. His eyes met hers, questions written in them. She nodded and he shrugged, then handed them over to Fletcher.

"You let your wife keep the purse, Mr. Granger?" Fletcher said with a smile.

Nathan chuckled good-naturedly. "'Tis she who lets me spend it, Mr. Fletcher."

Fletcher laughed. "Well said, Mr. Granger, well said indeed. Ah, here is Mrs. Fletcher now."

A plump woman with a kind smile approached, as she wiped her hands on the apron she wore, and tsked at Moira's drenched and ill-looking state. "Oh, you poor dear! Let me get you set up properly with a bath and some fresh clothes. Mr. Fletcher will make sure some food is sent up to you."

Moira nodded meekly, even as her stomach rumbled.

"The room does face the stables, I am afraid, Mr. Granger," Fletcher said with a worried expression. "The smell, I fear, might…"

"Not to worry, Mr. Fletcher, that will be more than adequate."

"My lads will bring the bags up straightaway, sir."

"Thank you very much," Nathan said with a nod.

Moira tugged on his sleeve and, in a weak, weary sounding voice that was not like hers at all, whispered, "Fred! Fred!"

He nearly burst out laughing, but managed to keep a straight face as he leaned down to her. "What, my love?"

She put her lips near his ears and hissed, "If you let them bring me nothing but broth, I can assure you that a live flaying and being covered with honey will be the very least of your concerns."

He swallowed back another laugh, but nodded. "As you wish, my love. I will see you later."

She gave him another fierce warning with her eyes, and then allowed Mrs. Fletcher to take her up to their room.

Nathan turned to Fletcher. "I think a tray should be sent up to her, Mr. Fletcher, when she has finished her bath. But she does not handle broth well, so perhaps something hearty? I worry for her constitution, and anything of substance would do her some good, I should think."

"Of course, Mr. Granger, of course," Fletcher said, nearly

stumbling over himself in an effort to be of use. "And now would you please let me get you a drink, sir? Something to warm your bones?"

"That would be excellent, thank you, Fletcher. And will someone see to our horses?"

"Of course, Mr. Granger," Fletcher told him, bowing slightly.

Nathan nodded in approval. "I thank you, Fletcher. It is so rare to find such excellent service and comfort." A bit over the top, but not untrue.

Fletcher grinned so wide Nathan was afraid his face would crack under the strain. "Thank you, Mr. Granger, that is such a comfort to me. May I have some food brought to you? And would you care for a seat near the fire? We have a few other patrons staying with us this evening, many of them very pleasant indeed. You can be assured of some fine company."

Now that was what Nathan was looking for. Time to spin the Granger's story a little bit deeper.

"I confess, I had hoped for some. You see, Fletcher, my wife and I are traveling in search of her brother. She has not heard from him in some time, and they were so very close. She is making herself sick with worry over him." Moira was going to kill him if she found out what he was saying, but if he could get some good information on Charles' possible whereabouts, he might have something to placate her with.

"Last we heard, he had been in this area," he continued, speaking in a low, but earnest voice. "Do you think that some of these good people might be able to assist us?"

Fletcher's eyes widened and he nodded repeatedly. "Oh, I am sure they could, sir, I am sure they could. Come, let me introduce you to them. Such fine men and their manners are so engaging, sir, I feel certain that they will be most obliging."

Nathan smiled to himself as he allowed the still-talking Fletcher to lead him towards the small group of men by the fire. Regardless as to the outcome of his search for information tonight, they were at least certain to be well treated and cared for.

And he was fairly positive that was one more thing that he and Moira could agree on.

Chapter Seven

"What in the name of all that is holy are you wearing?"

Moira turned at Nathan's shocked and very nearly screeching voice. She looked down at herself, then back up at him. "A shirt and breeches. Why?" She tugged the cap on her head into place and put her hands on her hips, staring at him with concern.

He could not manage to close his mouth, and staring at her seemed quite rude, so he just covered his face with one hand. "Why are you wearing a shirt and breeches, Moira?" he asked from behind his hand, his voice muffled.

"I should think that obvious," she said with a snort. "I do not think the patrons, nor the Fletchers, would approve of a woman in a skirt climbing out of their window and sleeping in their stables."

Now Nathan could not ignore her indecent clothing. He removed his hand and stared at her in horror. "What?"

"I am sleeping in the stables tonight," she said slowly, as if he were the sick creature in the marriage and not she. She gave him a bemused smile as she picked up the sheet rope she had made.

"No, you are not!" he said coming towards her.

"Yes, I am," she argued, as she danced out of his way and up onto the windowsill, rope in hand.

"Moira, be reasonable!" he protested as he watched her, more than a little nervous about her being on that ledge, and more than a little disturbed at her wardrobe, and even more than a little outraged by her statement.

"I am being reasonable, Nathan," she said calmly as she opened the window and leaned out, tugging slightly on the sheet rope to test it.

"This is the furthest thing from reasonable," Nathan said coming over and taking hold of the rope. "This is the definition of lunacy."

"Poor Mr. Granger has a lunatic wife," she pitied with a smile. "What will he do?" She started to ease her way down.

"Moira, please," Nathan begged, everything in him knowing this was beyond wrong.

She gave him a look. "Nathan. Today you said you accept that we are equals. Equals take turns. You slept in the stable last night, I shall do so tonight. I have no qualms about this, so I do not see why you do."

"You don't have qualms about anything," he muttered, running a hand through his hair. "Moira, it is not proper!"

Her look turned even more severe, if that were possible. "Surely we have argued on *that* topic enough for one day. I have left you some stew and bread, if you are hungry. I will be back up in the morning, so you may leave the rope as it is. No one will see it back here, and the rain has stopped."

"Moira..."

"Good night, Nathan!" And without another glance up at him, she very skillfully made her way to the ground and headed for the stables.

Nathan watched her go in anguish. How could he possibly let her sleep in the dirty, dank stables and hay while he enjoyed the comfort of a room and a bed? It went against every principle that he held close to him. But how could he fight a woman who was so infuriatingly determined to do exactly what she wanted when she wanted and without any consideration for the inconvenience of others?

He ran a hand through his hair and turned away from the window, agitated and anxious. What if she was discovered in there?

What if something happened to her? What if their whole scheme was found out because they were no longer convincing as husband and wife? What if…

He had to stop with the "what if" scenarios or he was going to drive himself mad. Moira would be fine. She was clever enough to avoid discovery; she was indomitable enough that anyone who may come across her and wish her harm would flee in the face of her wrath. She would be fine for one night.

He knew all of this was true, but it only served to make him feel guiltier than he already did. He moved to the window again, and shut it only slightly, keeping it open enough so that he could hear if anyone would shout for help. He would be able to get to her quickly if she needed him, and that, at least, was a comfort.

He looked around the room for some sort of distraction, anything to take his mind off of the woman that was surely going to be the death of him and her incredible ability for conceiving foolhardy ideas. He saw her dress from the day spread out before the fire, no doubt nearly dry already, and the hated bonnet on the floor next to it, along with her jacket. Next to them was a neatly folded nightgown, no doubt the best the Fletchers had to offer. That was apparently not to be used tonight.

Involuntarily, his thoughts went back to the extraordinary ensemble Moira had chosen to don that evening. He had to swallow in spite of himself at the memory of how her legs looked in those breeches. They had not been a tight fit, thankfully, but even so, he had never imagined how long and trim her legs would actually be. He had not thought of her legs at all before now, and it seemed a perfectly good waste of human creation to hide them.

"Steady there, Nate," he muttered, desperately trying to clear those less than appropriate thoughts from his mind. Moira deserved better than his gawking. Then again, she did bring it upon herself. "Oh, now really," he scolded aloud, "it's not as though she wore them so you could stare like an idiot."

That was true, but even so, he was a man.

"I am a gentleman," he reminded himself aloud as he paced a bit.

Gentleman or not, they were some exceptionally fine legs…

"I'm a gentleman, I'm a gentleman, I'm a gentleman," he mumbled over and over, pacing and rubbing his hands through his hair in agitation. This was getting entirely out of hand. "I am a bloody gentleman!" he finally bellowed, his voice ringing off of the walls.

Faintly, he heard from somewhere else in the building, "Well, all right, then! Don't get so excited!"

He growled in frustration and moved quickly around the room. Excited, that was a good way to put it. He was too excitable, he needed to be controlled. After all, Moira was not something to stare at; she was a curse sent from all of his enemies past, present, and future to torment, agitate, and infuriate him. She tested his patience, his resolve, and his character, and he did not know how long he could last under these circumstances. There was only so much a man could be expected to endure before enough was enough!

Rationality soon swept over him as he sat down moodily in a chair before the fire. There would be no giving up, there would be no abandonment, and there would be no overpowering her opinions and claiming authority over her. She had spirit, that much was evident, but it was fragile, much more so than she probably thought. Any overbearing actions on his part would send her storming off on her own. And he would no longer be able to help her. She would be closed off to him forever. He could not do that to her.

And so he would just have to endure her maddening traits, wearing breeches and sleeping in stables now being added to the ever-growing list.

He groaned and pushed himself out of the chair. There was a pitcher and bowl of water in the corner, and he took the chance to splash some of the cool water on his face. If Moira was so determined to be equals, he would let her sleep in stables. He would act as though he had gotten over it, pretend as though he did not care what she did. He could fight down his desire to shake her, though it was becoming a more tempting thought by the minute. She could think that she had everything in control, that would not trouble him.

But so help him, if at some future day, someone said "There

goes the appalling Earl of Beverton, who once let a woman sleep out in the stables while he himself took the only bed," he would hunt down Moira and, married or not, would put her over his knee and give her a paddling that would surely send him to prison.

He stripped off his shirt and loosened his trousers, then sat on the bed and removed his boots. Well, if Moira was the least bit cross tomorrow morning, he would be only too happy to remind her just whose idea it had been for her to sleep out there.

It would serve the hellion right.

Moira woke refreshed and cheerful the next morning, and stretched amidst the hay, rolling a bit. She was quite used to sleeping in such conditions, as she enjoyed sleeping in the fresh hay of her neighbor's barn on a regular basis. If one knew how to make the accommodations comfortable, one could get a perfectly good night's sleep in such.

She sat up and pulled at some stray pieces of straw that had embedded themselves in her hair, wondering if Nathan had gotten over his shock. She grinned at the image of his expression last night. She wondered which had surprised him more: her outfit, or her determination to sleep in the stables. Whichever it was, he would have to get over it.

She picked up her blanket and shook it out, sending bits of hay flying off in every direction, which made her giggle, for some reason. Then she tucked it under her arm and walked over to the inn, where her sheet rope could still be seen hanging from the window. It was still fairly early, so she did not expect that many of the patrons would be stirring as yet. She did hope Nathan would be, however. It would be a trifle awkward to be sneaking back into their room while he was still asleep.

At least he had kept the window partially ajar. She had fully expected him to shut it in protest of her actions. That would have made things difficult, but not impossible.

It just went to show what a decent man Nathan was, and reaffirmed to her once again that she had made the right choice in choosing him as her travel companion.

She took hold of the sheet rope and began to climb, thankful that the brick of the building was rough enough for her to get a decent grip with her boots. They were not exactly designed for such activity, and it would be far too easy to slip if she were not careful.

She reached the window and opened it the rest of the way, then peeked at the bed. Sure enough, it was empty. She grinned and hauled herself into the room, landing rather inelegantly on the floor, which made her snort in laughter again. She quickly stood and pulled the sheet rope in. She could unknot it later, right now she was famished.

She turned towards the fire and let out a shriek that she immediately covered with her hand.

Nathan stood by the mirror and wash bin staring at her, the lower half of his face covered with shaving soap, and entirely shirtless. Entirely.

"Good morning," he said staring at her, his eyes amused, and a small, almost imperceptible half-smile quirking on one side of his mouth beneath the soap.

"Good morning," she managed from behind her hand.

"I take it from your laughter that you slept well, regardless of the hay?" he asked, his voice innocent as if the fact that he was standing before her half naked was nothing.

She nodded quickly, her mouth still covered.

"That is good. Now, if you do not mind, I should like to finish my shave."

She nodded once more slowly, and he turned back to the mirror, but not before she caught the flash of a grin that crossed his face.

Goodness sakes, the man had quite a build. She had once thought him ordinary looking? Was she *blind*? She doubted a sculptor could have done a more complete job on him. She should have known he would have been well formed, and had wondered about it several times, but she should not have thought about it at all. She should not have even contemplated anything of the sort with him. And she most definitely should *not* be staring at his back in such an outré fashion, particularly not when he could very plainly see her in the mirror, should he have chosen to, which she suspected he did. She would have done if she were him.

She gave a very accurate quarter turn and sat down on the bed, facing the window, and away from him. She could feel her cheeks flaming and the burn from them helped to bring some sense to her terribly addled brain. He was merely a man who kept himself in good condition. There were many such in England, she knew. Why, some of her own farming neighbors had worked without shirts on occasion and they were exceptionally well formed. It could not be shocking that Nathan, who had, after all, served in the army, would be so as well.

Even so, she could not help but to sneak the occasional peek back at him as he shaved. If he noticed, he did not comment on it, which she was grateful for. She could only take so much mortification in one morning. She did take note of a rather dangerous looking scar below his right shoulder. It was faded and the skin stretched, but she could only imagine the damage the original wound had caused. Had he a similar scar in the front? She couldn't remember; her brain had been slightly occupied when he had been facing her so. Where had he received such a scar? What hand had caused it?

Before she could think more on it, he turned towards her, his face now devoid of soap. "Well, if you have quite recovered yourself, Mrs. Granger, I think you had better get yourself out of those fetching breeches of yours and into a dress. We would not wish to scandalize our fine hosts, now, would we?"

She almost shook her head stupidly in response, but caught herself. Oh, now, wait a minute. Who said that he got to be all superior this morning? He had been just as startled by her appearance last night as she had been by his this morning, except he had words and she did not. That was changing now.

She smiled sweetly at him. "I rather like my *fetching* breeches, but if you think it best, Mr. Granger, I will certainly change out of them. But I do believe you ought to cover your… self as well. We would not want poor Mrs. Fletcher to faint away before breakfast, now, would we?"

Nathan's eyes narrowed as he stared at her. "Of course not. But

I would not have been so indecently dressed had I known I would be receiving visitors this early."

"But a wife is no visitor, Mr. Granger," Moira said coyly, standing from the bed and moving over towards her dress.

"A wife does not sleep in the stables either," he pointed out, watching her warily.

She shrugged, and picked up her dress, shaking it out. "If the wife does not object to sleeping in stables, and can sleep rather well in them, then why should the husband complain? Surely he would appreciate the benefit of a night well spent in comfort without a wife to inconvenience him."

"Because the husband *cannot* sleep well knowing that the wife is out in a cold, dank stable with the animals, open and exposed to all elements and God knows what else, when she should be safe and warm inside!" he shouted, as he strode over until he was directly in front of her.

She looked up at him, tilting her head slightly. "You did not sleep well?"

He released a gust of air and his voice took on a very forced calm. "No. I hardly slept at all."

"That is a pity," she said softly, her eyes flicking down to the scar on his chest. "I slept very well indeed." Her eyes shot back up to his and she quirked a brow at him.

His eyes held hers for a moment, then he quickly turned from her. He picked his shirt up from off of the floor and dropped it over his head. "Well, hurrah for you, then, Moira," he said as he began tucking the ends of his shirt into his trousers. "As I said, I did not, so forgive me if I am not so cheerful. If you have no objections, I will go and see what our hosts have prepared for breakfast. Perhaps you will get back into whatever your character was before coming down yourself?"

She folded her arms and glared at him. "I know my character, Nathan, as do you. She was your creation, after all."

"Yes," he retorted, sitting down to put his boots on, "and because of that, you received a hot bath and some decent food, but I do not hear you being grateful for any of it. All you could do was sneak off to the stables." The last of his words came out in a grumble, and he shook his head.

Moira could see the agitation from last night was still rampant in Nathan. What a poor man to have to deal with her and her eccentricities while trying to be proper. She heaved a sigh and walked over to him, taking hold of the bedpost near him. "You are right. Thank you for encouraging them to take care of me so well, even if she did fuss overly much. And the food was excellent. I wish we could have equal quality at all of our stops."

Nathan set his now booted feet down and looked up at her. He offered her a reluctant smile and stood. "You are welcome. I am sorry that I made you sound so very ill."

She returned his smile and leaned her head against the hand on the bedpost. "I deserved that one. Margaret was dreadful. Celia is a fair compensation."

He chuckled and leaned on the post himself. "Do you think we will ever get through a night without fighting?"

"Hmm," she mused, looking up at him, "probably not. Perhaps that should be our task tonight. But then, it might make for a very dull evening."

He grinned at her. "You may be right. Whatever would we do?"

For a moment, they just smiled at each other, not feeling any need to speak. An odd sort of pleasant tension filled the room, and the air about them suddenly seemed a bit thinner.

A bell sounded downstairs, and they sprang apart as if burned.

"I should change," Moira hastily said, backing away.

"Yes, of course," Nathan answered, moving for the door, "and I should get downstairs and see what food there is."

"I will join you shortly."

He nodded and left the room quickly, not looking back at her.

Moira took a deep breath from within the room and changed as quickly as she could. Fighting with Nathan always left her with a strange feeling of exhilaration, but what had happened just then… That moment when the fight had been forgotten and they had been simply been Nathan and Moira, with no hurts or worries to plague them.

It had been a rush of feelings she was not prepared for, but she was not certain she could identify any of the emotions involved.

She had to push all of that out of her mind now. She had to become Celia Granger again. Her nose wrinkled up at the name, but there was not time to think up a better one. She pulled the cap from off of her head and brushed her hair out as best as she could, then plaited and pinned it up neatly. Her cheeks still looked too rosy for an ill woman with delicate health. She moved to the wash bin and splashed her face with some of the cool water, wishing that Nathan had not made her out to be quite so ill as he had.

She looked at her reflection for a long moment, her thoughts awhirl. She took a few steadying breaths, then reached for the cursed bonnet on the floor and headed for the door.

It was only a matter of minutes before Moira joined Nathan in the main room of the inn, looking very proper and demure in her dress and bonnet. From all appearances, it looked as though Mrs. Granger had received some truly good care during their stay. Her eyes were bright, her cheeks ever so slightly tinged with color, and her smile warm. Nathan was relieved that her good mood was going to continue on. She played at shyness as she took the seat across from him, but when she met his eyes, he saw her amusement in them.

He winked at her and her small smile flickered into something bigger for only a brief moment, and then she was back as the docile Celia.

"My dear Mrs. Granger!" Mrs. Fletcher's voice cried out as she appeared as if out of nowhere.

Moira's smile held steady, much to her credit. "Mrs. Fletcher."

"Oh, my dear girl, you look so refreshed this morning!" Mrs. Fletcher cried, taking her hands. "It must have been the tea that I brought you! That was it, was it not?"

"It may have been," Moira allowed in a very small voice, but with a gentle turn of her smile. "I am feeling much better this morning, and it is all thanks to you and your excellent care."

Nathan tried not to laugh as he started on his meal, but when he received a sharp kick to his shins, he sobered. "Yes, I cannot thank you enough, Mrs. Fletcher. My Celia has not looked this well in some time."

"Oh," the woman fluttered, placing a hand to her chest, "I am only too eager to help where I can. Now do let me pack you a little something for later. You cannot search for your dear brother without the proper sustenance!"

"Oh, you are too good, Mrs. Fletcher," Moira said in a very grateful sounding voice, but Nathan caught the tick of her lips that indicated she was trying not to laugh.

"Not at all, not at all," she tittered as she went off in search of some food for her new favorite patron.

"Well played, my dear," Nathan murmured as he took a drink. "You are becoming quite the actress."

"Oh, you have no idea," she responded, taking a bite of her food. "That tea she made me drink tasted very much like how I imagined grass tastes."

He chortled into his own meal and swallowed quickly as to avoid choking. "Well, you are a good sport for going along with her."

She shrugged. "She is kind hearted and I cannot fault her intentions. What about you? Shouldn't Mr. Fletcher be seeking you out to volley you with his desires to serve?"

He grimaced, and shook his head. "I have already seen good Mr. Fletcher this morning, and he has other patrons he has now moved on to. But a speedy departure once we have our parcel of food might be advisable. They might bring you more tea to keep up your constitution."

"Tossing that tea off of the Tower of London would keep up my constitution much more than drinking it would," she muttered darkly, making him laugh again.

"Do you know, Mrs. Granger, I think you are becoming quite vivacious," he commented, leaning back in his seat. "Perhaps we should stay here for a few days and see if we can't get you back to robust."

The look Moira give him would have frozen an entire company of soldiers in their tracks.

He chuckled and held up his hands in surrender. "Very well, then, we'll go on. Let's just finish eating and then take our leave."

They did so speedily, for the Fletchers looked as though they were about to descend upon them once more. They took their leave as fast as they could manage, which was not very fast considering their hosts, but once they had the parcel in hand, they were able to convince the Fletchers that they really had to be going. Nathan cast one last look at their table to be sure they had collected all of their belongings, and noticed a sum of money on the table that he had not placed there. He looked to Moira, who was not paying any attention to him at all as she started towards the horses. Again she had paid for everything, and paid generously. He had questioned last night when she had simply given him the coins for their stay, but she had insisted. To now have more money to give to the same place was odd.

Not that he was disapproving, for he thought they certainly deserved some additional compensation. But if they were going to keep on this way, he was not sure how much she would be able to afford to give out and still have enough for his promised pay.

He had no intention of taking any money from her, regardless of what she thought. He had no need for it, and she would need all of the funds she could once they found her betrothed.

He did not understand why she was so determined to pay, or how she was able to do so without worry.

But he was determined to find out, if for no other reason than to assure himself that she was not putting herself into financial ruins for this missing fellow of hers that was, more than likely, not willing to do the same for her.

And if Nathan needed to help financially to make sure that she did not, then he would do so, never mind his own attempts at privacy.

Moira was worth it.

Chapter Eight

"Might I ask you a rather personal question?" Moira asked when they had been riding for a while.

Nathan looked very surprised, but not at all hesitant. "Of course."

"I don't want to pry," she told him earnestly, praying she would not offend.

He smiled. "If you are, I will tell you, or else I will pass on the question."

She nodded, then bit her lip in hesitation. It was a terrible habit, but she tended to do so whenever she was nervous or uncertain. Her aunt had tried to forbid her from doing it, but she had not been successful. Someday, she supposed, she would wind up gnawing her lip quite off. But there was nothing for it.

"When you were… well, when I happened upon you suddenly this morning," she corrected with a slight blush. She had recollected the memory quite often, but that little fact would remain her secret.

He waved off her embarrassment, but said nothing.

"I noticed that you have a scar on your back and chest that appear to be from the same wound. If it is not too personal, would you tell me how you got them?"

Nathan sighed and hesitated, and Moira could see the internal struggle that was waging in him. His expression was one of anxiety and of pain, his brow furrowed.

"Is it really so painful to talk about?" she asked quietly as she watched him.

"Not painful," he said slowly, "just not very pleasant."

"If you want to pass, Nathan, you can." He owed her no explanation, and she should never have asked.

He shook his head, as if suddenly deciding. "No. No, I will share it. But I warn you, it's not a very good story."

"With a scar that looks like that, I hardly expected it to be," she told him with what she hoped was understanding.

"I was nineteen when I joined the army," he began. "I was mad with the glory of it all. I had lived a very dull life up to that point, or so I thought, and the idea of being in that uniform, of battling for King and country, sweating and fighting and sacrificing on the field of battle, was all I could think about. Of course, once in the army I learned that there were very few battles, if one was doing the job right…" He trailed off and shrugged. "It was not as glamorous as I had dreamed."

"But safe," Moira murmured almost to herself.

He nodded. "I did not understand the fortune that was ours. But after two years, it was time for battle and we were not ready. I had a few men under my command, but they were boys, really. Many could not even manage to fire their guns properly. I was terrified that I would lead them into something from which they would never return."

"A legitimate concern, I think," Moira soothed with a smile

He did not return it. Suddenly it occurred to Moira that the worst was yet to come. "I was… called away for a time… and when I returned, I found my men improved in battle essentials. At last, we would be able to be a proper force for the army. The day finally came when we could face battle, and we were ready. But our foes were numerous, much more than we had anticipated, more than even the reports had indicated. We were completely outnumbered. Looking back on it now, we should have retreated, waited for reinforcements. But there was no thought in my head but to attack. We would not turn from our duty. I would not abandon my responsibility."

Moira listened carefully, a feeling of dread welling up in her. It was as though Nathan were back in those harried moments before the battle, and she was not here at all. His voice was distant, his eyes unfocused. Half of her wished that she would make him stop, but the other half silently urged him on.

"I turned to my men," he continued in the same tone, "and gave my orders. They knew that my orders were to be obeyed without question; it is the nature of the army. But when I sounded the call, none moved. My highly trained and dedicated soldiers would not do it. They had talked boldly of the brave actions they would perform when called upon when they were safe around their campfires or boasting to young ladies infatuated with nothing more than the regimentals on their back, but when faced with an opportunity to prove themselves, they would not. I was enraged."

She could only imagine. If there was one thing about Nathan Hammond that she knew well, it was his high opinion of duty. The idea that an entire company of men refused to do theirs would have offended him beyond reckoning.

"I called them all cowards and a disgrace to the banner they held so proudly. I said that if I could not have men that would do their duty and put the good of others before themselves, then I would go before them at the expense of my own life, as was the call of a soldier in His Majesty's army. I turned from them and went to my horse."

Moira's mouth gaped as he spoke, never imagining that this was what had happened. Surely he did not… *surely* he would not have…

"And then I sounded the call once more, and rode towards our enemy. On my own."

A gasp of horror passed Moira's lips before she could stop it, and she brought a hand up to cover her mouth, but Nathan paid her no heed. "They didn't follow you?" she asked, wondering if he would even hear her.

He shook his head in response. "Not at first. I believe they stood there for a moment, unable to believe what a stupid thing I had done. But the moment the first shots were fired, they abandoned their fear and charged after me. I suppose I ought to be grateful that they felt any sort of attachment to me at all. It would have been many bullets in me as opposed to only one otherwise. At the time, however, I would not have cared. The moment the bullet shot through my chest, I felt justified in my action. I had done my duty and paid the price for it as well. But once the fire spread through me and I fell to the ground, I realized what a fool I had been, and instantly I mourned the lives I knew I would lose." He shook his head slowly and exhaled. "And then I lost consciousness and woke up some days later at a camp in Bedford where surgeons had been tending to me night and day. They should not have fought so hard for someone so foolish."

"How many lives were lost?" she whispered.

He smiled grimly. "Only two. One was a hardened veteran whose heart gave out moments after battle, and the other was a fool who rushed out to defend me before being fully recovered from illness. Apparently, our company's incomprehensible actions terrified the enemy and they feared our strength would overwhelm them." He snorted softly in derision. "It was a lucky chance that they were. Disaster would have been inevitable, but on our side alone. Our commanding officers were so impressed with our astonishing victory that they gave me a commission and honored the entire company."

"Nathan…" Moira murmured in an almost breathless manner. Such pain and depth of regret was unexpected, and his determination to run himself down was disconcerting for her, knowing what a strong man he was at all other times.

He either did not hear her or was simply ignoring her, for he went on. "My wound was grave enough to prevent me from taking command in such an active role again. I didn't mind, I was hardly in a position to lead anyone. But I didn't want to resign my commission. I had no prospects outside of the army, no hope of anything else to do in my life. I was therefore to be used to search out companies and soldiers that had either gone missing or had not been heard from. I was a reckless rider with a drive that was well suited for the hunt." He finally looked at her, his eyes hard and his jaw tight. "That is how I came across your Mr. Carpenter and several others at times. I was able to track them down and… *convince* them to return to their regiment. I became well known for it, but it did not endear me to the men I found under those circumstances. It was late last spring, almost six years after receiving my wound, when I decided that enough was enough, and I left the army."

"No wonder you wished to remain hidden," she murmured faintly.

He offered her a stiff smile. "So that is the rather extended story of my scar, Moira. As I said, not a very pleasant tale."

"What could possibly have led you to do something like that?" she asked, utterly baffled still at his daring actions.

Instantly, his expression shuttered and his eyes darkened. "Pass," he muttered, looking away.

It was one word, just one simple word, and one that she herself had insisted upon and had used, but that one word spoke volumes. What could be worse than what he had already shared?

"Does it still hurt?" she asked in small voice, determined to keep him talking, if at all possible. "Your scar, I mean."

"No."

Moira bit her lip again, wishing she had never asked about any of it.

No doubt Nathan was very much looking forward to returning to his former life of privacy, away from annoying women and invasive questions that he had been more than obliging enough to answer.

But Moira could not help but admit, if only to herself, that she thought more of him now that she knew him better than she could have possibly imagined she would. And for that alone, she could not regret her actions.

The silence dragged on and on, and in it Nathan found only painful reminders of the past and the knowledge that he was a fool. Neither one of those things would make Moira very comfortable, should she have known, and he had had quite enough of it.

"Can we talk of something else, please?" he asked softly with a sigh.

Moira peered up at him from beneath her long lashes, biting her lip. "Would you rather I be silent? I have forced you to talk quite enough for one day, so I would more than understand if you would care for some peace."

He surprised himself by smiling. "No, as a matter of fact, I would not care for silence. I don't want to reflect any more today."

She returned his smile with a bright one of her own, and his spirits lifted at the sight of it. "Well, in *that* case…"

"Oh, good heavens," he moaned in mock-agony, "what have I just done?"

She frowned at him. "Hush, you. I have one simple question."

He raised a brow. "And that is?"

She made a face. "Do I really have to wear a bonnet to be proper?"

He chuckled, more amused than he thought he would be. "Yes, Moira. You are quite shocking without it."

"I shock everybody, that has nothing to do with my headwear."

His chuckles turned into full laughs and it took him a moment to recover.

"Surely country rules are not so stringent," Moira added, still looking discontented. "I can be more casual here, yes?"

He was not going to answer that particular question, as her definition of casual worried him slightly. "You only really have to wear them in London, I suppose. That is where fashion and propriety matter the most."

She suddenly looked a little whimsical. "I don't remember London." She shrugged one shoulder. "It would be nice to see it with adult eyes and appreciate it properly."

"I will take you," he said instantly, offering her a smile. He would enjoy taking her about the city, showing her the sights that had fascinated him in his youth, and letting her experience the wonders that could be had there.

She looked up at him sadly. "When would we be able to do that, Nathan?"

That shook him out of his pleasant imaginations. She was correct. They were traveling to find her betrothed so that she could be married and start the life she had been waiting years for. They would never be free to associate outside of public settings. He would never be able to show her London or any other place he might want to.

He knew all of this, and had known it, but even so, the recollection of it made him sad.

"Perhaps you are right," he said quietly, not bothering to hide the fact that he was disappointed. "But you must go back at some point, you know. You would have a wonderful time there."

"Yes," she murmured, "I'm sure I would."

Her downtrodden expression only served to add to his own sense of regret. It was time for a subject change. "Might I ask you a question now?"

She smiled at him and nodded. "If you would like."

"I was just wondering," he began, hoping she would be as open with him as he had just been with her, "why you are so insistent on paying for everything. I have been keeping track, Moira, and if we continue going as we have been these past few days, the whole endeavor is going to be very expensive. Are you sure that you have the funds you require for all of this?"

"I am sure," she said reassuringly, her smile a bit stiffer now.

"How?" he asked immediately. "I mean no offense, but from the state of your dresses and your boots, which are rather worn and well-mended, I have a hard time believing it."

Moira sighed and looked away, suddenly pensive.

Nathan cursed himself and shook his head. "I apologize, Moira. It is none of my business. Forget that I even asked."

"No, no, Nathan, there's no need to apologize," she said, turning back to him. "I am only trying to think of how to say this properly." She bit her lip again and looked down for a moment, then brought her eyes back up to his. "I am rich."

His disbelief must have shown, for she nodded. "I am not just rich, though. I am what some would call obscenely wealthy."

Her earnest words rang true in his mind, but he didn't see how it was possible.

"I suppose I need to start at the beginning," she said on another soft sigh, adjusting herself slightly in the saddle. "My parents were very wealthy. They were at the height of society in

London, and I believe were quite the popular set as well. I have very little memory of life in those days, as I was quite young. My brother and I were rather spoiled, I think, but not in a bad way. At any rate, when I was eight years old, my parents and my brother were killed in a terrible boating accident…"

"Wait," Nathan interrupted, his heart stilling in his chest, his eyes going wide, "wait. You're one of *those* Dennisons?"

Moira gave him an odd look. "I'm not entirely certain what that means, but I suppose the correct answer would be yes, *those* Dennisons."

He gave a low whistle and ran a hand through his hair. That changed things drastically. Robert and Anne Dennison had been one of the wealthiest families in all of England, not just London, and had been the toast of society right up until the day they died. It was a terrible tragedy to lose a couple that everybody thought so well of, and for them to lose their son and heir as well had set more than a few pairs of eyes to crying. Many forgot that they also had a daughter, but most wondered what would happen to that fortune of theirs now that they were gone, and no one knew.

Now Nathan did, and suddenly everything began to make sense.

"Anyway," Moira continued, graciously ignoring his strange outburst, "I was eight years old when they died, and had no one to really care for me, and no need for a fortune that large. So my father's solicitor, who was a great friend, decided to put it all into trust until I turned twenty-one, or until I was married, whichever came first. But I was not permitted to speak of it to anyone at all until either of those things occurred, or I would lose it all. Then I was sent away to live with my mother's older sister Miriam, who was neither a pleasant woman nor any sort of competent mother. But she knew about the inheritance, and she took me in more for the sake of hoping that when I reached the age requirement that she would get something."

Nathan listened carefully, knowing that there were things in her answer that she would rush through that were actually very important bits of her past that he wanted to know very much, and he was right. She gave no details of her parents or her brother, and did not speak much about her aunt. The money she talked freely of, which told Nathan that she could have cared less about it.

"So that is why I have money, but no wardrobe," she said with forced lightness. "I had to make these dresses myself out of the fabric that Aunt Miriam let me have. I have only had my fortune for a year or so, and I have no idea what to do with it."

Now that Nathan could believe rather easily. "So I take it that Charles knew nothing of this?"

She shook her head. "Not at all. To be fair, I had no idea myself just how large it was. But I have always wondered if he would have known, would he have left the way he did?"

There was no way to answer that except for saying, "I don't know." Nathan would like to think that the answer was no for Moira's sake, but a man's pride was a tricky thing. Depending on the sort of man that Charles actually was, it might have made things worse. He was not entirely certain what he would have done, had he been in that situation. It was something he had never had to consider.

He chanced a question along a different path. "What do you remember about your parents?"

A more pensive look crossed her face as she thought. "I remember that my father smelled of hay quite a lot, but in a pleasant way, not a smelly one. I remember him reading to me in the library before bed. I remember my mother smiling all the time, and her and Father laughing so hard they could hardly speak over something that I did not understand, but I remember the laughter. I remember going with my mother to a dress shop and watching her try some things on. I thought she was the most beautiful woman in the world."

She smiled at the memory, which made Nathan smile as well.

"If your parents were who I think they were," he remarked, "then your mother was widely considered to be one of the most beautiful women in England and your father owned the finest stables in London. They were both the envy of all society."

Her smile grew. "Really?"

He nodded, fighting his desire to laugh at her child-like wonder.

"That makes a lot of sense. When Uncle George, that's my father's solicitor, came to me last year to discuss my holdings, he mentioned the stables, which are under the care of a Mr. Grant. I still own the stables in their entirety, but he recommended I retain Mr. Grant as their caretaker." She shrugged and smiled. "I had no desire to run stables myself, so I agreed. I do not have a head for finances, so anytime that I can get others to do things for me is a blessing."

"Very wise," Nathan said with a grin. "And what do you remember of your brother?"

"Robbie was twelve when he died, but he was a horrible tease," Moira mused with a fond smile. "He used to tug at my curls any chance he could. He would jump out at me from behind corners and doors and it never failed to give me a fright. But he could also make me laugh at anything at any time. I remember one day hiding out in the barn and crying about something that I had been scolded for, and suddenly, there was Robbie. He sat down next to me and put his arm about my shoulder, and not three minutes later, he was tickling me and I giggled until I could not breathe."

"You loved him very much, didn't you?" There really was no question; it was plain to see that she still held very strong affection for him.

"I worshipped him," she said softly, her eyes misting a bit. "He was my hero. Everything he did was brilliant in my eyes." Suddenly she closed her eyes and looked away. "I still miss them very much," she whispered.

"I know," he said gently, putting a hand over hers where it sat on the saddle horn and squeezing it. "I know."

Her blue eyes met his dark ones, and he nodded at the questions there. "My father died when I was fifteen, and my mother only six years ago. There is not a day that goes by that I don't think of them."

She nodded her thanks, and sniffed back the few tears that had begun welling up.

"Can I ask you something else, Nathan?" she asked as she wiped at her eyes with her sleeve.

"Of course."

She smiled at his simple response. "You had said that you can speak French fluently."

He nodded. "I can."

"Did you learn that in the army?"

Again, he nodded. "It seemed appropriate to learn it as many of our deserters would make for the French coast. There is nothing the French love so much as a British traitor."

She shuddered delicately. "I can only imagine. But what I was really wondering is this; would you teach me?"

He looked at her carefully. "Teach you French?"

"Yes, if you please," she said with a smile. "I would love to speak other languages. Besides, would not the mark of a truly refined lady be the ability to speak several?"

"I suppose," he said slowly, eyeing her cautiously. "What other languages would you learn?"

She shrugged. "Oh, probably Italian and German, as is appropriate. Perhaps Latin or Greek. Would those be beneficial?"

He snorted and shook his head. "Only if you are a scholar or a bluestocking."

"So you do not know Latin, then?"

Now, how should he answer that? He had spent a good number of years in schools where Latin was very strictly emphasized, but how many common men could say the same? He opted to tell her the truth, even if it was a gross understatement. "I know a little. Enough for church, at least."

Nathan braced himself for her accusatory finger as his almost-but-not-quite-the-truth slipped out and brought in religion at the same time, which would undoubtedly be revealed to her as not entirely correct when he found himself suddenly struck by lightning.

But Moira said nothing, and he relaxed.

"So, will you teach me French?" she asked with an innocent smile.

He returned her smile and nodded. "If you wish to learn, Moira, then I would be glad to teach you."

Her smile grew into a grin, and she looked positively delighted.

At that moment, she could have asked him to bring her the moon and he would have found a way to do it.

"All right, Miss Dennison," he said in his best teacher voice, which made her giggle, "let us begin. The first thing you need to know is the French alphabet."

It was much later when they finally reached an inn to stop for the night. The day had been an odd mix of frustration and amusement as Moira had struggled to grasp the French language. Nathan had been patient and corrected her as gently as he could, but honestly, the simple basics of a language should not have been that difficult for anyone.

What made the whole endeavor worth it were those rare moments when she exceeded his expectations and surprised herself in the process. She would smile and laugh in elation and he was helpless but to join her. She was learning, however slowly the process was coming, and her pride and sense of accomplishment were nearly as rewarding to Nathan.

He only prayed she would not need to use her newfound French skills for quite some time.

"Can I have another turn at telling our story, *s'il vous plait*?" she asked with a grin, her accent actually quite good.

He rolled his eyes, but smiled all the same. "*Oui, mademoiselle*." Then he threw her a mock frown. "But make it a good one."

She nodded, her eyes twinkling. "Oh, have no fear, I will."

In spite of her words, Nathan had a great deal of fear all of a sudden.

But he swallowed his protests and dutifully helped her off of the horse and followed her into the inn, which was rather crowded and loud.

"I am terribly sorry to bother you, sir," Moira asked in a very soft voice when they approached the innkeeper.

The man turned, obviously haggard, but his expression cleared at Moira's smile. "How can I help you, miss?" he asked with a slight incline of his head, obviously completely oblivious to Nathan's presence.

Moira blushed prettily and ducked her head. "It's ma'am,

actually, sir," she said shyly as she took Nathan's hand, which sent a surprised jolt through him. "My husband and I have just come up from Devon and need only a place to rest for a time before continuing on to Preston. Have you any rooms available?"

Her voice was so weary and earnest that Nathan almost believed her himself.

The innkeeper smiled kindly and waved them over to a table. "I shall check the books for you, ma'am."

"I am so sorry to trouble you," Moira said as they followed. "I can see how very busy you are and I hate to be an inconvenience."

He waved a beefy hand in the air. "No trouble, no trouble at all. I only hope we can accommodate you." He pulled out a ledger and brought it over to them and scanned the page. "I have one room left, but 'tis a very small room with only bed for one." He looked up at Nathan finally, and his eyes widened slightly as he took in his size. "I am afraid, sir, that it will not do for the both of you."

Moira turned to him with luminous eyes that held him captive in spite of his knowledge of her act. "Oh, George, what will we do?" she asked in a would-be tear-filled voice, placing a hand on his chest.

It took Nathan a moment to think of something to say, but he covered her hand with his and smiled. "It will be fine, Hannah. I have spent many nights in the stables before when I was in the army. A bit of straw will not bother me a bit. It is better that you are warm and comfortable and safe in here."

Her mouth twitched and her eyes narrowed ever so slightly, but she sniffled and nodded, then buried her head against him. "Only if you are sure, George. You know I hate to be parted from you, even for one night."

Nathan had to fight hard to refrain from bursting out laughing. He wrapped his arms around Moira, whom he could feel shaking with her own laughter, and rubbed her back gently. "I am sure, my love. You are weary and there is a warm bed here for you." He looked to the innkeeper, who was watching them with interest. "We will take it, if you please, sir."

He nodded and bent over the ledger. "And what is the name?"

"Rupert," came Moira's muffled voice from Nathan's chest.

She turned and faced the man. "George and Hannah Rupert."

Nathan made a noise and she elbowed him swiftly, clamping her lips together as the man nodded and wrote the names down.

"Very good. Allow me to show you to your room?" He indicated the way, and they both nodded, taking only short breaths through their noses.

Somehow, they made it to their room with straight faces, and thanked the innkeeper for showing them up. But the moment the door was closed, they both gave in to their laughter, their sides aching from the restraint. Nathan covered his mouth as Moira indicated they should be quiet, even amidst her own giggles and snorts. He nodded, his eyes beginning to tear up a bit with mirth.

When they had both calmed, he sat on the floor against the tiny bed facing her as she took a chair. "What came over you down there, Moira?"

She shrugged with a smile. "I haven't a clue. I pretended that Hannah Rupert," she broke off for another snicker between the both of them, "was a beautiful woman who commanded attention with one look, but was as sweet as cake. She is also very attached to her husband." Here she grinned at him, and his chest tightened in response.

He snorted, even as his heart stuttered. "Obviously. I thought I would have to pry you off of me down there."

Moira chuckled even as she removed her boots and set them aside. "Just playing the part, Nathan. You were quite convincing yourself."

He nodded his thanks and leaned his head back against the bed, staring at her fondly. "But you had one thing right; Hannah Rupert is a beautiful woman."

She scoffed at him and shook her head, still smiling. "Oh Nathan, please. Regardless of how wonderful she is, Hannah Rupert is still me."

"Yes. Exactly."

Moira's smile froze and color raced into her cheeks faster than he thought was possible. She looked away and said nothing.

"Moira?" he asked with some concern.

She shook her head, biting her lip hard.

He crawled over to where she sat until he was on his haunches before her, and put his hand over both of hers where they rested in her lap. "Moira," he said again, this time with some firmness, though as gentle as he could manage.

She looked at him finally, and he saw that, though her eyes were damp, no tears had fallen.

"What did I say?" he asked softly.

"You… you said I was beautiful," she managed, her voice thick.

His brow furrowed as he looked up at her. "I don't under…" He stopped himself as understanding hit him and his expression cleared. "You don't think you're beautiful."

She looked away once more, and it broke Nathan's heart a little. How could a woman as bright and vivacious and stunning as Moira think so little of herself? He had known she was beautiful before he had even met her, and that opinion had only strengthened as he had come to know her, and he was now in a very precarious situation indeed.

But what could he tell her? That he and all of his friends had been stunned silent at the sight of her? That the innkeeper downstairs had been astounded by her not because of her role-playing, but because of Moira herself? That she had the maddening ability to stop his heart with a smile or a laugh and he had no control over it? All of those things would sound like pure flattery, and she would not care for that at all.

Slowly, almost hesitantly, Nathan reached out and cupped her cheek, turning her face towards him, waiting for her eyes to meet his before speaking. "You should, you know," he said softly when they did, stroking her cheek ever so slightly. "You really should."

He stood then, and headed for the door. "I will go see what they know about Charles here. Good night, Moira." He exited and closed the door softly behind him, glancing in just long enough to see her cheeks still tinged with color, and to hear her reply softly, "Good night, Nathan."

Chapter Nine

"Moira! Moira! Wake up!"

Moira was shaken awake by a very excited Nathan, and it took her a long moment to realize that it was still night. "What is it, Nathan?" she groaned, burying her head into her pillows again.

"You have to come down right now," he said, shaking her once more, then going over to where her dress and boots sat. "And by right now, I mean right now."

"Unless there is a fire, Nathaniel," she mumbled into her pillow, "I most certainly will not come anywhere right now."

Nathan grunted and headed back over to the bed. "You most certainly will," he retorted as he grabbed the bedcovers and threw them off of her, turning back to her clothing as she squealed at the cold.

"Nathan! I could have been indecent!" she screeched, scrambling for a blanket to cover her.

"It would have served you right." He shrugged and tossed her dress at her. "Now get dressed and come downstairs."

She glared at him as she shook out her dress with the one hand she was not using to cover herself. "Why am I coming downstairs in the middle of the night, Mr. Rupert?"

"Because, Mrs. Rupert," he said impatiently, "there is a man downstairs who knows something of your brother."

Moira stilled in bed. "Charles?" she whispered as she stared up at him.

Nathan nodded, a slight smile quirking at his lips. "The very same. Now, are you coming down or must I dress you as well?"

She frowned at him and indicated with her finger that he should turn around. He did so with a slight roll of his eyes, and placed his hands on his hips, toe tapping against the floor. In a mere moment, her dress was on and she was working at the buttons. "All right, now give me my stockings and boots!"

He did so and averted his eyes as she put her stockings on.

"Oh, for pity's sake, Nathan, it is only my ankle," she scoffed as she pulled them up and slid her feet into the boots.

"I think we should attempt to preserve some sense of propriety somewhere," Nathan said unrepentantly. "Ankles or not, a gentleman never looks."

She snorted. "Bother with gentlemen. All right, I'm ready."

He turned back to her and cocked his head. "You are not going to fix your hair?"

She leveled a look at him. "You dragged your wife out of bed, Mr. Rupert. I hardly think they will expect me to be ready for an audience with the King."

He shrugged, and opened the door for her, then followed her out. "Now, this man said he met Charles in Preston some months ago, but he still remembered him. I told him I had to fetch my wife so she could listen in as well and ask questions."

She nodded absently and began twirling a strand of copper hair around her finger, biting her lip repeatedly.

He noticed and took that hand in his own. "Relax, Moira. It's going to be all right."

She met his eyes, still gnawing at her lip a bit.

He offered her a smile, and squeezed her hand. "I'm right here."

She smiled briefly and nodded, squeezing back.

As they entered the taproom, Moira's hold on his hand tightened and Nathan smiled in spite of himself. He knew she was not nearly as calm as she appeared. As anxious as she was, he was grateful for the opportunity to have her hear this with him as they found out more about Charles. It would set her at ease, and give her some hope for the remainder of their journey.

They approached the table where a pleasant looking middle-aged man sat. He stood at their approach and took his hat off, brushing at his hair as he did so.

"Hannah, this is Mr. Francis," Nathan said with a nod. "He was up in Preston some six months ago, and he remembers your brother."

Mr. Francis bowed. "Mrs. Rupert."

Moira curtseyed in response. "Mr. Francis. It is a pleasure."

"The pleasure is all mine, I assure you," he said with a smile.

Moira indicated that he sit as she and Nathan did so. "So you know something of Charles?"

He nodded. "Yes, ma'am, I do. I had just come into port from Spain, where I had spent some months visiting a cousin. I had never been to Preston before, and knew nothing of the city. Your brother was working at the docks and saw my confusion, and offered his assistance."

"That sounds like Charles," she murmured with a smile, still gripping Nathan's hand under the table.

"He was very helpful," Mr. Francis continued with a nod. "I was there for three days and every day he was there if I needed him. He assisted me in getting my affairs in order and helped me to find the men I needed to speak with. He was very pleasant, ma'am. You have a fine brother there."

"Thank you," Moira said, her eyes warm. "I have not seen him in quite some time. He…" She looked to Nathan, as if unsure of what exactly she ought to say.

He squeezed her hand softly and smiled. "He wanted to make his own way without assistance from the family. I am sure you can understand."

"I do. I have a brother like that myself."

Nathan nodded. "Hannah and I were away when he left and he

gave no forwarding address for her to reach him. Would you have one?"

Mr. Francis shook his head. "Sadly, I do not. Allenford said he was looking for a permanent place of residence, but had not been able to yet."

Moira clutched Nathan's hand tightly. "Did he… did he seem happy?"

Nathan glanced over at her, his hand very nearly going numb in her grasp. He smoothed his thumb over her hand, hoping to bring some measure of comfort.

"He did, Mrs. Rupert, though a trifle worried, if you'll forgive me."

"Worried about what?" Nathan asked, leaning forward slightly.

Mr. Francis sat back, shaking his head. "I could not say. We did not discuss matters beyond our business, but I wondered if it might be a woman."

Again, Moira's hold on Nathan's hand flinched. If she got much tighter, he would not have use of it for quite some time. "A woman, eh? But you did not see one with him?"

"No, but as I said, we were strictly business. But when a man looks worried about something, chances are that it is a woman, is it not, sir?" he commented with a light laugh.

Nathan returned it half-heartedly. "You could be right, Mr. Francis. You could be right. What do you think, darling? It's about time for Charles to settle down, I think."

"Yes," Moira said with a smile that did not reach her eyes. "Yes, I think he should. I do hope I get to meet her before he does, however. A sister must give her blessing, you know."

Mr. Francis nodded sagely. "That I do. My own sister threatened to have me drawn and quartered if I did not wed someone she approved of. But I showed her." He grinned at the both of them. "I married her best friend."

They all laughed and Nathan pushed off from the table. "Well, I think you should go back up to bed, Hannah. I will try to get some particulars from Mr. Francis so that we may expedite our search for Charles."

She nodded without argument, even silently, which was an even bigger indication to Nathan that she was troubled. He led her back over to the stairs up to their room and turned her towards him. "Are you all right?" he asked softly, looking at her closely.

Again, she only nodded.

Nathan lifted her chin to look at him. "Really?"

She let out a breath slowly. "I don't know yet. Fair enough?"

He smiled a little, tapping the underside of her chin. "Fair enough." He moved a hand to her hair, which hung so beautifully down her back, and twirled a few strands a bit. "I think you are right, you should leave your hair down on occasion. It suits you."

She smiled and a slight blush reached her cheeks. "We are in public, Mr. Rupert."

For a moment, he had forgotten that. But now he looked around briefly and saw not a few eyes sneaking in their direction. "So we are," he murmured, turning back to her. "They think we are adorable."

She snorted lightly. "Not at all. They think we should stop now."

"Only because it makes them jealous."

"Or nauseated."

He restrained a laugh and gave her a mock-severe look. "Now is that any way for a wife to speak to her husband?"

"It is if the husband is being idiotic."

He rolled his eyes a bit and smiled at her fondly. It delighted him to see her return it. Unable to help himself, he leaned forward and pressed his lips to her forehead, lingering just a touch longer than he meant to. "Good night, darling," he whispered against her skin.

Almost too softly for him to hear, she replied, "Good night." Then, without meeting his eyes, she went up the stairs, their fingers separating at last.

As Nathan watched her go, he clenched his hand almost involuntarily, then looked down at it. Her hand had fit so perfectly in his; they had felt so natural together. He had not even minded her death grip on him; instead he had found himself oddly enjoying every minute.

He closed his hand and walked back to the table where Mr.

Francis sat, watching him in amusement.

"You are obviously very attached to your wife, Mr. Rupert," he said with no small amount of humor.

Nathan thought about denying it, but what was the use? He knew the truth, and Mr. Francis had seen it. "I am, Mr. Francis," he said in a low voice, though he could not help smiling as he did so. "It would seem she holds an odd sort of power over me."

"That is as it should be, Mr. Rupert," he laughed as he toasted him. "As it should be."

The next morning was a relatively silent affair as the two rode away from the inn. Nathan had not slept well in the straw of the stables, and Moira had not slept well in the comfort of the bed. The cause for such awkwardness was lost on Nathan, but something needed to be done about it. The silence was eating at him, and he felt time weighing heavily on them both.

"There is something else I want you to know about me."

Nathan looked at Moira in disbelief. There were about a thousand other things he wanted to know about her, and she only thought of one? He wet his lips and then said, "I'm afraid to encourage you, but go on."

She smirked at him, then sat up straighter. "When I was a little girl, I thought I was going to grow up to be the Queen of England."

Nathan could not help the bark of laughter that escaped him at her response. *That* was something she thought he needed to know?

"Why are you laughing at that?" she said, even as she grinned. "It is not so uncommon a thought."

"No, I am sure it's not!" he laughed. "I can just see you practicing your coronation and greeting your loyal subjects."

She sniffed at him. "I did, and I was very good. I would have been a wonderful, wise, and benevolent queen, adored by all."

He shook his head, smiling. "So when did you realize that you would not become queen?"

She glared at him in a very regal fashion. "Who says that I won't?"

He snickered, which made her giggle, and soon they were both laughing, for reasons they could not explain.

"Oh, I needed a good laugh," Nathan said on a sigh. "Thank you for that."

"You are more than welcome," Moira replied cheerily, "but that was not why I brought it up. I just thought you might want to know what Little Moira imagined herself doing."

"I did want to know, actually," he said with real honesty. "I wondered if you were the princess type of little girl or if you favored being a knight of the realm."

She smiled. "While the action of the knight of the realm was appealing, I was always more interested in the fashion of a queen. My brother was content to play the knight, and took to defending me quite seriously. I never so much as stubbed a toe."

"I should hope not!" Nathan replied in a very shocked tone. "A knight who cannot protect his queen is a useless fellow indeed! No bruising or bloodshed may come to the queen, or else the knight who failed his duty must lose his head."

Moira laughed and looked over at him with delight. "Were you a knight of the realm, then?"

"No, alas, I was far less scrupled," he said with a sad shaking of his head. "There were no knights in the Hammond household."

"So what, then?" she asked, obviously determined to make him share as well. "What did little Nathan spend his days pretending?"

He ducked his head, suddenly shy, which made her smile grow even wider. "Oh, come now, Nathan," she scolded playfully. "It cannot be any worse than me honestly thinking I would grow up to be a queen."

"Well, all right," he said, resigned to the fact that she would not give up until she knew all. "Do you know the legend of Robin of the Hood?"

"The one who robbed from the rich to feed the poor?" she asked with a furrowed brow.

He nodded. "The very same. I imagined myself to be Robin, battling the evils of Prince John and his minions, determined to protect King Richard's honor…" He trailed off with a smile as he reminisced. "Spencer and I would play in the woods behind our home for hours on end. Our father would have to come out and find us or we would never have eaten. We insisted on finding food in the woods, but he used to say, 'Even outlaws can eat at a table,' and so we would."

Moira pursed her lips thoughtfully. "Why do I get the feeling that you received your fair share of scrapes and bruises?"

He grinned widely. "But of course I did! One could not be Robin of the Hood without climbing a great many trees, and one cannot become adept at climbing a great many trees without falling out of an even greater number. And then there was the archery, and sword fighting, and carriage seizing…"

"My goodness," Moira said with a laugh, "you must have been filthy little urchins indeed!"

"We were," he moaned. "Mother would be so appalled with the pair of us. She would call for Mrs. Whitcomb, the housekeeper, and set the task to her of getting us presentable again." He shuddered at the memory. "I don't believe my skin will ever be the same after the scrubbing she gave me."

"I'm afraid that I cannot pity you," she said, shaking her head. "You have not known the pain of a scrubbing until you were receiving one from my aunt Miriam. I made the mistake of following one of the neighbors' dogs on one of the days I was allowed to leave the garden, and when I returned to the house, she was so enraged she made me strip right then and there and set me in a washtub of freezing water she had used for dishes and scrubbed my skin with the same bristle brush."

Nathan's amusement vanished in a sharp burst of pain. "Wait a moment. One of the days you were *allowed* to leave the garden?"

She shrugged without emotion. "Most days I was not permitted to leave our property. That changed when I turned sixteen, but by that time I had nowhere to go, so most of the time I remained anyway."

"Moira, was your aunt… I mean… did she…?" He could not bring himself to complete an entire sentence, to even formulate the questions he had swirling about. There was too much horror involved in them.

"I would rather not recall those days, Nathan," she said softly, her expression pained. "It is done and I am here, well and whole."

"Please," he begged in a low voice, "I only wish to help." He could not explain it, but at the moment, he *had* to know what she had endured.

She took a deep breath, and released it slowly. "Very well, but only if I can say it quickly, and without interruption, and then never speak of it again."

"I promise. Never again." He held his breath, wondering if he would be able to bear whatever it was she was going to share with him, but if she had borne it, then he could bear to hear the telling of it.

After a moment's hesitation, Moira began to speak rapidly and in low tones that Nathan, even with his excellent hearing, had to strain to catch. "When I came to live with my aunt, the only thing that prevented her from complete neglect was the inheritance she knew I was to receive. I became her servant girl in every respect, except for wages. I spent many nights locked in a closet instead of my bedroom, which was not much bigger, because of some childish mistake I had made. I received beatings on regular occasions, and most of the time I did not know the reason, not that Aunt Miriam required a reason. We never discussed my family unless she was ranting about the inconvenience of their deaths. All the good memories I had of them I held onto with all that I had. When I had been well-behaved enough to venture out, I was spurned by most, and those that did not instead chose to mock me. I suppose my aunt had spread some rumors about me and no one doubted them."

She finally took an audible breath and swallowed. "My aunt died almost three years ago, and that is the end of it."

Nathan could not believe what he had heard. He had figured that her childhood had not been pleasant, given the losses she sustained so early, and from what she had already told him about her aunt, but he had never imagined anything so cruel. How many nights had she cried in the darkness of her closet or bedroom, wishing for any other life but her own? How many injuries had she sustained without deserving any of them? How much had she suffered in silence with no end in sight?

Abruptly, he reined Mercury in, stopping in the middle of the road. Moira turned to look at him, stopping Flora as well. "Nathan? What is it?"

He dismounted and walked over to her without speaking. He reached up and took her waist, then lifted her off of the horse and set her down on the ground. Before she could say anything, he pulled her into his chest and wrapped his arms around her tightly.

"I am so sorry," he said quietly, holding her close.

Slowly, hesitantly, she brought her arms around him. "It happened a long time ago, Nathan."

He nodded against her, his heart still beating too hard for comfort. "I know. But there was no one to hug you then. Now there is."

Chapter Ten

The rest of the morning was spent in cheerful reminiscing and recounting of childhood tales of daring deeds that would shock any proper members of society. And Nathan's stories were even worse.

"I have a confession to make," Moira said later that afternoon.

"Oh for heaven's sake, now what?" Nathan asked, but with a smile.

She glowered at him. "Well, if you are going to be all snippety about it, then maybe I won't tell you after all."

"I am not snippety!" he said as he laughed.

She rolled her eyes. "Please. Even your friend Colin would say you are snippety."

"Colin would say anything if he thought it would bring about a juicy piece of gossip," he remarked dryly, causing Moira to snicker in response. "But come on now, and tell me."

"Will you be snippety about it?"

He shrugged. "That all depends."

"On what, may I ask?" she scoffed.

"On what your confession is and on your definition of snippety."

She quirked a brow at him, but did not comment. "Very well.

My confession…" She hesitated a moment, then exhaled. "I had no idea how I was going to find Charles when I met you. Not an inkling. I had no plan, no guidance, and no set course. All I had was my determination to do something and the fact that you were the best person to help me find him, and I had not thought beyond that." She managed a wan smile. "I was completely bluffing when I came to you and I just thought you should know that."

Nathan watched her for a moment, knowing what it must have cost her to admit such a thing. He considered teasing her about it, but he decided against it. "I know."

"You know?" she asked in confusion. "How could you know that?"

"Because, my dear Moira, when I approached you after that little speech you gave me, you looked absolutely terrified. I knew then that you had no idea what you were doing." He offered her a kind, rather amused smile. "But I knew that you were trying your best to pretend that you had everything worked out, so I let you think you succeeded."

She stared at him, mouth gaping open for a moment. "So you knew all along?"

He nodded. "I knew all along."

"Well, then, why in the world did you agree to come?" she cried, looking rather more frustrated than anything. "I was completely clueless! You would have been better served staying right where you were and telling me to shove off!"

He bit back a grin and tilted his head slightly. "Perhaps I liked that you told me off before I had said five words. Perhaps I liked that you could shut up my friends so effectively just by standing there. Perhaps I thought your story was touching and wanted to help. Perhaps I am really a gentleman and could not allow a lady to be traveling alone. Perhaps you fascinated me and I wanted to know more. Perhaps I wanted to tell you to shove off, but I just couldn't do it."

Her wide blue eyes stared at him for a long moment. "That is a rather lot of options," she said carefully. "Which is it?"

"All of them at once," he said in a low voice, looking away from her. "And they rotate which is the primary reason constantly."

"That sounds confusing," she commented, almost to herself.

He snorted and shook his head. "You have no idea."

Moira wet her lips, then spoke softly. "Well, for whatever it is worth, I am glad you came with me."

He smiled and glanced over at her. "So am I." Then his smile turned slightly devious and his eyes twinkled. "Most of the time."

"Most of the time?" she protested in indignation. "When do you regret it?"

"Oh, shall we make a list?" he asked with a knowing quirk of his brow.

"I think we should, yes," she insisted. "I have been an excellent traveling companion. I have not complained once, which is more than I can say for you, I might add."

"I beg your pardon!"

"Don't deny it," she overrode impatiently. "I have paid for everything, and will pay you rather generously when we are through, and thus far, we have not had to suffer overly much."

"Speak for yourself," he muttered under his breath, half-hoping she would hear it.

If she did, she gave no indication. "So let us proceed with your so-called list, shall we? What devastating trials has poor Nathan had to endure because he agreed to come along on a poorly planned expedition with Moira?"

"Well, let me see," he said with a sigh, as if he had to think back. "There was that first night at the inn with Margaret and Rupert."

Moira shuddered. "I will give you that one."

He nodded his acceptance, and continued. "The first night you snuck out to the stables."

She shook her head. "No, I won't allow that. It was more than fair, and, as you had the stables last night, I will take my turn tonight."

"But…" he tried to protest.

"No," she insisted, shaking her head more firmly, giving him a look. "Do not argue with me. I am doing it."

He growled in frustration under his breath, his mind spewing all sorts of irritated expletives that made him feel only marginally better. "Your complete lack of ability or care to be ladylike."

As if to emphasize that point, she snorted in a rather unladylike fashion. "That is simply the way I am, Nathan. Eventually, you really will have to get over that."

"You say that as if it were a completely normal thing to do."

She sighed, and looked over at him. "How long are we going to fight about this?"

"Oh, probably forever," he quipped, grinning. "I am determined to be a gentleman and you are determined to be independent. I am not sure anything can be done for either of us."

"I am trying, you know," she said quietly, offering a small smile. "I am trying to not be so difficult. Well, trying not to *make* things difficult for you, I suppose."

"I appreciate that. In return, I will… allow you certain liberties without commenting or reproaching." That was really as much as he could promise. It went against his very nature to do it, but if she were going to make a concession, than so could he.

"So you will let me sleep out in the stables tonight?"

He refrained from grimacing, but only just. "I don't think I could 'let' you do anything, Moira, as I have absolutely no control over you whatsoever. You will do whatever it is you want to do regardless of anybody else. But I will not object, if that is what you want."

She smiled with a suspicious light in her eyes. "You mean you will not object vocally. I can see it in your face that you object wholeheartedly."

"Vocally, then," he conceded. "I will keep my feelings to myself on the subject."

"Thank you, Nathan."

Her voice was full of warmth, and it softened his resistance. He could not remain mad at her, not even for a second.

"Just promise me that you will be safe out there, all right?" he asked, meeting her eyes seriously. "Find a corner or something away from foot traffic and hide yourself well."

She nodded instantly. "I promise. I will not take any chances, I give you my word."

Relief washed over him, however briefly. "Thank you. Now, I

have an idea."

"You have an idea?" she teased, looking shocked and worried.

"I do get them occasionally, you know," he told her defensively.

"Oh, I am so sorry," she said, holding up her hands in surrender.

"Hrmph. What I was *going* to say is that we should play the Favorites Game."

Her brow furrowed and she looked completely lost. "I have no idea what that even is."

"It is quite simple. One of us picks a topic, and then we each say our favorite thing in that topic." He smiled at her with a hint of pity. "It was a favorite childhood game of ours for long journeys. Our mother taught it to us. Did you not have any games like that?"

"I cannot remember," she said sadly, but with a smile.

Feeling suddenly a little uncomfortable, he cleared his throat. "Well, then, you can pretend this one was. So any questions?"

She brightened a bit and thought for a moment. "Any topic at all?"

"Any topic at all," he said with a grin. "Shall I go first?"

She nodded excitedly.

He shook his head in amusement at her child-like enthusiasm. He had not played this game in years, but suddenly, he was just as thrilled to play it as she was. Her eagerness was infectious.

"All right," he began, looking over at her. "Ready? Favorite Shakespeare play."

"'Much Ado About Nothing'," she said promptly.

"Really?" he asked in surprise.

"Yes, really. It puts me into hysterics every time. Yours?"

"Henry V."

"I should have known," she laughed. "My turn. Favorite color."

"Green."

"All greens? Or just some?"

"Most shades of green."

"Mine is blue."

He grinned. "All blues?"

She rolled her eyes. "Dark and light blues, particularly."

"Very good. Favorite article of clothing."

"Are you serious?" she asked, looking at him in surprise.

He shrugged. "Why not? It seems as good a question as any."

She did not look convinced. "A wrap, then. That is my favorite."

"All right. Well, boots are mine."

She laughed merrily, and he smiled at her laughter. "What is so funny about that, may I ask?" he asked in mock-indignation.

"Of all the things you wear," she said in between breathless giggles, "the hardest to get on and off is your favorite?"

He rolled his eyes. "It's not that funny. I always envied my father his boots, and it was a great day when I was able to wear my own. They remind me of him, I suppose." He trailed off slightly as he remembered his father, and that first day of wearing boots, and he found himself feeling a trifle sad.

Moira sobered at his expression. "That is a good reason to have them be a favorite. Memories like that are priceless." One side of Nathan's mouth quirked up at her response. She smiled fondly at him. "Come on. Let's keep going. Favorite Greek god or goddess."

They arrived rather later than they had planned at the inn that night, but thankfully, the innkeeper and his wife were still awake and more than happy to see them.

"Have you any rooms available?" Nathan asked as they were ushered in.

"Yes, sir, we have a few. Would you and your lady like one to share or separate?"

Moira and Nathan shared a quick look, and Moira blushed slightly, which made the innkeeper chuckle.

"Sharing it is, then," he said with a knowing look. "What are the names?"

"Matthew and Felicity Cresswell," Nathan said, putting an arm around Moira and smiling back.

"Very good. And will you be wanting some food tonight, sir?"

"Only something light," he assured him, not wanting to put anybody out. "Perhaps just some bread and cheese?"

The innkeeper nodded and indicated that they sit at the table and wait for him to return, then rushed off to procure some food for them.

"This might be our easiest time yet," Moira hissed across the table.

Nathan leaned forward. "Sometimes less is more," he whispered.

She quirked a doubtful brow. "Sometimes indeed. Less is never more when it comes to food. Bread and cheese, Nathan? Honestly, I am starving!"

"Shh, keep your voice down," he shushed, amused in spite of himself. "And my name is Matthew, as you are well aware, Felicity." He gave her a pointed look at sat back.

She huffed in frustration and folded her arms. "Yes, of course, Matthew, *darling*," she said with as much sarcasm as she could. "But the point of the matter is that I hardly think this meal is going to be substantial enough for me."

"Then I shall be certain to make sure that you receive a fine breakfast in the morning, all right?"

"All right," she grumbled, not at all sure that would help things.

Nathan was really very amused by her antics. Was she always this grumpy when she was hungry, or was it just because she was tired from their journey? Somehow, he suspected it was both.

Before he could ask her about it, however, the innkeeper was back with a warm loaf of bread and some cheese for them. Moira obviously restrained herself, but Nathan could tell that she really would rather have attacked the whole thing instead of waiting for him to cut it for her.

"Is there anything else I can do for you before I go to prepare your room?" the innkeeper asked with a smile.

Moira shook her head, giving him a dazzling smile of her own. "No, I thank you, this is more than enough."

The man blinked, gave an unsteady smile, and nodded, then ambled out of the room.

Nathan chuckled, which made Moira look at him questioningly.

"What?" she asked.

"You should not do that," he said with a smile.

"Do what?" She frowned. "I didn't do anything."

"*Au contraire*," he said, wagging a finger slightly. "You confounded that man so completely that he probably does not know which way is up and which is down."

"What?" she laughed, taking another bite of her bread and cheese. "I smiled at the man."

"Yes, exactly. I don't think you are aware of this, Moira, but the smile of a beautiful woman is a very powerful and dangerous thing to a man."

"Well," she replied in an off-hand manner, not meeting his eyes, "if that is the case, then he should only be merely confused by mine. I will admit to being mildly attractive," she said, holding a hand up to Nathan's protests, "but I cannot admit more than that. It would be incredibly vain, as well as incorrect."

"Moira," Nathan scolded in a low voice.

She looked at him finally, obviously not willing to hear more.

He met her eyes, and held them, wanting to ensure she understood him. "Slightly confused is what happens when you are merely standing there, Moira. When you smile, you blind all around you, and leave them happy to be so. And I am not being facetious or flattering. That is truth."

"Please," she murmured, looking down, cheeks flaming.

"I am sorry if that bothers you," he said, trying to meet her eyes again, "but you ought to know these things."

"But I don't know that you should say them," she whispered, her eyes flicking up to his once, and then away again.

Nathan's heart stilled in his chest. He was the one making her uncomfortable, not his words. She was correct; he should not be the one complimenting her, telling her what a great beauty she was. That was for her betrothed to do. But the git had been gone from her life for so long, and there was no one left to tell her these things.

Still, it was certainly not Nathan's place.

He smiled kindly at her, in spite of the emptiness he was beginning to feel. "Can't I say these things as a friend?"

Her shoulders relaxed a bit and she finally met his eyes fully. "I guess I should allow for that. I am sorry, I…" She shrugged. "I'm not accustomed to compliments of any kind, from a friend or not. I'm not accustomed to friends at all."

Nathan swallowed back a lump in his throat, and put his hand over Moira's on the table. "Well, you have a friend now, and I will compliment you as I see fit, because that is what friends do. So you will just have to accept it."

Now it was she who rolled her eyes and grinned. "Oh, very well. But if I gain a large ego from this, I will blame you entirely."

"Not to worry," he assured her. "I will stop before your ego can go anywhere."

"Pardon me, Mr. Cresswell, Mrs. Cresswell, but I have your room all ready for you," said the innkeeper, suddenly appearing as if out of thin air.

They rose from the table and Nathan led Moira to the stairs. "I think I will stay down here for a while, Felicity," he said taking her hand. "I should like to have a drink and possibly discuss your brother's whereabouts with this fine gentleman, once he returns from showing you the room."

The innkeeper nodded hastily, and Moira bit her lip slightly. "I don't know if I can wait for you, Matthew. I really am quite fatigued."

He smiled and kissed her hand. "Very well, then. I hope that you sleep well, and are warm and comfortable. And safe."

Moira smiled at him warmly, her eyes telling him that she understood exactly what he was saying with his words. She went up on tiptoe and placed a gentle kiss to his cheek, lingering for a moment. "Good night, husband," she whispered.

He swallowed hastily, and stammered out, "Good night, wife."

Moira stepped back, squeezing his hand once, and then she turned and followed the innkeeper up the stairs.

Nathan waited for her to get all the way up before he turned and released the massive breath he had been holding since he did not know when.

He had not suspected that Moira would kiss him. Ever. And she had done it willingly, without prompting, and without need. Whether or not that meant anything was something he could not even consider.

And the touch of her lips on his cheek had sent every single one of his senses reeling. Even now, his heart was racing at the memory, and cohesive thought was very nearly impossible.

This was not good.

"Nate, I think you are in trouble," he murmured aloud as he ran a hand through his hair. "I think you are seriously in trouble."

He shook his head, trying to shake off the sudden shaken state he found himself in. He moved back over to the table and sat down, and put his head into his hands, wondering just what was happening to him.

Chapter Eleven

True to his word, Nathan made sure that there was a fine spread for Moira in the morning. She was a good deal more pleasant than she had been the night before as she came down from the room, properly dressed and looking rather well rested.

"Good morning, Felicity," Nathan said standing as she approached the table where he was.

She smiled warmly at him. "Good morning, Matthew. I didn't see you this morning."

He held back a grin at her secret meaning. "Yes, I was up rather early. I did not wish to disturb you."

Moira clamped her lips together, her eyes dancing. "I appreciate your thoughtfulness."

He inclined his head and indicated that she sit down, which she did. "And how did you sleep, my dear?"

"Oh, very well," she said brightly as she watched him fill a plate for her. "It was warm and comfortable, rather as if we were sleeping at home."

He gave her an incredulous look, but she only smiled. "Well, I do hope this breakfast will be enough to satisfy you, dear. I am not certain that last night's meal was substantial."

"It is more than adequate, thank you," she replied, her eyes showing real gratitude.

Nathan cleared his throat awkwardly and nodded. She really need to stop smiling at him, to stop looking at him like that, to stop being so grateful for things he did. A man could only take so much.

"Did you sleep better this time?" she asked softly, completely oblivious to his consternation.

"Yes, I did. Perhaps I am learning how to relax better." He threw her a lopsided grin that made her chuckle.

If he were being truthful, he would have told her that no, he had not slept well. Better than the last time she slept out in the stables? Perhaps. But did he sleep well? Not at all. How could he when he was very much afraid that he was falling in love with her?

It had been after midnight when that realization hit him. It explained everything: why he had been so confused lately, why she could have knocked him over with a blink of those gorgeous blue eyes, why every time she said his name was like music to his ears. He was falling in love with Moira. He should try to resist, he had determined that he *would* try. Knowing as he did, and had known all along, that they were going to find Moira's betrothed so that she could marry him and get on with her life… that made things more difficult.

That would make being in love with her agony.

He suddenly realized that Moira was looking at him, an odd expression on her face.

"What?" he asked, a bit defensively.

She swallowed and frowned. "You are not eating anything."

He shrugged it off. "I am fine."

"No, I refuse to sit here and eat this delightful breakfast alone. Either you eat something or I will stop and we will leave right now."

The tone of her voice cracked his pensive mood and he could smile. "You sound like my mother," he grumbled, taking a piece of ham from her plate.

She grinned in response. "Then I fully expect you to listen to me, is that understood?"

He rolled his eyes as he chewed. "Yes, Mother." She was a rather overbearing woman, when she wanted to be, but he appreciated the break in his cloudy mood all the same.

"When you have finished," he said after a while, "I think we would do well to hurry along today. We know that Charles is in Preston, or was six months ago, at least, and so our need for questions is not as great as it once was. We've been taking our time, but I think now we must move forward. That is, if you agree?"

Moira seemed to freeze in place for a moment, and she stared at him with wide eyes. He wished he could read them, see what was going on in her head. But if he truly wanted to keep himself from falling in love with her, he needed to stop dwelling on her entirely. He needed to keep his distance. Where he could.

She managed a smile. "I do. We should proceed with all possible speed. I am anxious to find Charles, as you can probably imagine."

Nathan could not imagine, but he nodded as if he could.

"I'm ready now, if you are," Moira said, standing up swiftly, not looking at him.

"Very good. Let me just find the innkeeper and pay him."

"Oh, don't worry about that," she snapped, pulling out her reticule. "I am funding this whole venture, so I will pay him."

"You don't have to," he said softly, wondering at her tone. "I can…"

She brushed passed him and headed directly for the innkeeper, who had just come out of the kitchens again.

Nathan watched as she approached the man, who smiled broadly, and took her offered money. He saw his eyes widen and flick back to her, as if he could not believe it. At her nod, he closed his fist around the coins and bowed deeply. Moira curtseyed and turned, met Nathan's eyes, then swept outside.

What had he said that had set her off? He frowned and followed her outside and noted that she was standing rather impatiently by Flora, waiting for him to help her up. His heart softened a bit at that. She was obviously mad at him, but she was still willing to allow him to help her onto the horse.

Without a word, he formed a lattice with his fingers and helped her up. Once she was situated, she turned Flora and started down the road, not waiting for him.

Well, he had said that he wanted to speed things along, in a way. Now, it appeared, they would be.

And it was all for the best, really.

The silence was deafening.

They had not said a single word in hours, not even to themselves. Moira kept her mouth firmly shut, eyes strictly forward, and her jaw was clenched so tightly that her teeth were beginning to ache. But she refused to give in. Why bother forging a friendship any deeper when it was not going to last anyway? It was hardly worth the effort from either of them.

She glanced over at Nathan surreptitiously again, she had been doing so every now and then for a while but he had not caught her yet, and saw that he still looked the same: slightly troubled, weary, and somehow still very handsome. She jerked her eyes back to the road. No, he was *not* handsome.

Of course, he is, scolded the little voice in her mind. *Some would call that a gross insult to find him merely handsome.*

She wished that voice would be silent as well. She did not need any more distraction than she already had, and when her own mind was fighting against her will, things got more than a little harried inside.

A noise from up ahead caused her to lift her eyes a bit. There was a carriage off to the side of the road, one wheel obviously broken, and three people stood outside of it.

She looked more closely, and saw that one, an old woman, sank onto a piece of luggage, looking very tired and haggard.

The other two were men, and they were arguing about something, and rather loudly at that. The younger of the men was waving his arms dramatically, while the older one stood with his arms folded, shaking his head.

"What on earth?" Nathan muttered from beside her. He nudged Mercury on a bit faster, and she matched them. "Can we help you?" he asked as they approached.

The older man turned, looking vastly relieved. "I certainly hope so, sir. We've broken an axle, as you see, and I'm trying to explain that there is nothing I can do, but it's pointless. I haven't a clue what this frog-eater is saying. Ruddy fool only speaks a handful of English words, if you can call them that. Sounds like a bunch of French gibberish to my ears."

Nathan's brows shot up and he turned to the younger man, who was red faced and seething. The man instantly started rambling off a stream of angry French, waving his hands just as vividly as before. Nathan dismounted and tried to calm him, in his own excellent French, but the man was not about to listen. He continued to rant and rave quite forcefully.

It was almost comedic to witness. There was Nathan, trying to be calm and placating, but obviously fast losing patience; then there was the Frenchman, angry and agitated and determined to be anything but calm, and interrupting Nathan so often that Moira doubted Nathan completed a full sentence. And then there was the coachman, who was contentedly leaning against his broken carriage, smoking his pipe.

The only person left was that old woman, ignored by the group, sitting all alone behind the lot of them, staring off at nothing. She was dressed from head to toe in black, with the obvious veils of mourning. The lines on her face were not particularly deep, but there were quite a few. Her eyes were dim and downcast, and no one marked her.

Moira heaved a sigh. She would have to reveal a particular secret that she had never intended to. Things were getting to be ridiculous. They were never going to solve anything if this incessant bickering was going to continue. She slid as delicately as she could off of Flora, and marched past the arguing men towards the old woman.

"*Bonjour*," she said gently as she approached, taking a seat on the trunk next to her. "*Je m'appelle Moira. Les hommes sont impossibles, n'est-ce pas?*"

The old woman's eyes lit up and she turned to face Moira. "*Oui, Mademoiselle Moira! Ils n'écoutent jamais!*"

Immediately they began a conversation filled with laughter and venting frustrations, all in rapid French. The old woman, Nicole, was traveling with her grandson, Louis, who had inherited his father's temper, and all she wanted was to find some place to rest her feet, but he would not listen to her. They were headed to London so she might stay for a time with a younger sister, who was married to an English baron, and she was exhausted already.

Moira nodded, then took Nicole's hand and turned to face the men, only to find all three of them staring at her in stunned silence, mouths gaping identically. "Nicole does not care about the coach or anything else," she announced to the silent gathering. "She just wants a place to rest her feet before they push on to London."

Nathan closed his mouth and turned to Louis, and spoke to him quickly, then turned to his horse. "I am going to fetch a hack to take the two down to the village we passed not too long ago. They should be able to find boarding there."

Moira nodded and relayed the message to Nicole, who nodded gratefully, then glared at her grandson, who started sputtering.

"Stay here," Nathan ordered brusquely as he looked at Moira.

She gave him a look of her own. "Where am I going to go, Nathan?"

He fought for control as he mounted Mercury, and glared right back at her. "Devil if I know," he gritted out.

Her eyes flashed and she opened her mouth to argue, but he spun the horse away and rode off at a gallop, kicking up a great deal of dust as he went.

Moira made a noise of frustration, and then felt an old hand take hers. She turned to see Nicole, full of understanding, smiling at her. "*Les hommes*," she sighed, shaking her head as she patted her hand.

"*Oui*," Moira replied with a shake of her own head. "*Les hommes*."

Nathan was not gone very long before he was back with the news that a hack was on its way. He was ready to move on immediately, but Moira was determined not to depart until Nicole was situated comfortably in a coach.

Now he was pacing around waiting for that blasted hack to

show up. He was furious. Not only were they unable to proceed at all because of her determination to stay with these people, but she had lied to him. She spoke French! Not only that, she spoke it perfectly! Her accent was absolutely flawless. Even Louis was impressed by it, and it was that alone that made the lad shut up.

Why the act then? Why had she made him spend that entire afternoon suffering through a lesson in French basics when she could have taught him a thing or two? He kicked at a patch of grass, glaring over at her as she chatted with Nicole and Louis, but mostly Nicole as they were both upset with Louis, and pretending as though he were not here at all.

He was so angry with her at the moment that he could hardly stand to look at her, let alone remain silent for this long. But at the same time, he could not *not* look at her. He had to. It was an involuntary reaction to being around her. And if he were being totally objective, she was not even looking especially lovely today. Her hair was a mess, her dress was dirty, and she looked worn out. But that did not matter. In his eyes, and he was well aware how biased they were, she was the most stunning creature he had ever seen.

And that was irritating.

At the sound of approaching wheels, he turned, sighing in relief. The coach had arrived, and they could be on their way. He nodded to the coachman, who returned it, then hopped down to help the former coachman with the trunks.

Nathan helped Nicole into the coach, then moved aside so she and Moira could kiss cheeks and express their farewells. Then Moira stepped back and Louis, still grumpy, climbed in and sat on the side opposite. In a matter of minutes they were gone, and Nathan and Moira were alone again.

They looked at each other briefly, then moved as one to the horses. Nathan silently helped Moira up, and then he stood there glaring up at her. For the longest time, she did not look at him.

"What is it, Nathan?" Moira asked finally. "You have been glowering at me for most of the day now. What have I done?"

He laughed incredulously. "What have you done?" he cried. "You can speak French!"

She met his eyes coolly. "I never said that I couldn't."

He could not believe what he was hearing. "I spent," he began as calmly as he could manage, "an entire afternoon, a very painful one I might add, teaching you French, or so I thought! Why in heaven's name would you pretend you couldn't speak it?" His voice had lost its calmness at some point and to his surprise, he now found himself shouting at her.

Moira narrowed her eyes and tightened her grip on Flora's reins. "I don't know, Nathan," she said in a scathing, sarcastic voice. "Perhaps I just wanted *you* to teach me." With a swift kick into Flora's side, she rode off, leaving Nathan standing in his place and staring after her, his mouth gaping open, eyes wide, anger gone.

She wanted *him* to teach her? That did not make any sense to him. Why would she want him to teach her anything, especially something she already knew? He was not anything special, nor was he as gifted in the language. There was no reason she should want him specifically.

Unless… unless she was starting to have some feelings for him as well.

He staggered in his place and gripped Mercury's reins for support as all of the breath left his lungs. That could not even be possible, could it? A beautiful woman like her, who already had a betrothed, would not be interested in plain Nathaniel Hammond. The Earl of Beverton maybe, but not Nathan as he was, stripped of title and fortune and breeding.

She could not possibly feel anything towards him beyond their circumstantial friendship and near constant vexation.

And yet… Could he have imagined the warmth in her eyes when they laughed? Hadn't she been just as still during those moments when their acting became a little too intimate? Didn't she react to seeing him shirtless the same way he had reacted to her in breeches? She had shared private, personal things with him as he had with her. They were close, there was no denying it.

Could it have been something more on her part, as it undoubtedly was on his?

Suddenly, he remembered to breathe, though it was not at all refreshing, and cleared his throat rather awkwardly, forcing the burning hope in his heart to subside. It was possible, but it was not probable. And it would not change a thing. She was engaged. They were searching for her love. Once he was found, she would be gone.

He mounted Mercury and raced to catch up to her. Whatever time they had left together, he did not want to spend it fighting or angry.

It felt like ages before he caught her, and she made no effort to look at him. "Moira, I'm sorry," he said as he slowed.

She sniffed and wiped at her nose with her sleeve, making him smile in spite of himself. "So am I."

"I should not have yelled at you for being fluent in French," he said, shaking his head. "It sounds ridiculous, now that I say it out loud, doesn't it?"

She laughed a little. "Perhaps, but not as ridiculous as me pretending I couldn't speak French just so you could teach me."

He grinned. "You were appallingly bad. I thought there was no way anybody could be that terrible at learning a language."

"And you were right," she responded with a sigh.

"But, Moira, your French is excellent. Where did you learn?"

She looked over at him and shrugged. "Is it too odd to say that I don't know? For as long as I can remember, I have been able to speak French. I spoke it to my dolls, that way Aunt Miriam would have no idea what I was saying. There must have been a French governess or a maid or something when I was younger, but I cannot recall."

That was not so surprising, given the tragedies of her past, but Nathan chose not to comment on that. "Well, wherever you picked it up, it is flawless."

She smiled demurely. "Thank you. I am sorry for being so angry with you earlier."

"It was a very long morning, wasn't it?" he asked with a wry grin. Then he sobered. "Moira, I don't want to fight."

"Neither do I," she murmured, dropping her eyes.

"Then let's stop," he said simply.

She met his eyes, smiling a bit. "Maybe if you were not so irritating…" she said lightly, with a shrug.

"Me?" he cried with a laugh. "Forgive me, but have you met

yourself? You are hardly a paragon of meekness."

"Well, you had already established that I am the most infuriating woman on the planet," she protested. "Shouldn't you have adjusted your behavior to accommodate mine?"

"Hardly! I only gave you the title for the sake of argument. I never thought you would be flattered by it!"

They bantered for much of the remainder of the day, and by the time they had decided they should stop for the night, even after making considerably less progress than they had hoped for, they were in high spirits.

Moira had no sooner stepped into the taproom of the inn that night than she was mobbed by the innkeeper's wife and two daughters, both of whom appeared too young to be present in such a place.

"Oh, my dear, you must be so weary! Are you staying the night? Do say that you are, we shall look after you considerably well. I shall draw you a hot bath and Molly here will see to it that your dress is washed and pressed for you, while Sally will bring you up a hearty dinner!" She finally took a breath as she waved to the rather crowded taproom full of men.

Moira looked back at Nathan, who was smiling to himself. "Darling?" she queried with an insistent tilt of her head.

"Do not fret, Jane," he said coming over and patting her on the back, then smiling at the other women. "I should like for you to get some proper rest tonight, and these fine women seem to be more than able to help you with that. Not to worry, dear, I will take care of everything."

She narrowed her eyes at him, but she could not help but to be amused. "If you are sure, Michael. I would hate to inconvenience you."

He shook his head and smiled in what would appear a loving manner. "Not at all, my dear. I will be up much later, long after you have gone to bed."

She nodded, sighing in resignation. "Very well. Ladies, I would be pleased if you would direct me to an available room and that hot bath you were speaking of."

All three women squealed in delight at the prospect of having a real lady in their inn, and herded Moira up the stairs.

She threw a panicked look at him, but he just smiled and waved her on. She heard his laughter as they left and swore to make him pay for it.

Up in the room, Moira was dreading what the bath would be like. She was already being fussed over, and they were only at the dinner stage. They had stripped her of her gown and put her in a fresh one of theirs, which fit surprisingly well, and were now trying to get her to eat something that smelled so terrible that she just knew that if one spoonful touched her lips, she would be ill.

"No, please, Mrs. Clarke, I cannot," she begged, holding up a hand.

"Oh, but you must, child," the round woman scolded, holding the bowl out to her. "It is just the thing to cure the weary state of your body from a long day of traveling."

Moira doubted that very much indeed. "Please, I am sure it is wonderful, but I just…"

"Oh, do eat up, my lady," Molly said with a pleading look in her eyes.

She could not eat it. She would not. But how to make them leave her be about it? Frantically her mind raced and she seized upon the first thing that came into her mind.

"I am with child," she blurted out, covering her stomach.

The women in the room froze, mouths gaping. In the next instant, the bowl clattered to the ground and she was swarmed by them, hugging and squeezing and screams of joy.

"Darling girl! Is this your first?"

At her nod, Mrs. Clarke screamed again. "Oh, dear child, I was so dreadfully sick with my first. Sally, take this away and bring her something else that will not make her ill!"

"Yes, Mama," the girl said as she rushed out with the food she had just brought in.

"Your husband must be so pleased!" Molly squealed, taking a hand.

"Or does he even know yet!" Mrs. Clarke said with a gasp. "You look so thin, you cannot be very far along."

"He…" Moira began.

"He doesn't know, does he?" Molly interrupted with yet another squeal.

"Well…"

"Oh, you must tell him, indeed you must," Mrs. Clarke insisted, pulling Moira from the chair.

Moira's heart stopped in her chest. "Now?" she managed to squeak out.

"Yes, yes, now," Molly insisted as she dragged Moira to the door. "Mama is quite right, there is no time like the present."

She could not even manage to say another word as the two women spoke over each other about how delighted he would be and how delighted they were, and things only got worse when Sally rejoined them and offered her own opinions and prostrations on the subject. A horrible feeling of dread welled up inside of Moira as she saw the number of people in the taproom. Not only would she be unable to pretend she had told Nathan, but now she would not even be able to tell him in privacy. They were going to make a grand spectacle of this and Nathan had no idea it was even coming.

Please let him act happy, she wished with all of her might. She could only imagine the horror that the Clarke women would express were his reaction anything less than jubilant. She shuddered at the thought.

Nathan looked up in surprise as the boisterous Mrs. Clarke and her daughters dragged Moira into the center of the busy taproom.

"Quiet, please! Everybody, quiet! I beg your pardon for interrupting your evening, gentlemen," Mrs. Clarke said with a wave of her hand.

Nathan eyed Moira carefully, noting that, although she appeared calm on the outside, her eyes were panicked, her fingers were clenching each other, and her teeth were clamped on her lips so hard they were white.

"Our dear Jane here has something she needs to tell her husband, and we want you all to be witnesses!" Mrs. Clarke continued joyfully.

Nathan read the apology that flashed across Moira's eyes, and tried to ask what for with his own, but before he could, all of the men behind him shoved him forward so that he was only a few feet from Moira. "Uh..." he stammered, rubbing a hand on his trousers, "what is it, Jane?"

The entire room went deathly silent, as if what was about to be said were of grave importance.

"D-darling," Moira said in a trembling voice that sounded so unlike hers it worried him.

"Well, go on and tell him, dear!" Mrs. Clarke urged, grinning.

Moira took a deep breath and steeled herself. "I am with child."

The collective gasp that went up from the room would have been comical had Nathan not felt as though something large and heavy had been swung into his chest. The first thought that entered his mind was a blatant denial, knowing it was impossible. The following thought reminded him of their act, and he knew he somehow had to respond quickly.

"Are you certain?" he asked quietly, his voice hoarse as he stalled for time, the anticipation surrounding them almost tangible.

For a moment, she looked ready to deny it, but at his almost imperceptible nod, she nodded once, and then again.

He knew what he had to do. What any sensible husband would do with such news.

But he was no husband.

And yet...

He took a deep breath, and stepped towards her until there were only a few inches in between them. He put both of his hands on her shoulders, and drew her in for a kiss.

The moment his lips touched hers, he was lost. Though the room had erupted with cheers, he did not hear them. Her lips were yielding and molded to his far too easily. He could not breathe, could not feel anything but the sensation of his mouth on hers. Somehow, one of his hands made its way from her shoulder to her cheek, and he touched it gently, caressing it with his fingertips. He let go of his hesitation and gave himself up to it, unable and unwilling to resist her.

After what felt like an eternity, and yet was entirely too short, he pulled back, staring at her as he struggled to breathe or to think. Her eyes were wide and luminous, and she looked just as tossed about as he felt. For a moment, all they could do was stare at each other. Then Moira smiled.

At that smile, he knew.

He was in love with her.

He always had been.

Then he heard the roar of the crowd around them, and was jolted back into reality.

"Smile," Moira hissed through her teeth, her smile turning fixed. "You are supposed to be happy."

He shook himself and grinned broadly at the gathering, most of whom clapped him on the back and shouted their congratulations.

"I'll be taking the missus back up to bed now, sir, if you don't mind," Mrs. Clarke said as she took Moira's shoulders.

He nodded, unable to say anything. He met Moira's eyes once more, and at her own nod, he released the breath he forgot he was holding.

His newfound friends brought him more celebratory drinks, and for quite some time, they carried on in that manner.

It was not until much later, long after Mr. Clarke had gone to bed, and once the taproom was empty and he was alone, that Nathan was able to think clearly as he sat before the fire, staring absently into it.

He loved her. He loved Moira. Why deny it any longer? It was far too late for that. Fighting it would be futile. That kiss had told him everything he needed to know. He knew he would never forget that moment, mind racing, breath pounding, heart soaring.

And he would never, as long as he lived, forget the feel of her lips on his.

His thoughts returned to her smile… That soft, secretive, almost wondering smile she had smiled as they caught their breath. Had that been for him? Or had it been nothing more than an act, a show she had put on for their utterly rapt audience?

He didn't know, and he couldn't ask. But he would keep that smile locked away in his mind when all of this was over. It would haunt him forever.

The reminder of what he had lost.

Chapter Twelve

They made their escape from the "helpful" intentions of the Clarkes as early as they possibly could the next morning. The night had been extraordinarily painful for Moira, first with having to announce her supposed pregnancy to a room full of strangers and pretending that Nathan was the father, and then having to sustain herself purely on a lukewarm soup, and *then* enduring the attentions of the women during the bath they insisted on helping her with. At least they had been as good as their word concerning her dress, which was now as clean as it had ever been.

The only part of the night she did not regret with her whole soul was the kiss that she and Nathan had shared in that busy, crowded taproom.

It was probably the one thing that she *should* regret. But she didn't.

The moment she had seen Nathan this morning, anxiety had surged and consumed her. He had not said a word to her, and his eyes were dim and troubled, with lines that seemed permanently etched into his brow. Sensing that he did not wish for conversation, she had maintained silence for as long as she could. But now they were alone and had been riding for quite some time, she could not take this awkward tension any longer.

"I am so sorry that I told them I was pregnant, Nathan," she burst out, her words flying rapidly. "I have no idea what came over me. They were trying to feed me this awful looking something or other that had such a putrid stench that I knew if I had to eat it, I would be violently ill. So the only way I could think to avoid that would be to claim that I was with child, because no one would feed something so foul to a woman with an especially sensitive stomach, and once I said that, they insisted that I come and tell you right then, and I couldn't get out of it. I know it must have been dreadful for you, and I…"

"I apologize for kissing you."

Moira stopped her babbling instantly and froze. "W-what was that?" she asked, feigning deafness. Surely he had not actually said what she had thought she had heard him say.

He cleared his throat, and spoke louder. "I said I apologize for kissing you."

Moira's heart seemed to stop and her eyes began to burn. He regretted it. That was why he looked so tired, and why he was not himself. He wished he had not kissed her. He was so miserable about it that he had not been able to sleep. For some reason she dared not identify, that stung sharply.

"Oh," she murmured. It was all the reply she could manage, and she wished that it had not sounded so small.

"It wasn't proper," Nathan went on, as if he had not noticed how still she had gone. "It was a rash decision and an assault on your virtue. It should not have happened and I am sorry for it."

Moira looked away for a moment, closing her eyes against the welling moisture within them. She needed to remain calm; it would not do to become a water pot in front of a man who found kissing her disagreeable. She took a measured breath in and released it slowly, feeling some of the tension leave her body. She forced a smile and turned back. "Oh, Nathan, there's no need to apologize for that. What I was going to say before you interrupted me was that I was grateful that you had such quick thinking. Don't be troubled about it anymore; I was not offended in the least. You did what you had to for the sake of protecting my reputation, and I thank you for that."

Nathan's heart sunk and he almost snorted in derision. Her reputation had been the very last thing on his mind when he kissed her.

"It was my own fault you had to anyway," Moira said quietly, her voice heavy with regret.

That stung worse than anything else. His regret extended only so far as it made her uncomfortable. He could never regret the kiss itself.

But if she were lamenting it, if he had affronted her in any way, then he owed her more apologies than he could ever give.

"I don't blame you, Moira," he assured her, fighting back the desire to hit something. "You reacted in the way you thought best for the situation, you could not have foreseen how they would react."

"No, I couldn't," she sighed, her smile growing. "They were impossible to fend off, and I did try."

"I believe it," he said, finding himself somehow able to smile despite the pain. "The look on your face when you came down was priceless. I only wish you could have seen it."

She groaned and shook her head. "I was absolutely petrified, Nathan. But, in spite of everything, I didn't have to eat that horrible food, and so it worked out well enough."

"And that is all that matters," he affirmed with a nod, the familiarity of their banter easing him.

"Hardly, but it was important," she laughed. "Now, I have a question for you."

He quirked a brow at her, trying to hide the slight nervous twinge he felt. "Is it even your turn?"

"Who knows?" she asked with a roll of her eyes. "I am just going to pretend it is. Nathan, what do you want most out of life?"

His mouth popped open in surprise. That was a question he was not even sure he knew the answer to, let alone something he expected she would ask him. What did he want most in life? Oh, that she would somehow not marry Charles Allenford, that she would not care that he was actually an earl, that his brother would speak to him again, and that he would always be surrounded by family and friends that loved him. But that probably was not the answer she was looking for.

"Too personal?" she asked with a wince, misinterpreting his silence.

"No," he said slowly, shaking his head a bit, "it just requires a bit of thought." He sighed and considered his words carefully. "All I really want, I suppose, is to know when I leave this world, that I have done some good in it."

Moira nodded, smiling to herself. "That's just the sort of thing I thought you would say."

"Is it? I would hate to think that I am predictable."

"You are certainly not predictable, Nathan," she said with a laugh. "I think I know you fairly well by now. It does not surprise me at all that what you want out of life is not even for or about you, really."

"I think there is a compliment in there," he teased, "but I could be mistaken."

She shook her head and smiled. "If there is, it was entirely by accident, I can assure you."

"What about you, Moira? I will ask you the same question." He suddenly found himself wanting to know what she wanted out of life, what her hope for herself was.

"I only want to be happy," she replied. She shrugged and smiled. "That is hardly as selfless, I know, but…"

"It's better," he interrupted, finding himself a bit humbled by her simple admission. "You didn't ask for anything at all, really. You can be happy in a variety of ways, and you don't care which. That is a good thing to want, Moira. And you deserve whatever happiness comes to you."

"Thank you," she said shyly, ducking her head a bit. Then she grinned mischievously. "And that was full of compliments, Nathan. You are getting careless."

He changed the subject immediately. "So your middle name is Patience?"

"Oh, I wondered when you were going to bring that up!" she

cried, putting a hand to her brow. "I thought I said you weren't allowed to speak of it."

He shrugged. "You said it yourself, I'm not predictable."

"That is no excuse," she argued, waving a finger at him. "I knew you wouldn't let it go."

He smiled unapologetically. "So, are you going to share? Or must I become very annoying about it?"

"Become?" she muttered with a snort. "You have yet to be anything but. Very well. Patience was my grandmother's name, but my father could not stand her, so he was constantly apologizing for letting Mother name me after her. We used to make up pretend middle names for me."

"And which was your favorite?"

"Elizabeth," she said with a fond smile. "It always sounded so grand and elegant to me. I longed to be an Elizabeth."

He smiled in return. "It would have suited you."

"That's what my father said," she laughed. "He used to call me Moira Elizabeth, even when Mother forbade him to."

"Then I will ignore the name given you at your birth, and think of you as Moira Elizabeth as well," he promised.

"Really?" she asked, still grinning.

He nodded. "Really."

She seemed so delighted by the notion that Nathan almost laughed. But she said nothing else, as if she were more than content just by that detail alone.

In spite of her contentment, Nathan couldn't help wondering when she was going to ask him about the question he had passed on. He repeatedly looked over at her, knowing it had to be forthcoming. Yet she looked as satisfied as could be.

Finally, he couldn't stand it anymore. "Well, aren't you going to ask me?"

She looked at him in surprise. "Ask you what? Your middle name?"

"No," he said, confused by her confusion, "about what I said not to talk about, since I asked about yours."

She shrugged. "No, actually. You said you didn't want to talk about it, and it seemed a trifle more important than a distasteful middle name, so I had no intention of asking about it ever."

"Honestly?"

"Yes, honestly," she replied matter-of-factly.

He stared at her in awe. She was entirely serious. This was not a ploy to get him to talk about it out of some bizarre sense of reciprocation. She was not going to ask him about something that he had said he did not want to share.

But oddly enough, he didn't want to hide it from her any more. Limited though the information might be, he wanted her to know.

"I'm going to tell you anyway," he said suddenly, bringing Mercury closer so he would not feel as though he were shouting.

"Nathan, you don't have to," she told him, her eyes sober and clear.

"I know, and I appreciate that," he responded with a smile. "But we have each passed on one question, and you were gracious enough to share yours anyway, and I would like to do the same."

She watched him carefully for a long moment, and then she nodded. "If you are certain, I would be honored to hear it."

"I don't know if honor is the word to use," he told her with a shake of his head. "It's not something I am proud of." He sighed heavily, and began: "I am the older of two sons. No other children. My father and mother had a very good marriage, and in fact, that is my mother's ring you have been using."

"What?" Moira gasped, looking down at the simple band around her finger.

He nodded. "I wasn't going to tell you that, but it seems silly not to now."

"I had no idea," she murmured, her eyes still trained on the ring.

"Well, now you know. At any rate, they were very happy, and raised us well. My father was a strict man, but never cruel. He encouraged us to always better ourselves, and to do something useful with our lives, regardless of circumstances. He had expectations for us to meet, and responsibilities that we were supposed to bear." Nathan smiled sadly at the memories, then cleared his throat and looked back at Moira. "He died when I was fifteen, and I was left to care for Mother and Spencer. Mother was never very well after that, but she was always kind. We took great pains to see that she was well cared for while we were away at school. One of the neighbor girls, Anna, was particularly very good to her. She became her companion, and a constant friend. In due course, Spencer and Anna formed an attachment, and I was more than pleased to give my consent for them to be wed when they were old enough. After I had been in the army for two years or so, I received word that Mother was very ill, and I rushed back."

"When you left your men," she said in recollection.

He did not respond to her comment. "I arrived to find her close to death. Spencer was a mess, and Anna was distraught. I sat up with Mother all that night, and Spencer relieved me early in the morning, so I could sleep for a few hours. That continued for a few days. But one night, during Anna's watch, I could not sleep. I went in to Mother's room and found Anna holding her hand and crying. I went to comfort her, she was the closest thing to a sister I have ever known, and she turned to me. I held her for a few moments while she cried, and Spencer came in and saw us. He started yelling at me for talking such liberties with his betrothed, which I denied emphatically.

"Soon we were arguing, him blaming me for my absence to some ridiculous army when Mother needed me, and me telling him that if he had stopped spending all of his time mooning over Anna then he could have been of more help. All the while, Anna sat there and heard every word, still holding onto Mother's hand." He was forced to stop by the sudden rawness in his throat. "Suddenly, Anna screamed and began to sob, and our fighting ceased. At some point during our arguing, Mother had slipped away. We had been too involved with hurling the most injurious things we could at each other, that we had not even said our goodbyes. Spencer cried out his despair and sank into one of the chairs, but I couldn't move. I couldn't speak."

He swallowed back the pain that was as fresh and raw as it had felt then, and shook his head. "We had a graveside service for her a few days later, but I don't recall any of it. The only thing I remember from that time is three days after the service, when my brother came into my study and overturned my chair while I was still in it. As I looked up at him from where I had fallen, he said, 'Now I have lost the only women I have ever loved. I hope one day you know what that feels like'."

"Women?" Moira asked, interrupting gently. "Plural?"

Nathan nodded, the motions jerky. "Anna decided she could not marry him after all. I'm not sure if it was our fight as Mother died, or if it was the pain of memory, but she broke things off and her family moved to Shropshire."

"Poor Spencer," she murmured softly.

"He left shortly after that, and I haven't seen him since," Nathan continued, as if she had not spoken. "We have not communicated at all. That is why I was so determined to act so foolishly that day in the army. I had thought only of what I wanted and not of what was needed. I had abandoned my responsibilities at home, and in doing so, I had turned my back on the duty owed to my family. My brother had lost everything dear to him because I was too careless to have a clear thought in my head. And now he hates me."

"Oh, Nathan," she said, reaching over to put a hand on his. "I'm sure he doesn't hate you. He was angry and hurt, and probably hating himself more than you, but you were the most convenient outlet. You must not blame yourself anymore."

He shook his head. "You didn't see his face, Moira. There was hatred in his eyes."

"Perhaps in that moment he thought he did, Nathan, I don't know. All I know is that you need to fix that relationship."

"How can I? It seems fairly impossible at the moment."

"I can't tell you how, Nathan," she sighed, looking away and removing her hand. "I don't even know. All I know is that I would give everything I have for one more day with my brother, even if we were to spend it fighting."

He winced at her soft words. "I'm sorry," he murmured.

"I am not the one you need to be apologizing to," she said, giving him a very serious look.

"But I tried to!" he cried, throwing his hands up into the air. "He doesn't want to be my brother! I have received no word from him, and no hint at any sort of reconciliation. It does not even matter that he was in the wrong, and…"

"Oh, Nathan, don't you see?" she interrupted with a pitying smile. "It's not about who was right or who was wrong. It's about putting the past where it belongs, letting go of your pride and hurt and anger, and realizing that all that matters is each other. You would be surprised at what sort of miracles can take place when one only has the courage to take a first step in the right direction."

They were forced to take shelter at an inn midway through the afternoon as a storm swept through the area. They barely made it in before the thunder and lightning began. Thankfully, there was a room for them, should they need to stay for the night, which it was beginning to look like they would. Not that Nathan was about to complain, he was not in any further hurry to get to Preston than they needed to be. Torturous as it was, he wanted to spend as much time with Moira as he possibly could, regardless of the setting or situation.

After they had eaten, and when it became apparent that they would not be able to go anywhere that night, they took refuge in the room that they had been given. Moira now sat by the window staring out at the rain as it lessened, and smiling at the dispersing clouds.

Nathan was sitting on the floor by the fire, content just to look at her, not really caring if she noticed. It was her turn for the stables tonight, and he knew she had no intention of giving that up, storm or no storm. He had learned that it was best not to fight her when she had made her mind up. But watching her now, seeing the simple pleasure she took in the aftermath of a storm and the appearance of the stars from behind the clouds, he could not let her leave. He could not be apart from her.

Not tonight.

Her future did not involve nor concern him, and could not, but he was just selfish enough to want to pretend that for one night, it could. He wanted to watch her wake up in the morning and see how long it really took her to fall asleep at night.

He didn't want her to go.

She looked exhausted, but somehow still so beautiful. She had let her hair down hours ago, and he loved the way it flowed down her shoulders. He loved how it curled only at the very ends. He loved that she was sitting with her knees tucked into her chest with her skirt draped so modestly over them. He loved that she was barefoot, and that her boots had been the first thing to go.

It was amazing to him how easy it was to admit to himself that he loved her. He could not help loving her. It was the most natural thing in the world.

She made him want to be better; she challenged him, encouraged him, teased him, taught him in ways that he never dreamed anyone would or could.

He could not have expected any of this, not for a man of his nature and expectations. But he realized now that, secretly, he had been lonely for a long time. He was tired of the days and nights alone. He had spent a good portion of his adult life wondering about love, and now he had found it, but couldn't have it. The irony made him ache in places he did not know existed.

He had shared more of himself with her than he had with anyone. She knew him better than any other person ever had. How could he give her up when all of this was over? For what had to be the thousandth time, he cursed her betrothed. And yet, had the man not been foolish enough to leave her, then their own paths would never have crossed. He would never have met her, never known the sweet fulfillment that she brought to his once lifeless heart.

He could not let her go.

Unless he knew she would be happy. Only then might it be possible for him to do so. Even then, it would hurt like hell, and he knew it.

But tonight, she was here. He would never ask her to betray her betrothed, but tonight he needed her near him.

"Stay with me tonight."

She turned towards him with a jerk, her eyes wide, her cheeks flushing slightly. "What?"

"Just tonight. Don't go out to the stables. Stay."

Her expression was impossible to read, and his heart stopped.

"Why?"

For a long moment, he debated his answer. The truth would not be wise nor fair, not when they were so close to her… their… journey's end. But neither could he lie. He opted for a different truth.

"It's late," he said with a shrug. "The stable will be damp and chilled, the streets flooded. I cannot let you sleep out there like that. I can't have you taking ill. The innkeeper and patrons all think we are married, so…" He could see her indecision, her wariness in her eyes, but he could also see a glimmer of something else he did not dare identify. "I won't touch you," he murmured. "That's not what I mean. Just… please stay tonight. I… I need you to stay."

She continued to watch him steadily for a long moment, then she nodded slowly and turned her gaze back to the sky, her face still flushed. His heart soared within him, and he closed his eyes and sighed softly. Tomorrow would come and they would be themselves again. But not tonight.

Nathan wondered if he would regret this; being so close and so far away at the same time, glimpsing heaven but never allowed to touch it. He didn't care, he decided. He had tonight. He would not regret it.

He could not.

Nathan spread out his bedroll in front of the fire, still hardly able to believe that Moira had agreed to stay tonight. She was already situated in the bed, watching him work, looking rather content. She was supposed to be trying to sleep, but she wasn't.

He smiled to himself as he worked quietly. "Aren't you tired at all?" he said softly as he turned his head to look at her.

She shrugged lightly. "Of course, I am. But I told you that it takes me forever to fall asleep."

"So you did," he allowed as he laid himself down on the floor.

Moira blew out the candle, and the light in the room was restricted to the coals of the fire. Nathan put his hands behind his head and leaned back. As ridiculous as it sounded, though he was on the floor and she was high on the bed, he loved that he wouldn't be apart from her tonight. He grinned to himself. He was becoming such a lovesick fool. His friends would have washed their hands of him, had they known.

"Nathan?"

He turned his head towards the sound of her voice. "What?" he asked softly.

"Why did you bring your mother's ring for me to use?"

"I wish I knew," he said on a sigh. "I don't keep it on me, or out on display, or anything sentimental like that. I was only thinking of how we could travel without trouble, and being married seemed to be the easiest, and the moment I thought of that, I thought of the ring." He hesitated, and then ventured, "Does it bother you?"

"No, not at all," she replied at once, though he was not entirely certain he believed her. "I was only curious."

He considered that for a moment. "Well, I'm sorry I don't have a better answer for you."

She didn't reply, and he wondered if she might actually try to sleep now. He knew it would be some time before sleep came to him, but he wouldn't push conversation if she did not wish for it.

It was not as though he didn't have a great many things to think about, should he need to pass the time.

After a long while, he heard her moving about on the bed, and then heard a frustrated sigh. "Aren't you asleep yet?" he asked, laughing a bit.

"I told you," she hissed back, "it takes me a long time. And when I say a long time, I mean a long time."

He chuckled and turned on his side though he still could not see her, and propped his elbow up, resting his head in his hand. "Shall I try to help you sleep?"

"Only if you don't move from your current position," she quipped sharply.

He choked back more laughter. "I promise I will stay right here. I could tell you some of the grand adventures of Nathan Hammond and his merry band of idiots."

He could almost hear her smile "Now *that* sounds like a selection of stories to interest me."

"There are some rather fine tales to be told. Let us begin with the story of how Duncan was once bested by a milk cow."

And off he went, spinning all sorts of tales from his past, embellishing only slightly. It wasn't long before Moira was snickering into her pillow, and Nathan had to put his fist to his mouth to keep from laughing out loud. He told as many stories as he could remember, about all of them. He even told her stories he had sworn on pain of death never to tell. By the time he had run out of stories, Moira was laughing so hard she couldn't breathe, and he was not much better. They were continually hushing each other, and the need for silence only made the temptation to laugh that much greater. When they had eventually calmed, they had talked only a little longer about banal things, and it was not long before he could hear Moira's breathing deepen and the rustling ceased.

Nathan rolled to his back and closed his eyes, sighing painfully.

What he would have given to have more nights just like this.

Chapter Thirteen

Nathan jerked awake sometime in the night, utterly bewildered as to where he was, why he was on the floor, and what had woken him. Gradually, sense and reason returned to him and he recalled his situation. He was in the room at the inn, and Moira had stayed. He was unable to help the stupid, sleepy grin that crossed his face at the recollection.

It was still very dark, almost darker now than when he had finally fallen asleep, and he heard no noise, nothing that should have disturbed him. He rubbed a hand over his face and tried to get comfortable again, feeling his body relax and his breathing deepen.

Then he heard a panicked whimper and his eyes snapped open once more.

Was that what had woken him? Or was it just by chance?

Suddenly, there was a brief, but piercing cry from the bed somewhere above him.

"Moira?" he whispered to the dark, not sure if he wanted a response or not.

She made no reply but the sound of tears and frantic movement. He got to his feet and walked as quietly as he could to the bed. The sheets were tangled about her, and her eyes were still closed in sleep, though the sheen of sweat was forming on her skin.

"Moira?" he asked again, reaching out to touch her shoulder.

"No," she half moaned, half whimpered, burying her face into the pillow. "No, no, no."

"Moira!" he said a little louder, shaking her shoulder.

"Come back," she cried, thrashing slightly. "Mama, don't leave me! No!" Her cries dissolved into helpless, heaving sobs that even her pillow could not stifle.

Nathan's throat constricted and he almost groaned himself as he shook her harder.

"Moira, wake up. Moira, it's only a dream, wake up." He had to dodge a swinging fist, and switched to a much simpler, yet infinitely more painful approach. He sat on the bed against the headboard and pulled her hard against him, smoothing her hair. "Moira, Moira, shhh. It's all right. It's only a dream."

She pushed against him, her breathing ragged and choked. "No, no! Mama!"

"Shh," he soothed, holding her tightly and rubbing her back in wide circles. "Moira, it's all right. I'm right here. Wake up."

Abruptly, her flailing stilled and the resistance ceased, and with a gasp, she woke. Nathan released her immediately, but took hold of her shoulders so he could see her.

"N-Nathan?" she stammered, blinking at him.

"Are you all right?" he asked softly, staring at her closely.

She looked around quickly, fear and distress still etched on her features. Then she realized what he had asked and nodded. "Yes, I'm… I am fine. I'm sorry I woke you up."

Nathan did not like the way she attempted to reassure him, nor did he believe her. Her voice was quivering, and quiet tremors shook her.

"Moira," he said gently, his hold on her shoulders tightening.

Her lips clamped together and she avoided his eyes. "Nathan, please," she choked out, her breathing shallow.

Without a word, he pulled her against him again.

"Please," she whispered, weakly pushing at his chest.

He shook his head and held her more tightly. "No, Moira. You don't have to be strong right now. You can cry. I'm here. It's all right."

She was silent and still for a brief moment, then he felt her body shudder and curl against him. Her tears were quick to follow, and they rapidly fell onto his shirt, but he didn't care. In short order, she was trying to muffle sobs against his chest, clinging to him. He held her close, murmuring into her hair, rubbing her back, and trying in vain to soothe the pain that she was feeling.

He had never felt more helpless in his life.

Eventually, Moira fell into a slumber so deep she did not move at all. Nathan pulled blankets over the two of them, made sure there was a pillow behind Moira in case she should move, and settled in for what was destined to be the longest night of his life.

Moira awoke gradually, enjoying the sensation of a night well slept. She stretched her legs out, pointing her toes and groaning. She really had to learn how to sleep in a different position rather than curled into a ball. Waking up in the mornings was getting painful.

Suddenly her toes brushed against something that she did not expect. Another leg? Why would there be another leg in the bed with her? Her heart froze in her chest as faint memories of the night before flittered through her mind. Her nightmare… waking up in the dark and… Nathan… She gasped and covered her mouth, then slowly turned her head around to see behind her. As she feared, still slightly propped against the headboard, still asleep with his mouth slightly gaping, was Nathan.

She hastily turned her head back, shutting her eyes with a soft hiss. She had suspected that when she had agreed to stay, and how her heart had sputtered when he had asked, that he would be witness to one of her nightmares, but she never imagined how bad it would be, or how he would respond. She had fallen asleep in his arms last night, and it had been the best comfort she had ever received.

She quietly got out of the bed and tiptoed over to where a fresh dress lay on the chair. Without making any noise at all, she changed into it, avoiding as much exposure as she could. What if he woke up and saw her changing? That would be a perfect way to continue the awkward moments this morning. He would already have questions about the night before, she could not bear any more embarrassment than that.

Sinking into the chair, she put her face into her hands. That dream last night had been the worst in some time, now that she recalled it. Sometimes she could remember, other times she only knew she had had one, not the content of it. Regardless, they drained her strength and she was always so exhausted the morning after enduring one, so it was fortunate she had been able to sleep for so long this morning.

She took hold of her hair and began to plait it, sighing softly. If she knew of a way to ward off nightmares, she would have tried it with great enthusiasm. Anything would be better than dreams that plagued her nightly.

She glanced over at the bed and, with a jump of surprise, found Nathan awake and watching her, his dark eyes slumberous but steady. How long had he been doing that? He did not look startled or embarrassed, but the manner in which he stared at her was disconcerting.

Shaking off her shock, she flashed what she hoped was a convincing smile at him. "Well, hello there, sleepyhead! Were you planning on joining the living any time soon, or would you like more time to explore the insides of your eyelids?"

He smiled faintly, but didn't move. "I was dreaming," he said softly, his voice touched with a bit of wonder.

I never dream, Miss Dennison. She froze as the recollection of his words entered her mind. It had shocked her then, and she had been completely baffled as to how someone could possibly go through life without ever dreaming. But all of that was nothing compared to what she was feeling now. She would not even begin to imagine why he had suddenly dreamed last night. The prospect was far too dangerous.

"You were?" she breathed, her voice far less steady than she had intended it to be.

He nodded, his eyes fixed on hers with an intensity she had not seen in them before.

"About what?"

"You."

All of the breath seemed to evaporate from her lungs. Still he did not look away, did not even appear to blink. She swallowed hastily and tried to smile. "I hope I was amusing."

"You were maybe four or five," he told her, his voice low and gruff with remnants of sleep, "and you were up in a tree. I was around ten and running through the woods as if I was Robin of the Hood again. You were the Maid Marian, and I had to save you."

"Did you?" she asked quietly, wishing she could look away from him.

"I don't know," he replied in the same tone. "Did I?"

Now she had to look away; there was no pretending she did not understand him. Of course, he wanted to save her. Of course, he thought she needed saving. Of course, he wanted to protect her. That was what Nathan did. That was who he was. The protector. The defender. Robin of the Hood.

"Moira," he said softly, and she was helpless to turn back, only to find him sitting on the end of the bed, rather than lying on top of it. "What happened last night?"

Her throat suddenly dry, she swallowed and shook her head.

"Moira," he said again, not making any moves towards her. "Please. What happened? What was that?"

"A nightmare," she said bluntly, holding herself as still as possible.

"Yes, that much I figured out for myself," he said, and she could hear him smiling, but still she kept her gaze averted. "What was it?"

"I saw my mother," she whispered, unable to resist telling him. "She was dying. I couldn't save her. And then she was suddenly gone and I couldn't find her."

"Do you have nightmares often?" Nathan asked gently, when it became evident she was not going to elaborate.

She nodded. "Every night."

He rocked back in surprise. "Every night?"

She finally looked at him, a bitter smile on her lips. "Ironic, is it not? You don't dream at all, except for last night, and I have nightmares every night." She let out a hard bark of laughter. "It's almost comical."

Nathan did not smile. On the contrary, his concern seemed to increase. "How long has this been going on?"

She sighed and toyed with her plait a little. "Years. I don't remember when they began, but they come every night. "

"Are they always the same?"

She shook her head. "I dream about my parents most of the time, but I also dream about Robbie. And Charles. Sometimes I dream of being back in that dark, cramped closet and no one can hear me. Other times I am lost and have no idea which way to go, and I cannot find anyone to help me."

"I'm sorry," Nathan said softly.

"This is why I was so glad to sleep separately," she told him, giving an apologetic smile. "It was not so much that I had to sleep in the stables, but because I didn't want you to know about the nightmares. I usually wake up on my own and once I have calmed myself down, I can go back to sleep without any trouble." She swallowed harshly and her voice turned raw. "But sometimes I can't. Sometimes it is too real, and I am too scared. All of my fears come to life every night. The worst of it is that when I wake up, I am still alone, and all I have are my nightmares."

"And me," Nathan added, his eyes warm and friendly.

She smiled faintly, her heart burning with pleasure and pain. "Yes, and you. While it lasts." Then she sighed, and forced back the gloom. "So now you know my biggest fears."

He seemed to consider that, and Moira wished he would say something, anything, to ease the tension in the room.

"I have a terrible fear of public settings," Nathan suddenly said aloud, still watching her.

Her brow furrowed in confusion, and then she understood and allowed herself a small smile. "Have you?"

He nodded. "I become very anxious when I must be a part of a large gathering, or when I am expected to perform in some way or another in front of people that I don't know. I am quite good at conversing with people one on one, but when it comes to groups…" He trailed off and shuddered. "I will take working on a farm any day over a crowded ballroom."

"You fear being on display?" Moira asked, touched that he was sharing his fears with her now.

"I suppose you could say that," he allowed. "If I had to put a name to it, I would say that I have a fear of saying or doing something that will be perceived as wrong by those who don't know me. I fear public opinion." He paused for a moment, and then sighed reluctantly. "And spiders."

Moira stared at him for a heartbeat, and then quirked a brow. "Seriously? Spiders?"

He shrugged. "Give me snakes or ghouls or rats, and I am fine, completely unperturbed. But if you put a little spider into my line of sight, I will break out in a cold sweat."

"Do you scream?" she asked with a devious grin.

"Never," he said firmly with an emphatic shake of his head.

"Really?"

"Yes, really."

She narrowed her eyes and stared at him for a long moment. "I don't believe you," she said finally. "I think you scream."

"You are never allowed to meet Geoff," he muttered, standing up from the bed and rubbing his hands on his trousers.

"Why not?" Moira asked with a laugh as she went back to pinning up her hair.

"Now telling you that would be counterproductive, and give you far too many ideas, and I refused to be baited by you," he scolded with a smile. "Shall we go down to breakfast?"

She nodded and walked over to the door, where he escorted her out and took her hand. "If you tell anybody about you-know-what…" he warned in a low voice.

"Oh, really, who am I going to tell, Nathan?" she interrupted with a hiss.

He gave her a look. "Knowing you, anybody you can find."

She laughed out loud and tugged on his hand, pulling him into the room where a good many patrons already sat eating.

Well, there would hardly be a need for convincing the public of their proper relationship, Moira thought as they sat down themselves. The way Nathan was laughing, the way their hands were linked, combined with the ring on her finger, told everybody exactly what they already suspected.

If only it was the truth.

"I don't like the look of those clouds," Nathan said some time later, after they had been riding a while.

Moira looked where he was indicating, and shrugged. "They don't look too terribly imposing to me. Don't worry about the clouds." She flashed him a teasing grin. "Unless you are also secretly afraid of thunderstorms."

He glared at her in what he hoped was a menacing manner. "No, I just don't want to be caught out here in the middle of a storm. We are not near any shelter, and it would hardly be an easy thing to get our horses to behave if it storms."

That sobered Moira slightly, but she still smiled. "I think it will pass us by, Nathan. We had that large storm yesterday. I don't think we will have another one. Now, stop worrying and ride!" She took off suddenly at a mad gallop, laughing just as wildly.

He had no choice except to follow after her, but he grumbled about her lack of concern. Just because a storm had come yesterday did not mean that they would not get one today, and if she honestly thought that weather patterns actually followed a pattern, then she was not nearly as intelligent as he thought she was.

Urging Mercury on faster, he caught and passed Moira, earning a cry of outrage from her.

They continued to race back and forth, laughing all the while, until suddenly, the storm was upon them. And it was not some gentle spring rain. It was a torrential downpour with raindrops so large and falling at such a speed that the impact of one was almost painful. The wind howled and blew them about, nearly carrying away Moira's bonnet, which she had decided to don the moment the rain started.

"The bonnet?" Nathan yelled over the sound of the storm. "Really? I think it's a bit late for that!"

"Shut up, Nathan!" she bellowed as she hung onto her bonnet with one hand and Flora's reins with the other.

Nathan grinned in spite of the storm and turned back to the road, which was rapidly became impassable. Up ahead, he saw light coming from what looked to be a farm. He maneuvered closer to Moira and said, "I think we should make for that farm, see if they will let us take shelter there. Perhaps in the barn or something." He saw her face, and misread it. "It will be better than nothing, Moira."

"If you think I am going to be particular about where we take shelter, you are an imbecile," she said over the wind. "Flora is making me nervous. She is ready to bolt."

Nathan looked towards the farm, then back to their horses, who were whinnying and shifting anxiously, as well as getting their hooves stuck in the mud of the road. "Let's get off of them and make a run for it," he suggested.

Moira nodded and slid off quickly, her boots immediately sinking into the thick mud beneath her. She gripped Flora's reins tightly in her hands and tried to move, but found her feet to be stuck. "Nathan!" she yelled with no small amount of irritation.

"What?" he called back, his own level of frustration very high.

"I am stuck in the mud, Nathan," she bellowed, trying once more to free herself. "What a grand idea that was, getting off of the horses in the middle of the road. Did you think we would fare much better than they did in the mud?"

"I didn't hear you object!" he argued as he made his way over to her, clutching Mercury's reins in his fist. "Did you have any better ideas? No!" He drew out the "o" dramatically as he trudged through the mud. "'Don't worry about the clouds,' you said. 'It will pass us by,' you said. Well, are you happy now, Moira? I said I was worried about them, but since you were so sure they were nothing, we did nothing. I should just leave you in the mud and let you fend for yourself."

"Oh, who asked you to do anything?" she barked, shielding her eyes from the rain. "If you want to ride on ahead to safety, then be my guest! I can manage very well without you!"

He snorted as he reached her and bent down to examine her boots. "Yes, very well indeed, from the looks of things. You have things quite in hand, haven't you?"

She screeched in frustration. "Ugh, if I had the use of my feet, I would kick some of this disgusting mud into your face, Nathaniel Hammond!"

He glanced up at her through the rain, looking rather sardonic. "That is not very good incentive for me to get you out of here, is it?" Before she could respond to that, he began unlacing her boots.

"What are you doing?" she screeched.

"You are not going anywhere in these," he commented matter-of-factly. "They are only going to sink further and take you along with them. They must come off."

"So you are going to make me march all the way up there in my stockings?"

He sighed and looked up at her again. "Tempting. But you know me better than that, Miss Dennison." Without another word, he swept her up into his arms in one fluid motion, leaving her boots behind.

She squealed in surprise and held onto him as best as she could, and he grimaced as she wriggled in his arms. "Hold still, woman," he growled. "This is going to be difficult enough as it is."

She frowned up at him. "Well, my apologies for not being the size of a twig."

"That is *not* what I meant, Moira," he scolded as he slogged through the thickening mud towards the grass on the other side of the road.

"Oh, well, now you are claiming I don't understand you. That's a true statement, if ever I heard one," she drawled, reluctantly latching a hand behind his neck.

"Stop choosing to be offended!" Nathan cried, slipping a touch on the grass. "Do the whole world a favor and shut up!"

"You first!" she protested, tugging on Flora's reins as the horse tried to escape. "Why don't you try hurrying along instead of talking the storm out?"

"I could go a lot faster without you as an added burden," he informed her, "but as that is hardly an option, I am doing the best that I can."

Moira ducked her chin as her cheeks flamed. She was cold and sopping and obviously irritated, but it did not stop her from tucking herself a little closer into the moderate warmth of Nathan's chest.

Nathan tightened his hold on her, feeling her shiver against him. Her warm jacket was worn and too thin for a storm, but he had nothing better for her. His own jacket was hardly substantial and was far too wet to offer. "We're almost there," he said gruffly, wanting to comfort her, but not willing to let go of his argument.

"Good," she said shortly as the arm around his neck tightened ever so slightly. Then she growled and untied the bonnet from her head. "This bonnet is useless," she muttered, flinging it off into the storm.

Nathan looked down at her with a quirked brow.

"What?" she asked without concern. "I am already soaked through, it is not as though it was actually being of use. It was a tatty thing anyway."

"You cannot go with nothing." He shifted his hold on her enough to take his own hat from his head and place it on hers, but not before a steady stream of water fell from the rim onto her dress.

"You did that on purpose!" she cried as she tried to shake the water off, which did nothing but spray them both with droplets.

"I might have," he said with a shrug, "but now you have protection for your head and I do not, so my actions are negated by each other."

"That is hardly accurate," she mumbled as she adjusted the hat. "There was no need for protection for my already sodden head, and your hat is hardly worth wearing itself."

"You are welcome."

"Must you always have the last word?"

"Must you?"

She muttered under her breath, unaware that he could hear every word, and he bit back a grin at her choice of words.

"If you are going to be so poorly behaved," he said calmly, "I would be more than happy to carry you over my shoulder instead."

"What makes you think I would not prefer that over this?" came the immediate response.

Nathan sighed and shook his head, torn somewhere between terribly amused and irritated beyond belief. One thing was certain, miserable and cold and drenched as they were, he was rather enjoying having Moira in his arms. And protesting as she might be, she was making no effort to shift away from him.

It was an odd sort of peace amidst the strife.

The thunder and lightning came in earnest then and Nathan quickened his pace as much as he dared, fearing they would lose control on the horses.

Suddenly, three men appeared from the farmhouse rushing towards them.

"Do you have shelter for us?" Nathan called out to them.

"Yes, of course!" the youngest of the three called as he reached up and took Mercury's reins from him. "Mama is already making some hot tea and soup and my wife and sisters are setting to the rooms."

"Oh, we only need the barn," Moira insisted as an older man took Flora's reigns from her.

"Nonsense," he said as he put a comforting hand on her shoulder. "We have room."

"Besides," said the third man, also quite young, "Mama would never hear of it. She would put us out in the barn before she would let any guests do so."

"We are most grateful," Nathan said as they made their way to the house. "I'm Nathan, and this is Moira."

"Squire Joseph Cutler," the oldest man said. Then he pointed to the others. "My sons, Jacob and William. There are two daughters, a younger son, one son-in-law, my sons' wives, and three grandchildren inside, along with my wife." He smiled at them, in spite of the storm. "You may wish someone else had found you tonight, sir. It is hardly going to be peaceful."

"Oh, don't worry," Nathan commented dryly. "I've not had peace in quite some time now."

A sharp jab into his ribs from the woman in his arms left Nathan quite unable to comment on anything else for a while.

Chapter Fourteen

The squire's words should have been fair warning, but neither Nathan nor Moira could have expected just how true they were.

From the moment they had entered the spacious farmhouse, they were set upon by a rather demanding, yet impossibly sweet Mrs. Cutler, who insisted they call her Madeline. She bemoaned their sorry state and instantly rushed Moira upstairs and ordered the men to see to Nathan.

They immediately dried and warmed her thoroughly, then changed her into a frock belonging to one of the girls, though which one Moira couldn't have said. She didn't recall any of the names, despite having had hurried introductions.

They returned to the large room on the first floor where the remainder of the family and Nathan, now changed himself, were waiting. The room was positively bustling with people, both adults and scampering grandchildren, and Mr. Cutler stood against the wall near Nathan, and watched the gathering with a quiet smile.

She made a quick count, and with her and Nathan as an addition, there were fifteen people in this house, which was certainly large enough for a family, but hardly one of this magnitude. It was quite simply astounding.

She moved to stand by Nathan as Mrs. Cutler and her daughters returned to tend the food. "Do they all live here all the time?" she whispered as she reached him.

"Shh," he scolded out of the corner of his mouth, as he saw Squire Cutler's mouth twitch. "You are not nearly as quiet as you think you are."

She glared at him, but didn't comment.

"Don't worry, Moira," the squire said as he leaned near them. "We don't take offense easily in this family. We can't. The answer to your question is no, we do not all live here all the time. The married ones have homes of their own not too far away. Emma and Jack, that is our youngest boy there, are the only ones remaining. The others are here for Madeline's birthday, which is in two days. Her only request was for the entire family to be together for a week, and, as you can see, we are fairly bursting at the seams."

"I'm sorry to cause any further inconvenience," Moira said softly, feeling guilty and letting Nathan take her hand in consolation.

"It's no trouble at all," came Madeline's cheerful voice from across the room. "We have plenty of room for everyone, and I will hear no more about it! Now come and eat, all of you, before it gets cold!"

Moira looked to the squire, who only smiled and shrugged. "I never argue with Madeline, you know," he whispered as she passed him. "It would be impossible to get a word in."

They spent some time socializing with the family after they had finished the excellent meal, and it was a wonderful respite from the excitement of the last few days. They'd been questioned, rather gently, about their story, and rather than pretend marriage at this point, Nathan explained that they were cousins searching for Moira's husband, and it seemed to come far more easily than anything they'd tried yet. Faintly, she wondered why they hadn't done so before.

The family was very sympathetic to their plight, with some rather maternal tears from Mrs. Cutler, and the sons assured them both that they could easily reach Preston by nightfall tomorrow if they left in the morning.

Nightfall. Tomorrow night this would all be over. Moira looked over at Nathan, who returned it with a similar expression. After tomorrow, there would be no pretending a life with him, no familiarity of speech or argument, no more stories or questions… All of that would belong to someone else.

And they would never see each other again.

Suddenly, she could not breathe and her chest ached.

In Nathan's eyes she saw that he had not been immune to the words either, but what exactly he was feeling, she could not possibly know.

To be perfectly honest, she was afraid to.

As the dinner finished, the family suggested, quite energetically, that they enjoy some dancing. There was no arguing with the guests, but Nathan nearly groaned. The dishes were quickly cleared from the table and no doubt the speed with which they were cleaned was something that should have deserved a reward. In almost no time at all, the furniture was moved into other rooms and suddenly, the room was spacious enough to hold quite a large number of people.

It was only then that Nathan noticed a small pianoforte in a corner of the room. He wondered how much it had cost this family, who clearly had enough to get by, but not much beyond, for they did not even have help around the house. The instrument was old and worn, obviously much loved, but still in serious need of repair. If someone in this family could play half as well as the piano's use indicated, they deserved a better one.

Each of the girls took a turn playing as the rest danced, and it was hard to say which of them were more talented. Nathan begged off from dancing, as the numbers allowed him to, and he spent much of the time watching. One daughter, Sarah, if he recalled, was expecting and kept him amiable company.

"Not dancing, Nathan?" she asked with a smile as she looked up at him.

"No," he said instantly, shaking his head with a dry laugh. "No, I would not shame the present company with something so atrocious. I am much better at observing, thank you very much."

"That is not a very good reason, you know," she told him, her eyes dancing.

"But alas, it is the only one I have. You have a far better reason, I see," he said with a grin, his eyes indicating her stomach.

"Yes," she said with a warm smile, rubbing it once more. "I do not think dancing would be wise in this condition. But Clara will dance after a while, once she has played a bit, and then I shall take over. I have not quite the technique she does, but I make up for it in energy."

Nathan laughed aloud and faced the dancing again. "Now that I can believe."

He fell silent as he watched the dancing, eyes tracking one person in particular. Moira looked so alive as she danced. She laughed, and smiled, and her hair, long and luxurious down her back as he preferred it, fairly shimmered in the flickering light of the room. Instead of tiring after a dance, she almost looked more energized, as if the dancing was rejuvenating her.

She looked over at him on occasion, and always with the same little tilt of her head, inquiring, inviting, but not voicing the question. He was tempted, he really was. Dancing with Moira would not be like dancing with any other woman. He knew, without hesitation or previous experience, that he would never regret one dance with her, no matter how his lack of ability might jumble the whole thing into an unidentifiable mess.

He could watch her all day, dancing or not, but something about observing her dance made his heart warm. Charles Allenford could not have the slightest idea of what an amazing woman he was so fortunate as to be engaged to. Years of friendship, no matter how close they might have become, could not have compared to the depth and intensity of his emotion for her. For what she was. For how she affected him.

If it could have, there was nothing in the heavens or the earth that would have been able to take him away from her side.

He smiled as he watched her, loving the way her laughter rang like music in his ears. Suddenly, he needed to be the one making her laugh, making her smile, bringing that light out of her. He had so little time with her, and here he was standing against the wall watching her enjoyment.

Again she looked at him, again she tilted her head so adorably, and smiled at him. Instantly, he made up his mind. He looked down at the woman next to him, and, to his astonishment, saw that it was now Clara. It seemed he had watched longer than he thought. He smiled at the woman, and asked, "Would you care to dance, Clara?"

She smiled up at him. "I would love to, Nathan." She looked over at the dancing, and sighed. "They have almost finished this one, I fear."

"Well, then let us give them a finish to remember," he said with a grin as he offered her his hand.

She took it and they lightly joined the dance, and he found himself smiling the entire time.

As it finished, Clara's husband approached to claim her. "That is, if you don't mind dancing with your cousin, Nathan," he added pleasantly, ever so slightly out of breath.

Nathan looked to Moira, who was staring at him and smiling in a stunned amusement. "I don't mind," he murmured.

He walked over to her and bowed very properly. "If you would be so kind, Moira, I should very much like to dance the next with you."

She curtseyed very prettily, then said, "I thought you did not care for dancing."

"I find myself so entranced by your smile tonight that I dare to make an exception." His own words stunned him, but he would stand by them. Truth was truth, after all, and if she thought he was teasing, then so be it.

"Are you under my spell, then?" she asked with a tilt of her head.

"Entirely," he said in a low voice with an accompanying nod. "I am yours to command as you will."

Moira's eyes danced playfully as she fought to restrain her grin. "Then I command you to dance with me, Nathan, and enjoy it."

"If you insist."

She laughed merrily at his words and he smiled, unable to help himself.

It was, without a doubt, the best dance he had ever had. He

was not particularly skilled, but neither was he worried about that now. He could not worry about anything when he danced with her. He did not enjoy dancing, it was true. But if he could do this every time, he could come to be very fond of dancing indeed. As it was, he danced with her three more times before the entire company was too exhausted to continue.

And it was not nearly enough to satisfy him.

Nathan could not sleep. He lay on the bed in Jack's room, staring up at the ceiling, his thoughts awhirl. He kept seeing Moira's face as she danced, the light in her eyes as she smiled with real pleasure, her delight that he would join her regardless of his distaste for it… He would have to leave all of that behind him soon, and that knowledge left a bitter taste in his mouth that he could not expunge.

He heard a noise suddenly, and sat up, listening again. *No*, he prayed silently, *please don't let that be…*

But he heard it again, that panicked half moan, half whimper from the room next to him. He groaned and raced from his bed still fully clothed out into the hall. Heart pounding, he didn't even hesitate outside the door and pushed it open, entering the now-moonlit room and going to the bed instantly.

Moira was writhing as if in pain, her brow dampened with sweat, and her expression pained. She moaned with each twist of her body, and her head thrashed from side to side frantically. As yet, she was not forming words, but Nathan knew they could not be far in coming. She gripped her blankets and sheets in her hands, clutching and releasing them rapidly.

What could he do? He yearned to take her in his arms and hold her as he did before, but he held back. Reason broke in and he could not bring himself to do it. If he held her in his arms, even to comfort her in her dreams, he would never be able to get through the next few days. It was too much, too tempting, too close to his deepest desires.

He had to leave. Now. Before she said anything or called for anyone. If he waited any longer, he wouldn't be able to leave with any sense. And yet here he stood, only able to clench his own fingers convulsively, helpless against her fear.

Again she whimpered, and now came the tears as well. Nathan shut his eyes and swallowed painfully. He could not bear it. He could not ignore it, yet he could not act. He didn't know how he could give in without being swallowed up by regret later.

But inaction would kill him just as surely as action would.

Opening his eyes again, he looked back at Moira, and, gathering every ounce of strength and willpower he possessed, he allowed himself to bend down and press his lips gently to her clammy brow. "It's only a dream, Moira," he whispered against her skin. "It's all just a dream."

He winced against the powerful draw to stay, and pushed himself up and away from the bed and exited the room without a single glance back, shutting the door softly behind him. He leaned back against it and sighed harshly. Still he wanted to go back, every fiber of his being screaming that the woman he loved needed him. But it would be a disaster. It would destroy him.

He shoved away from the door and walked, not back to his own room, but down the hall and to the stairs. He would not sleep tonight, not for a long while at least. The night had cleared and the moon and stars were out in their full splendor, and he would need their majesty for some clarity in his own mind.

Tomorrow they would reach Preston. Barring an absolute miracle of biblical proportions, they would find Charles Allenford within hours of that. Then Moira would be where she belonged, and Nathan…

He shook his head at the choking sensation that enveloped him. He had no idea what he was going to do. What was left for him after Moira was gone? The very thought of it was bleaker than his darkest moments past. How could he possibly just turn her over to another man's care, knowing he felt what he did for her?

For one moment, one blissful, agonizing moment, Nathan allowed his mind to venture where it had previously balked at going. What if he told her everything, begged her to choose him instead? What if she said yes?

He imagined the life they would have together, days full of joy and nights that were no longer plagued with fear, the laughter of their children as they played, and the two of them as they aged together, still delighting in each other.

It was perfect. It was all a man could want and so much more. He had always imagined he would be the kind of man who would end up marrying out of necessity and not love. He would have children he adored, and he would grow to love his wife because of and through them, but never a romantic or passionate love.

Now he could not imagine how he would ever be able to go back to that, knowing what it could have been, had life been fair and just.

But life was neither fair nor just. He would be forced to adapt to his new situation, and make the most of it.

"How?" he asked aloud, begging the heavens for answers as he ran hand through his hair.

What was he supposed to do? Let her walk out of his life forever without telling her just how much she meant to him? Could he live with the knowledge that he had never tried for her?

He rubbed his arms in the chill of the night, but tilted his head back to catch more of the breeze on his face. "Help me," he whispered, closing his eyes.

"It seems to me," came a quiet voice from behind him, "that a man who needs to ask the stars for help is in quite a desperate place."

Nathan turned in surprise to see Squire Cutler walking up towards him at a leisurely pace, and watching him with interest. "We are in one," he responded as calmly as he could, turning back to face the stars.

"We?" the squire queried softly, coming to Nathan's side and looking out at the stars with him.

"My cousin and I."

The man chuckled and put a hand on Nathan's shoulder. "Son, if the two of you are cousins, then I am the King of the Belgians."

Nathan met his eyes, shaking his head at once. "Squire, I don't mean to contradict you, but…"

"Oh, don't even try it, Nathan," he overrode, squeezing his

shoulder briefly. "I can see the way you look at her, and it's not anything close to familial concern. You are in love with her."

Nathan held the gaze for a long moment, then looked away. "Yes." It was all he could say before his throat constricted rather painfully.

Again came a gentle squeeze to his shoulder. "I think perhaps, Nathan, now would be an excellent time to get a few things off of your chest."

Nathan nodded, swallowing with difficulty.

It took longer than he expected, telling their story. And he told the squire everything, even the things that Moira did not know. He told him everything about his title, his first impressions of Moira, about his friends urging him to go, how even then they could see what he could not. He confessed the pain at pretending to be married, and how it became harder each and every time to return to normal. He explained the truth about Charles Allenford, as much as he knew. He even told him about the faux pregnancy and kissing her in public and asking her to stay and her nightmare and falling asleep with her in his arms.

Finally, he reached the point they were at now, and what had forced him out of doors tonight. When all had been said, he fell silent, feeling rather drained. The squire had remained silent during the entire telling, nodding at parts, brow furrowed at others. Nathan was grateful for the lack of interruptions, as it made the telling easier.

"That is quite the story," the squire finally said, squinting up at the stars.

Nathan laughed without humor. Yes, it was rather, wasn't it? A story for the ages.

"How does she feel?"

"I don't know," Nathan answered, feeling rather raw and exposed at the moment. "If I did, maybe I could… maybe we could…" He broke off, knowing it was pointless to speculate at this time.

"I don't claim to know much of love," the squire said on a sigh, shifting his weight slightly. "I am a simple squire of little consequence, my lord."

"Don't call me that," Nathan begged with a quick jerk of his head. The very reminder of who he really was scalded him.

The squire ignored him. "But I know that there are at least two parts of love, for those who really and truly love another."

Nathan looked over at him and waited, sensing that he was not going to like this at all.

"The first is that loving someone sometimes means that it is better to give them up than it is to keep them."

"I don't know if I can," Nathan rasped, his voice hoarse.

There was only a slight smile of pity from the squire in response. "The second is realizing that nothing you want matters anymore."

Nathan grimaced in pain, the words felt like a lash upon the back of his already wounded soul, from which the stinging would never subside.

Amidst the pain, he felt the gentle squeeze of reassurance on his shoulder once more, and turned to find the squire already heading back to the house. His words echoed in Nathan's mind as he remained, his turmoil greater than ever.

Let her go? How could he possibly do that? Maddening as she was, frustrating and irritating as she had the capacity to be, Moira was the sunlight to his otherwise dreary world. When she was gone, it would seem even darker than it was before.

He sighed in dejection and walked further away from the house. What did it matter how he felt? There was no choice to be made here. Starting tomorrow, life would get darker, and it did not matter if there was light at the end of the tunnel or not.

For, while he was in it, the darkness was still dark.

The hole would still be a hole.

The pain was still pain.

Chapter Fifteen

Moira watched Nathan from her window as she sat in the window seat, wondering where he was walking to, and what Squire Cutler had said to him.

It had not been long that she had been awake, but thoughts of sleep were no longer prevalent. She had woken from her nightmare with a jerk to find the room empty, and only the moonlight was there. It streamed through the window brightly, casting long shadows against the floor. She had eventually caught her breath as the fear began to subside, but it took much longer to calm her mind.

That nightmare had been worse than any other of late. And it had not been about her family or Charles.

This time it had been about Nathan.

She could not bear to revisit the details of it. The feeling of horror still lingered, and she still clung to words she had heard in it. "*It's only a dream, Moira. It's all just a dream.*"

Yes, it had been a dream, but nothing had ever felt so real. She had not dreamed of Nathan before tonight, but it had been more terrifying than any of the others. Her panic had been real and all consuming, and she had never been so grateful to wake up from a nightmare. Vainly, she had hoped that he would be there to comfort her again, that he could sweep the hair from her eyes and tell her that everything would be right again, that nothing could hurt her.

But alone she had been when the dream had ended, and Nathan had been outside with the stars.

Then where had those words come from? Surely she could not have imagined it all; it was far too real for that.

Or had she?

It was possible, she supposed. If she had wanted something so badly during those moments, her mind might have conjured up something of the sort.

But she hoped that it was real.

There was something about that man that made her feel safe, that there was nothing to fear. She might fight against it, but part of her secretly thrilled whenever he demanded that she let him be a gentleman, or begged her to be ladylike. She knew that it was silly, but his level of respect for her, for any woman, she suspected, was one of the most attractive qualities about him.

And there were quite a few attractive qualities about Nathaniel Hammond.

He had this way of smiling when he was particularly amused by something but wanted to hide it. It made his eyes crinkle ever so slightly, and she had always heard the expression of "dancing eyes", but she had never seen it until now. And he always ran a hand through his dark hair when he was frustrated, and all that served to do was make it untidy, which was terribly becoming on him. His anxiety about public settings was adorable, his fear of spiders amusing, and his inability to be indifferent about anything never ceased to make her smile.

She stared at the place where she had last seen him and sighed. She wished he had come to her. He always knew how to put her at ease, and how to set her heart flying in the most shameful manner at the same time. After her nightmare the other night, when he had held her and told her that it was all right to cry, she had given in and done so. She had needed to cry it out, and he knew it.

He always gave her what she needed, even if she did not know of her need.

It was one of the things she loved the most about him.

She gasped as the realization washed over her and covered her mouth with both hands.

She loved him? How could she…? When did she…?

She shook her head as tears welled in her eyes. What did it matter when or where or how she came to love him? All that mattered was that she did, and she had not even known that she had started. She loved their fights, their laughter, their silly games, their pretend marriages, their teasing, their questions… She loved the way he watched her when he thought she wasn't looking, the way he lifted her spirits with a smile, the fact that he told her things he didn't even need to. She loved how she had felt in his arms. She loved the way he made her blush. She loved the way time stood still when he looked at her.

Somehow or other, he had taken a hold of her heart and she wasn't sure she wanted it back.

But what about Charles? She groaned and grabbed at her hair. Charles had been everything to her for so long. She loved him! He had brought joy into her life when there had been none. He had seen something in her when no one else had cared to. He always thought the best of everyone, even if they did not share his opinion. He was a good man, one of the best. He was her best friend. He was the man she had promised to marry.

And Nathan… Nathan was…

She looked out of the window and saw him reappear. His head was down and he walked slowly, still not turning towards the house. He glanced up towards the window and she sat back, hoping he couldn't see her from that distance. She held her breath, watching him intently, wishing she knew his thoughts. Finally, his shoulders sagged and he turned and continued walking in the direction he had been going, shaking his head.

Slowly, Moira released her breath and pulled her knees into her chest. What could she do? She couldn't forsake her past for something that had come on over the course of a week, no matter how fervent it was.

Nathan was one of the best men she had ever known. He had nothing to give but himself, and she suspected that had he a fortune of any sort, nothing about him would change. But he was right, they needed to move forward and find Charles. The sooner they did, the better. She could not in good conscience abandon him before finding him. What if he should reappear, having worked all this while for her and was at last ready to marry?

She had to go. She had to be loyal and faithful to Charles. He deserved no less.

But what about Nathan?

She wanted more time with him. She wanted to make sure she knew all of his secrets, and he knew all of hers. She wanted to see if he was as vulnerable to her as she was becoming with him. She wanted to know if it could be possible for him to love her.

Once they were separated, when she had gone with Charles, would he go on and find someone else to love him? The thought made her chest ache and her stomach clench.

She could not love him. She should not.

She was going to marry Charles Allenford, as she had been planning for years. She would be a good wife to him, and knew that he would be a wonderful husband. He would be a loving and devoted father, and their children would love and respect him in return. Their life would be very good, better than many people in the world could hope to have.

She bit her lip and shook her head, more questions flooding her mind.

Had Charles kissed her the way Nathan had, as if savoring a delicacy? Would Nathan have resented her fortune, when he had none? Did Charles think she was as beautiful as Nathan seemed to? Would a child of Nathan's take on his features? Would she always wonder if she had done right, regardless of her decision?

She rested her head against the cool pane of the window, and sighed. It would be best to pretend that she had not felt anything tonight. It would be best if she went on as she had been. It would be best if nothing changed from the original plan.

It would be best if her life continued on without Nathan.

He appeared out of the darkness again, and her doubts resurfaced. He had his hands behind his back, expression troubled. He did not look up this time, which she was grateful for. She just wanted to look at him for a while. She wanted to memorize his handsome face. She wanted to smooth those creases in his brow away. She wanted to kiss that frown away. She wanted to run out to him, beg him to hold her, and stay right here forever. She wanted to forget everything else but the two of them in this moment.

But that was not possible.

For one thing, Nathan was far too principled to allow her to break her promise to Charles for him. For another, she could not bear to injure Charles. Not after what he had done for her and been to her. She owed him another chance.

She would have to force her thoughts and feelings of Nathan away. She would have to become the perfect lady, one who did not abandon principles for a flighty romance. Time would soon mend the wounds, she was sure. Time could heal all sorts of things, and soon he would forget all about her and he would be but a fond memory to her.

He stopped for a moment, and she watched his shoulders heave with a sigh, and she felt herself do the same. What was the use? It did not matter that she could not or should not. It did not matter that it might be all on her side. It did not even matter that she was fighting it every step of the way.

"I love him," she whispered to herself, her heart swelling and breaking at the same time as she touched the glass. She loved them both, Nathan and Charles. She loved two men at the same time, with the same heart. She turned away from the window, buried her face into her hands, and sobbed.

What was she going to do now?

With a last wave to the squire and his family, all of whom had come outside to see them off, Nathan and Moira turned their horses back to the road they had tried to travel the day before. As yet, they had not spoken anything but pleasantries to each other, and Nathan, for one, was not in any hurry to change that.

He had eventually come to the realization last night that the squire had been right; he had to let Moira go where she needed to. Because what he wanted did not matter anymore. He did not matter anymore. Only she did.

It was a painful discovery, one that he was still reeling from, but even so, it was right.

Sleep had come, but it had hardly been restful. He had woken with the same empty feeling he had gone to bed with, and it still remained. His head was muddled, and his body ached as if he had been dragged behind a wagon for several miles.

He would have to be more careful with his behavior from here on out. He had to treat Moira as he would any other lady, and not as he had been.

Looking over at her now, Nathan's heart lurched a little harder than he would have liked. Though she was dressed very properly, and in fact, more nicely than she had been since that first day, something was not right. Some of the color had left her cheeks, and she stared almost blankly ahead of her, as if nothing ahead of them was worth pursuing. She looked resigned, but collected. There was an air of sadness about her, and he wanted to ask her about it.

But he couldn't.

Distance. He had to maintain distance.

He looked up at the bright sun in the morning sky and sighed softly. He knew his duty, and he would do it.

But oh, how it stung.

Moira could not even bear to look over at Nathan, though every sense she possessed was keenly tuned to him. She knew very well that she looked dreadful this morning, she had not needed Madeline to tell her so. She had assured her that fresh air and exercise and finding her husband would improve matters greatly, but she had no way of knowing if the sweet woman believed any of it. After seeing Nathan, how tired he looked, the way his face was fixed with a politeness that she instantly hated… she knew she had made the right decision.

It was better to pretend nothing had happened. It would make things easier when faced with the actual decision that she would have to make. If she were objective and open, and not emotional and conflicted, then things would work out as they should.

But once that decision was made, there would be no going back. Reaching Preston would change everything, but could she bear it?

She scolded herself silently. Of course, she could bear it. She would have to, wouldn't she? It was not as though she had a choice but to bear it. One can always bear what one must, even if one does not think there is strength enough to do so. Strength would find her, and she would endure.

As much as she would prefer to completely ignore the man next to her, she could not. She had no desire for their last day together to be one of silence and pain. Surely, they could converse a little. Even strangers could find a topic on which to spend some time ruminating.

She cleared her throat slightly before asking, "How did you sleep last night?"

"Tolerably well," he said with a smile she did not believe for one second. "Yourself?"

"As well as can be expected," she replied, not looking at him.

Which was to say, not well at all, but he did not need to know that.

"I think we were very fortunate in our hosts," Moira said, changing the subject abruptly. Her tone somehow had reverted back to the polite, unaffected tone she had adopted when they had first met, which seemed oddly appropriate.

Nathan nodded. "Yes, the squire and his family were very generous. I would like to do something to repay them."

Of course, he would. Moira's eyes burned with the threat of tears, but she shook them off as best as she could. "Yes, that would be only right. I shall take care of that once we reach Preston and have settled."

A frustrated exhale escaped Nathan's lips, and he glanced at her. "If you don't mind, I would like to take that responsibility and privilege myself."

"Oh, but I…"

"Please."

Moira met his eyes at last, and had no choice but to agree. "Very well then, if you insist."

"Thank you," he said, turning his eyes to the road again. Then she heard him mutter, "It is about the only useful thing I will have done this entire cursed trip."

"That's not true!" she protested, losing only a touch of her polite tone. "You have been invaluable, and…"

"You have paid for everything," he overrode without emotion or volume. "You have taken the lead in everything. It has all been your ideas, your words, your opinions, your fiancé, and your everything else. I was here purely for show."

"Stop," Moira whispered, wishing he would not talk of himself in that manner, or of her in such harsh and derogatory tones.

"Stop what?" he asked bitterly. "Stop telling the truth? Stop being an idiot? What?"

"Stop," she said again, tears threatening to rise and spill over.

Nathan shook his head and let out a sound of irritation. "The sooner we get to Preston, the sooner all of this will be over," he bit out, digging his heels into Mercury's side and riding up ahead.

Left behind and on her own, and having no desire to talk any more, Moira let her quiet tears fall as she rode Flora at the same steady pace. Had she somehow not made him feel useful on this excursion of theirs? He *had* to know how important he had been. She would have been lost without him, in more ways than one, and she doubted she would have ever made it this far intact. How could things go from so sweet during the dance the night before to so agonizing and angry now?

Her tears came steadily, and her heart continued to break. What was she to do? Part of her longed to comfort Nathan, the other part held her back. If she put distance between them, things would be easier later. When it was time to say goodbye.

Not easy, but easier.

After all, he was the one in such a hurry to get there now. She knew the road would take her there eventually, but he was the one who was riding fast and hard towards it. If he wanted to be rid of her so swiftly and return to his pleasant existence before she had come into his life, then so be it. She could let him go far more easily if she knew he wanted it.

And if his manners this morning were anything to go by, it was quite plain that he did.

She would like to have pretended that thought did not bother her.

But it did.

It was some time later when Nathan reigned in Mercury a bit and turned him to face Moira as she rode in behind them. She had been so lost in thought, all surrounding him, that it took some time for her to notice him. When she finally did, her eyes widened slightly, but she covered the reaction with a smile so weak it was hardly a smile at all.

And one look told her he did not believe it for a moment.

"I think we should rest the horses for a time," he said without fanfare or apology. "We will reach the city in a few hours, and I think they could use it."

Moira nodded and slid off of Flora before he could come over and assist her. She took the reins and pulled the horse into a path of green grass near a large tree. Nathan followed with Mercury, then set the hobbles on the horses. He stood there watching them as they grazed, while Moira took a seat against the tree, watching him.

Where had their jovial friendship gone? She longed to make him laugh, or smile at the very least. But she did not know how. Suddenly she had lost her sense of humor and smiles were few and far between.

Nathan stood with his hands on his hips, strong and defiant, but his eyes and expression distant. He suddenly let out a gust of air and went to rub down the horses.

From her position against the tree, Moira had an interesting view. Nathan brushed Mercury with ease and gentleness, murmuring softly to him. The flesh of the animal rippled in delight under his strong hands, and Moira found herself feeling a twinge of jealousy. The loving care and attention she was witnessing was once something that had been directed towards her, obviously in more appropriate ways. Though he stood perhaps only fifty feet away from her, Moira missed Nathan. She missed who she was with him.

She missed who he was with her.

She missed them.

She had not spoken with him since his outburst, had not even attempted to. It was far too painful to pretend that this friendship of theirs could go on. And she greatly feared that if she spent too long with him, joking and teasing and laughing as they once had, he would see her feelings for him in her eyes.

No, she would sit here and watch him openly, averting her eyes if he should catch her. There was safety in awkwardness, and less risk of being hurt. Less danger altogether.

A soft smile played on his handsome face as he spoke to Mercury, and he rubbed the horse's side in appreciation. He was so good with the animals, so gentle and caring, much the same as he was with people. Nathan was all that was good and right in the world, regardless of how low he thought himself.

Were he a man of high rank or fortune, the women would have flocked around him. Moira, for one, couldn't believe they were not already doing so. She hoped he would find a woman good enough for him, one that would appreciate the full measure of the man she would be so fortunate as to spend her life with. One whose children she would bear and raise. Who would hold her in the night.

She swallowed back the flash of pain and jealousy and sighed. What was the use of thinking about Nathan's future? It would only make things worse, and tempt that already fluttering part of her that was yearning to run full on at him and fling her body on his person, all the while crying, "Love me!" in the most pathetic of fashions.

But that little, stubborn part of her was contained for the time being. She had grown quite accustomed to restraining it, but much more of these quiet moments of reflection and she might need to do something drastic, like slap herself. That would certainly attract Nathan's attention.

Flora, apparently not satisfied with being left out of Nathan's ministrations, walked over to him, nudging his arm with her nose. *Clever girl*, Moira silently praised as Nathan laughed softly and turned to rub the horse's nose, now speaking to her in those dulcet tones that Moira so envied.

Envious of horses? The idea would have been laughable if it

were not so very sad, and so painfully true.

Nathan looked at her then, and instead of casting her eyes away as she meant to, she was helpless to resist the draw of the dark, mysterious depths of his gaze. He saw her watching him, and he stilled for only the briefest of moments, and then he smiled at her. A soft, gentle, warm smile in which she somehow found an apology, a reassurance, and an invitation all at once. Transfixed upon that smile as she was, she didn't know if she could trust herself to go to him. Would she reveal everything with one look in those eyes? Would she find herself yet more tempted to toss everything to the wind and ride away with him?

The thought terrified her. She didn't know if she could take any more vulnerability as far as Nathan Hammond was concerned. She was already so weak in that area.

He sensed her hesitation, and the smile deepened ever so slightly. Moira's heart gave a little lurch in her chest and she considered again. What if it was the last moment they would have together? It was only a friendly gesture, a peace offering between them, a pleasant note on which to end.

How could she refuse such a thing?

She finally returned his smile and pushed to her feet. The flare of pleasure in his eyes immediately assured her that she had made the correct decision, if for no other reason than to prove to him that he was forgiven and she was still his friend. His happiness was all the reward she needed.

He handed her a brush and together they set to work on Flora, working silently, but with smiles. It was an odd sort of synchrony they shared as they worked, her stroke, then his, long and even against the warm skin of the horse. She would be lying if she did not admit that having Nathan so close was the sweetest kind of torment.

It would be so easy to turn around here and find herself in his arms, so easy to turn her head and brush her lips ever so softly across the stubble of that chiseled jaw. His scent enveloped her, taunted her, so strong at the moment that it was the most poignant of fragrances. The warmth of his body so near hers was a heady sensation, and she could only find peace in her mind by counting as high as she could as fast as she could. First in English. Then in

French. Then back down again.

Aloof as to her current state of frenzy, Nathan switched direction and brushed towards Flora's flanks, while Moira continued along the neck. A cool breeze drifted between them, and Moira's mental count became slower as her sense began to return. She allowed herself a nearly silent sigh of relief and mentally congratulated herself on her success.

Just then, Nathan's hand brushed against Moira's, and ever so abruptly, the counting in her head came to a halt. She froze and looked at their hands, touching only by a small amount as they rested on the horse, and she felt Nathan still beside her. The sudden intensity of feeling was enough to take the breath out of her lungs and steal the warmth of her bones.

She was transfixed by their hands together, hers seeming frail and delicate next to his larger and more weathered one. She remembered the way his warm hands had tenderly enveloped hers, bringing her comfort with their strength; the way they had gently squeezed hers in consolation; the way that hand had brushed so softly against her cheek as he kissed her that night, leaving a delicious tingling sensation in its wake. Even now, her skin prickled with the memory of it.

Against her express wishes, her eyes turned to him, and found his trained on her, the power of them startling and disarming and dangerously alluring. A shaky breath caught in her throat and he heard it, those compelling eyes darting instantly to her lips. Suddenly, she felt the need to moisten them, but even her tongue could not move. He hardly breathed as he stared, then brought his eyes back up to hers. The torrent of emotions Moira was feeling was matched only by what she saw swirling in Nathan's eyes.

Now it was her turn to look to his lips, parted slightly and so near. Those lips had changed everything for her. What would it be like to taste them again, in earnest this time? Unconsciously, she found herself pulled towards him, drawn in as if by magic. Her eyes met his again, and she found herself completely lost, and she could not even mind being so.

An irritated snort and scuffle of hooves from Flora broke the moment, and Moira hastily stepped back, severing the connection of their hands and averting her eyes instantly, her cheeks flaming. She rubbed an arm as if cold and tucked a strand of hair behind her ear. "We should be going," she said quietly, her voice not nearly as steady as she would have liked. "We need to reach Preston before dark." She bit her lip, and chanced a brief glance up at him.

Nathan remained silent as he stood there, his hand still resting on Flora's back. It still seemed as though he had yet to breathe, and his dark eyes, now unreadable, had yet to move from her face. After an eternity, he nodded, only once. Then he took two steps towards her, set his hands at her waist, and hoisted her up to Flora's back as easily as if she were a child. So unexpected was his action that she barely had time to rest her hands on his shoulders before she was airborne. In the next instant, he was walking back over to Mercury, and her racing heart tried to remember its normal pace.

He mounted his horse, spoke softly to him, then nudged his heels in, and the horse moved forward. Not a word was said between them, and he did not look at her again after putting her up on Flora, but she had caught that look as his hands had been on her waist, that open, almost hungry look that spoke volumes.

He was not as settled as he would like her to think him.

He had some strong feelings towards her as well.

But what sort of feelings were they? She knew enough of the world to know that a man could be attracted to a woman without having any real attachment to her. She and Nathan were friends, but would he have been willing to throw that label aside and pick up anew, or was he merely acting on human impulses?

Moira realized that the point was moot as to his motivations. That moment between them had been a mistake, and one of her making. She had known better than to allow herself to be in such close proximity to him, knowing how he affected her, and still she had allowed it. Now instead of having a fond memory of two friends sharing a quiet moment of contentment, she would have a haunting remembrance of what almost was, what could have been, and what never would be.

Hot tears filled her eyes again as she stared at Nathan's retreating back. She nudged Flora along, fighting for control. How she wished she knew what Nathan was thinking and how he was feeling. Perhaps if she did, her own sufferings would be lessened.

She would have been quite wrong. If anything, Nathan's thoughts were more tormented, his heart more anguished. Letting go of Moira would be the worst thing that he had ever endured, or could ever in the future.

He did not know what would be left of him when she was gone.

Chapter Sixteen

It was nearly full dark when they reached the outskirts of the city, and it was not a welcoming sight. The buildings, dark and looming in the limited light, were almost eerie and even the faint light of torches was not enough to comfort anyone. Moira rode a little more closely to Nathan, who had not spoken more than three words together since they had come nearer to their destination. Now his face was set in a sort of grim determination, but he could not help but feel a surge of satisfaction at her sudden nearness. She was as uneasy as he was, perhaps even more.

He forced a tight smile and looked over at her. "Not quite the tranquility of Gillam, is it?"

"Hardly," she managed, looking around with no small amount of anxiety. "I'm sure it is not quite so imposing in the light of day."

"I would not be so sure of that," he replied, looking around with interest. "From what I have heard, this place will become quite the teeming town one day."

"How are we ever going to find him?" Moira whispered as she looked around.

Nathan's heart ached at Moira's tone, but he covered it with a brave attempt at a carefree grin. "We have come all the way up from Hampshire without any real direction, and now you worry about finding him in one town?"

She gave him a look. "It is a rather large town, and there are many places a man can hide."

"Ah, but you forget who you are with," he said, his eyebrows quirking with a teasing suggestion.

It didn't amuse her, for once, but instead made her tense and he detected a slight wince as she looked away. "No, I have not."

Nathan cursed himself and gritted his teeth together. This was going to be even harder than he imagined if he couldn't pretend things could still be jovial between them. All he had was his ability to cover emotions with jokes, and if even that would be taken from him, then he would be left with only sullenness and silence.

It had been an afternoon of emotional cacophony. First his resignation this morning about distancing himself from her, then lashing out at her in his frustration, then that brief, delightful moment of peace when he had actually managed to smile genuinely at her. He had been breathless with the anticipation as she read his invitation to join him. Then she had, and he exulted in his good fortune at being able to have one more moment with her near him, innocent though it may have been. Or perhaps not so innocent as he found himself blatantly trying to ignore the fact that she was so close he could smell the sweet perfume that was all her own. It would haunt his senses for many weeks to come.

Then their hands had touched and time itself ceased to exist. He knew he could not have misread her reaction; she was nearly as unseated by the moment as he had been. She had drawn closer, and he had not thought or sense enough to react other than to do the same, knowing that heaven awaited him there. If the horse had not been agitated by the lack of attention, who knows what might have happened. Nathan knew that he would have been powerless to resist, and that terrified him.

Moira's reaction after all of that was what stuck with him. She was ashamed and embarrassed, and her first thought was of reaching Preston, and, no doubt, her betrothed. It was then he had been reminded of his resolution to maintain a cool detachment, and not even the perfect fit of his hands on her waist could deter that. He had to ignore everything about her.

Which was not possible.

He was exhausted already, but he knew tomorrow would be worse. It would be relatively easy to find Allenford once they asked after him. They would no doubt find him tomorrow, and then Moira would at last be reunited with the man she loved. Already Nathan found himself itching to be gone. He dared not hope that his darkest wishes, involving a death, a secret marriage, or incarceration, might somehow be true. It was foolish to anticipate anything other than the outcome expected.

He could only afford to live in reality, not in wishes.

At last, Moira caught sight of a boarding house that was large and well lit. It looked as welcoming as paradise in the relative oppression of the dark and terrifying town. Nathan had seen it as well and rode for it, then reigned in Mercury. "It would be prudent to set up lodgings here," he said gruffly as he dismounted. "We can begin our search in the morning."

Moira nodded and slid off of Flora, her borrowed boots from the Cutlers hardly making a sound on the dirt. Without a word, she followed him into the establishment, wondering how they were going to arrange their sleeping tonight, and what their story was to be. She could not share a room with him again, not if there was a chance she could dream about him, and she had very little doubt that she would. And she could not bear to pretend to be his wife even for one more night.

But Nathan would know what to do. He always did.

A very thin man wearing an apron was wiping down tables in the taproom as they entered, and he turned to greet them with a smile. "Welcome to Mrs. Farrow's Boarding house. Mrs. Farrow is down in the kitchens at the moment, but perhaps I can help you." His cheerful, thick accent was one Moira was not sure she had ever heard before.

"Two rooms," Nathan said in a short voice, but not unkindly.

Moira almost looked up at him but decided to look down at her toes instead.

"Two, sir?" she heard the man ask uncertainly.

"Two."

"Would you like them to be adjoining rooms?"

"It doesn't matter."

Moira swallowed hard, his bitter, careless words unknowingly cutting a deeper gash into her heart. He sounded so cold and formal, and not like Nathan at all. There was to be no story, then; no pretense at concealing their purpose. No more laughter, no more pretending.

"And if you could send a maid to help the lady, it would be greatly appreciated," Nathan continued, taking out a few coins of his own and handing them to the man.

The man's eyes widened and he nodded hastily, rushing off to find one.

Nathan turned to Moira, his eyes cold and hard.

"Nathan…" she tried, wondering where he had gone, for the man before her was a stranger.

"Good night," he said in a low voice as he bowed to her for the first time since she had known him. Without another glance, he turned on his heel and strode out of the door, leaving her standing there in the taproom alone.

Sobs welled up within her chest, but she dared not release them until she was safely up in her room. She had no desire to make a complete spectacle of herself here, no matter how she was hurting at the moment. For now, she would just hold them back, let the tears flood her eyes, and wait for the privacy she yearned for so her heart could finally crumble into the thousands of pieces it was threatening to.

The dawn came too quickly for Nathan as he sat in the taproom, where he had spent the majority of the night. He had managed a few hours of sleep in the room prepared for him, though it could hardly be called sleep. It had been a strange sort of unconsciousness that had not been restful by any stretch of the imagination.

Today was the day he would lose the woman he loved.

He had asked around last night as to a man by the name of Allenford, and had received direction towards an area of the city that was somewhat better than he had assumed to find him in. Either Charles Allenford was wealthier than he had ever let Moira know, or he had certainly made a good living while he had been apart from her. Either way, it was not comforting, save for the fact that he could rest assured he would not be leaving Moira in circumstances so far below what she deserved.

Walking around the city at night had been oddly peaceful, but not consoling. It served for clarity of thought, and of purpose, perhaps, but not of heart. No, that was still as conflicted as before, and even now it objected very strongly to what he would do.

But his heart would have to wait.

His mind was in control now.

A creaking on the stairs brought his attention towards them, and he saw Moira coming down, her hair simply pulled back, her face fresh and rosy, and her gown neatly pressed. She looked as beautiful as he could remember seeing her, and it hurt. She saw him, and offered a small wave and a smile, and his protesting heart jumped into his throat.

How he loved this woman!

He forced down his heart and quirked a half smile back, and returned the wave. The relief in her eyes made him regret his actions of the night before even more, but he did not dare apologize, for once he began to do so, he would not be able to stop, and soon he would be apologizing for far more things than he wanted her to know.

She came over to the table he was at and sat across from him, folding her hands on top of the worn wood. "Good morning," she said softly, her voice smaller than usual.

"Good morning to you." Really, he did not have to be cold when talking to her, only restrained. He tried to put more warmth into his smile. "Shall I ask for some breakfast?"

She shook her head and tucked a stray strand of copper hair behind her ear. "No, thank you, I don't think I can eat this morning."

He frowned and gave her a look. "You must eat something. It's a big day for you."

"Precisely why I cannot," she murmured, picking at the skirt of her gown with one hand.

He started to reach for her hand, then thought the better of it and propped his elbow on the table instead. "You must eat something regardless. Let me call for something for you."

She shook her head more firmly. "No, I thank you. I will eat later, but for the moment, I would prefer not to."

He stared at her for a long moment, warring within himself. Part of him wanted to force her to eat something, so he could avoid worrying about her any more than he already would be, and the other part of him wanted to wash his hands of the whole affair and let her behave as she would, since she would not be his concern for very much longer. Finally, he allowed himself to nod. "Very well, if you are certain."

"I am," she affirmed, looking resolute, though her eyes still did not meet his.

"Well, I have found out the area where we can expect to find Mr. Allenford, so if you are prepared…"

"Yes, of course," she said quickly, jumping up as if she had been burned. "It may still be early, but it will undoubtedly take some time, yes?"

He nodded, oddly tempted to smile at the rapidity of her words, regardless of their topic. "Undoubtedly, but not too long."

"Excellent. Walking or horses?" she asked, suddenly all business.

He wished she would not be so very fixated on finding Charles right at the moment. It was more than slightly disheartening. But then, she loved the man, and that said enough about him to permit Nathan to accept the torment of the day. "I thought we could walk. It's not too far and the horses have had little rest in the last week."

She gave one firm nod and started for the door, her face set in determination. Nathan had no choice but to follow her, though he would gladly have remained in the taproom by the fire for the remainder of the day.

It did not take long at all for someone to know the name of

Allenford well enough to give quite accurate directions, and it was far too soon after that when Nathan, rather unfortunately, found himself standing in front of a modest looking townhouse, Moira nearly quaking at his side.

"Well," Nathan said to no one in particular, "this is a rather encouraging edifice, isn't it?"

Moira didn't respond, continuing to stare at the door, as if she could not contemplate such a thing.

"Aren't you going to knock?" he asked, forcing a teasing light into his voice that he did not feel.

"I find that now the moment is here, I am dreadfully ill at ease," she said, wringing her hands and biting her lip.

He swallowed his own nerves and nodded. "That is only natural. But you haven't come all this way to turn coward at the finish, have you?"

She sighed and straightened up. "No, I have not." With as much composure as he had ever seen her take on, she marched up the stairs to the door and knocked three times, then stepped back slightly.

After only a brief moment, the door opened and a middle aged woman with a kind smile stood there, a cap perched ever so slightly crooked upon her head. "Yes?"

"Is this the Allenford residence?" Moira asked, her voice shaking a touch.

Nathan wished he could be there standing next to her, offering strength and comfort. She was terrified; she may not appear to be so to others, but he could tell.

"Yes, ma'am," the woman replied, still smiling. "The master is not at home, but perhaps…"

"Who is it, Kitty? Let them in if you can, it's far too cold for anybody to be out there this early," came a woman's voice from behind her.

Nathan saw Moira stiffen, and felt himself do the same. Surely that was not…

"I have not got to that point yet, madam," Kitty said, turning to look back at her. "She merely asked if it were the Allenford residence, and I said it was, and that was as far as it got."

There was an amused, yet exasperated sigh, and then, "Well, for heaven's sake. You take William and I will talk with the young lady."

"Very good, ma'am," said Kitty with a curtsey as she disappeared.

"I'm terribly sorry about that," the other woman said as she came into view. "We have only just recently been able to have any help, and Kitty is a dear, but I don't know how much experience she has." She chuckled a bit, and smiled warmly.

Nathan was struck by the woman, and her openness. She had dark hair, and wide green eyes that he suspected were always amused. She was a touch on the plain side, if one were to be severe, but her obvious open temperament and friendliness made her so agreeable that one would hardly notice it.

"I apologize for keeping you out here like this. My husband is not at home at the moment, and the baby has only just…"

"Then you are Mrs. Allenford?" Moira interrupted, her cheeks a little paler than Nathan would have liked.

The woman's eyes narrowed a touch. "Yes."

Nathan fought back the urge to run up to Moira and steady her, for she looked positively ready to faint. "Mrs. Charles Allenford?" she somehow managed to get out.

Mrs. Allenford's face cleared and she laughed merrily. "Dear me, no. My husband is Mr. Peter Allenford, the elder brother. Charles lives with us, but he is no closer to marrying than my own child, I fear."

He was a right sight closer than she could have possibly imagined, Nathan thought as he sighed heavily, both in relief and regret. As traumatizing as it would have been for Moira to have Charles married, it would have made things so much the easier for Nathan.

"The second is realizing that nothing you want matters anymore." The squire's voice echoed in Nathan's mind and he closed his eyes against the desire to groan.

"My name is Moira Dennison, and I…"

"Moira?"

Nathan's eyes snapped open and he turned at the male voice he heard from somewhere down the street. A young man of no more than twenty-five stood stock still in the street, staring at Moira as if he had seen a ghost. An older man, obviously his brother, stood next to him and was staring between the two back and forth in abject confusion.

"Charles," Moira whispered, though it somehow carried as if she had spoken in normal tones.

For a moment, no one moved, and it seemed no one even breathed. Then suddenly Charles was running and Moira was coming down the steps of the house, smiling brightly. In the next instant, he had his arms around her and was swinging her around, both laughing merrily.

Nathan's heart stopped in his chest, and he suddenly found it difficult to breathe. What he had expected the dreaded reunion to be like, he could not have said, but never had he envisioned this. Nor could he have imagined how exquisitely it would hurt.

"What are you doing here?" Charles asked with a laugh as he finally set Moira back down.

"I came to see you, of course," Moira scolded impatiently, rapping him on the arm sharply. "I had enough of being alone, and came to find you."

A bit of the light in Charles' eyes died and he sighed, shaking his head. "I shouldn't have left you alone for so long, Moira. I'm so sorry."

Nathan snorted to himself in derision. Sorry could not begin to cover what the man ought to be saying to Moira.

"Charles," Moira said softly, "when you left, you said you were going to find work so that you could earn enough to marry on. Have you done so yet?"

Charles looked at her, his face draining of color a bit, and Nathan's heart gave a frightening lurch. But then he took Moira's hands in his own and raised them to his lips. "Yes, I have," he replied in a voice that sounded more hollow than grave.

It was answer enough. Moira nodded and smiled warmly. "You have filled out a bit, I think. Had your face not been so unaltered, I should not have known you again. I can no longer hide your scrawny self behind me."

That brought a laugh from her fiancé and he hugged her again.

"Moira, Moira, I've missed you! But come, I must introduce you to my family." He kept one arm around her and turned her to face his brother, who had come up behind them, and was only now beginning to smile. "Peter, this is Miss Dennison. Moira, my brother Peter Allenford."

They curtseyed and bowed respectively, and Peter took her hand, kissing it softly. "Pleasure, Miss Dennison. Charles has mentioned you before, of course, but his description of you fell far short of reality."

Nathan almost groaned in agony, but here, at least, was a man who knew what a rarity Moira was.

Moira grinned and accepted the compliment with a tilt of her head. "I wish I could say the same for you, Mr. Allenford, but he never mentioned you at all."

Peter flashed a glare at his brother, who shrugged. "I should box his ears for that, but I'm afraid that I cannot. He didn't know I was still alive, you see. He was told with the rest of the family that I went down with my crew at seventeen, but I had the bad timing, or great fortune, as you may wish to call it, of being ill at the time and was in Spain recovering. He only received news of me two years ago."

"Hence your desire to come to Preston," Moira gasped in realization as she turned to Charles.

He nodded, still smiling at his brother.

She shook her head at him. "I wish you had told me."

"I wanted to, but I couldn't be sure it was true," Charles said with only the barest hint of an apology in his tone. "At any rate, I see you have already met Gwen." He gestured back to his sister-in-law, who stood at the door still, smiling at them all.

"Yes, I have, though not formally." Moira turned and curtseyed properly, making Gwen smile even more. "A pleasure, Mrs. Allenford."

"Oh, please, call me Gwen," she called. "If you'll excuse me, I'll see to William now before Kitty goes mad."

Nathan was beginning to feel very out of place, and wished most heartily to be anywhere else. He was no longer needed, and certainly not wanted. He started to shift away, when he heard, "I would like you both to meet Nathan, who has been helping me to find you." With a groan, he turned and forced himself to smile just a bit, as would be polite.

The brothers shook hands with him, and he was pleased to find that both had a firm grip with strong hands. They exchanged pleasantries, and Nathan was relieved that neither man asked after his last name. He could not be certain who would know his name this far north, and revealing that bit of information now would not be wise.

"Well, I think we all have much to talk about," Peter said with a grin as he rubbed his hands together, "and it is rather chilly yet this morning. Miss Dennison, would you care to come in?"

She smiled and took his arm. "I should be glad to." She turned back to Nathan and for the first time in many minutes, looked uncertain.

"I will be heading back towards town, Miss Dennison," he told her, backing away with a bow.

She disengaged herself from Peter's arm and came towards him. "You're not leaving now, are you?" she asked, her eyes full of concern and a touch of fear.

How touching, he thought bitterly. *She remembers me.*

He smiled blandly, even as his eyes raked her face hungrily as if for the last time. "Not until the morning. I will not leave without saying goodbye, don't worry." He raised his eyes to the men behind her, then looked back down. "You seem to be well taken care of. I trust I don't need to have you fetched back to the boarding house tonight?"

"No, I'm sure they can see me there," she murmured, her eyes wide and slightly confused. "And I will arrange for your reward to be waiting you this afternoon at the bank we passed on the way in."

He nodded, instantly ignoring her words. There would be no reward for him. Not even a monetary one. She could use it however she liked. They could.

They. It was no longer Moira and Nathan. Now it was Moira and Charles.

"Until tomorrow, then," he said stepping back and bowing once more. He needed to leave now, before it was too late. Before it hurt any more.

She curtseyed a little, still watching him intently, not saying anything further.

He could not bear to have her look at him so, could not abide the potency and beauty of those eyes a moment longer. He turned and walked away, feeling as though he were leaving his very soul behind him.

Chapter Seventeen

Moira lay awake in her bed that night, feeling more than a touch of confusion, but a great deal of relief as well. Her reunion with Charles had been better than she could have hoped for. He was exactly the same as she had remembered, except for being larger and stronger, which was a fine improvement. They had talked and laughed for most of the day, and she had truly enjoyed reminiscing with him. They never spoke of marriage; the word had not even been said except for when she had asked about the money, but she was in no hurry. It had been so long since they had been together that some period of time to get reacquainted would be necessary before either of them could comfortably agree to finally marry.

She got along splendidly with Gwen, his sister-in-law, and adored his nephew William, who was only a year in age. Charles' brother Peter was actually a very reserved man and had hardly said anything once they were inside, but he was certainly agreeable in spite of it all. She was fitting in very well with Charles' family, and she could not deny that she was happy to be with him again.

And yet she could not sleep. She was fatigued, as they had spent a good portion of the afternoon out in the city. Charles had wanted to show her everything he could and she had enjoyed the day immensely. He was right; Preston had many things to offer. She could be very happy here without exerting too much effort. But with all the contentment she was feeling, still sleep would not come.

She released a huff of frustration and sat up, rubbing at her eyes. She knew the trouble.

Nathan.

She had not seen him since she had gone inside with the Allenfords, not even when she had gone walking about the town. Her first stop had been to request that the banker draw up a note for five thousand pounds, which caused his brows to shoot so high that she feared they would fly off of his face entirely. But once she showed him the letter she had procured from Uncle George, who was a rather well known man in London, there was no trouble at all. She informed the banker to expect a man asking after the reward sometime that day, praying there would be no difficulties about it. She still knew very little of the fortune she had inherited, and had yet to tell Charles of it. For some reason, she wanted to hold that information back a little longer.

It had been very peculiar, not seeing Nathan for almost an entire day. It was unsettling, at the very least. But she had it on good authority that he was still here, which was of some comfort. She had doubted his words to her that morning when he said that he would not leave without saying goodbye. That moment had felt very much like a farewell in its own right.

Though the time was drawing rather nigh, she was not ready to say goodbye to him. Not that she had much of a choice in the matter. She was engaged, and to a man she cared a great deal for. Beyond that, Nathan was not suitable for a woman of her apparent rank and fortune. Charles could barely be considered such, but if what Nathan had said was true, that society would be a much harsher critic of her than she would like, then she could not risk its aggravation further by marrying so poorly.

That was hardly a reason at all. It was a paltry excuse, and something that she felt dirty for even thinking. What did she care about society and their dictates on whom she could or could not have? But, in spite of her opinions, it was something that she really should not ignore.

And she needed to gather all of the reasons that she could, poor or not, to support her decision.

She had maintained her distance sufficiently well, she thought, save for that little incident the day before. They had been merely amiable acquaintances, with no hint of what lay beneath the surface. Tomorrow would be the severing of their relationship in its entirety, and there would be no more distance from anyone. There would be no need for it.

Why then was she so restless tonight?

She shook her head and got out of the bed, sliding her feet into her slippers and pulling on the wrap Mrs. Farrow had left for her. The kind, middle aged woman who ran the boarding house had been so comforting last night when she came up to assist Moira herself. She had offered her services in any way that she could, and even hinted that, should she have wished it, she might be able to find some warm milk down in the kitchens at night.

That would soothe her mind and relax her enough for sleep.

She tiptoed as quietly as she could down the hall, hoping not to disturb any of her neighboring guests. The stairs were rather worn and in some need of repair, and were destined to creak horribly, but if she stayed to the right side of them, she would be safe. Gingerly she trod, wincing with every step.

A faint light from the taproom stopped her in her place and she held her breath, pressed her back to the wall, and slowly peered around the corner into the main area.

Alone at a table near the fire, the same place he had been this morning, sat Nathan. He had a drink before him, but even from her position, Moira could tell that he had not touched it. He just stared at it, one hand turning it absently on the table.

He looked exhausted, much more so than he had been this morning. His eyes were vacant, hardly blinking at all. The man who normally looked so strong and vibrant without any effort looked as though he carried burdens far too great for him. It hurt Moira to see him like this, and she wished she knew what she could do to make those shadows disappear.

She watched him for what seemed an age, drinking in the sight of him. Aching and despondent though he appeared, he still was as strong and dear to her, he still made her heart tremble. She watched as he put his head into his hands, ground his eyes with his palms. It took all of her willpower to keep from flying to his side and holding him, comforting him, confiding in him…

But she could not. She should not.

After a few moments, she could bear no more. She turned silently and made her way back up to the room, her eyes burning with unshed tears. Strong, immovable Nathan was miserable. And she knew that, somehow, she was the cause. How could she live with that? How would she bear that in the coming days? Surely they could still be friends. Surely…

She shook her head frantically, interrupting her thoughts. It was impossible. For her part, she could not go back to being merely friends with the man she loved as much as him.

Tomorrow she would say goodbye to him.

Tomorrow would be the beginning of the rest of her life.

Without him.

She closed the door to her room and flung herself onto her bed, sobbing into her pillow for what she was about to lose.

Nathan was ready to go before the sun came up, but he was not about to wake Moira up to say goodbye to her. Her sleep was troubling enough; intentionally shortening it would be cruel. Especially since it was just for him.

He could just leave now. He could leave her a note explaining…

But no, even as he thought it, he shook his head. She deserved more than that, and, as much as it would hurt, he had to see her again. He had to say goodbye properly.

Or as properly as proper strangers do. His version of a proper goodbye with her would probably scandalize those who were paragons of propriety, even if she had not been engaged.

And she was definitely engaged, there was no maybe about it. She would be Mrs. Charles Allenford. Mrs. Charles bloody Allenford, who was untouchable to him. No amount of money, no loftiness of title could change that. She would be happy with him. That was all that mattered, really.

He was tightening his bedroll onto Mercury's back when he heard a noise from the door, and he turned.

Of course, it was Moira.

She was dressed, albeit rather plainly, and her hair was down completely. Her eyes were wide and somber, and it was all he could do to remain where he stood. How many mornings had she looked like this and he had taken it for granted?

"You are up rather early," she said softly, watching him adjust the saddle now.

"It would be better to get an early start," he said gruffly. "I have a long way to go."

"Yes, you do," she murmured. She inhaled quickly. "Nathan, I don't know how I can thank you for all you have done."

He could not bear her gratitude, not when he felt the way he did. He shut his eyes tightly, and forced himself to breathe. "It was nothing, Miss Dennison."

"On the contrary. I can never repay you for this."

He opened his eyes and turned to face her. "Be happy," he said plainly, meeting her gaze. "That is what you deserve. That is payment enough."

He saw her swallow hard and felt his own throat tighten in response. This was only going to get worse. He turned to mount Mercury, and had his foot in the stirrups when he heard his name from her again, and he hesitated.

"One last question before you go, if I may?" she asked, and he could almost hear her biting her lip.

Half of him screamed to refuse, but he knew it was fruitless. "Of course."

"Why were you really sorry for kissing me?"

Of all the questions she could have asked him, she had to ask him that one. "The truth?"

"I would appreciate that."

He closed his eyes, and slowly released a breath. What was the use of pretending anymore? She wanted the truth from him, and he was going to give it to her, no matter the cost. "Because I knew instantly that I would spend the rest of my life comparing any other kiss to that of Mrs. Charles Allenford, and I knew none would be able to measure up."

It was a long moment before she responded. "Oh…"

He shook his head at himself and mounted the horse, knowing he needed to leave before things got worse. He turned Mercury towards the road, then looked back down at Moira, whose eyes were shining with tears. How could he leave her?

"Moira," he started, his voice more of a croak.

"Oh! The ring, of course!" she cried hastily, her fingers scrambling to remove it from her hand. It took an awkwardly long moment, but eventually she had it off and held it up to him.

He opened his palm and she dropped it in, and it suddenly felt as though he carried the weight of his world in his hand. He hadn't thought to ask her for it, hadn't even considered it. He wouldn't have missed it. He stared at the ring, the perfect circle of gold that had been a symbol of everything he had ever wanted, and it had been hers from the very beginning of their journey. He didn't want it back. He wanted her to keep it. He wanted to throw it to the wind. He wanted…

He closed his hands around it, and swallowed back everything he felt. He looked at Moira, letting his eyes say whatever they would to her. "It has been an honor having you as a wife, Moira Dennison."

She blinked back tears and he saw one trickle down her cheek. "It has been an honor to have you as a husband."

They stared at each other for a moment, and then Nathan cleared his throat and straightened, shifting his eyes away. "Goodbye, Miss Dennison."

"Goodbye, Mr. Hammond," she whispered.

He nudged his heels into Mercury, but stopped before they had gone more than three feet. Something was tugging at his mind and his heart, and he could not leave Moira forever without asking her, without knowing the truth. He turned slightly in the saddle and met those eyes once more. "That night that I kissed you, you smiled. Was that for the benefit of our crowd, or was it for me?"

She looked startled for a moment, then smiled a small, sad

smile. “Does it matter?”

Did it? Did it really, considering everything? “No,” he said softly, shaking his head a bit. “No, I suppose it doesn't.” He touched the brim of his hat, and turned back, kicking the horse again.

As he started off, he heard something from behind him, something so soft it could have carried on the wind, something that he was undoubtedly not supposed to hear:

“It was for you.”

With a groan and shutting his eyes as fiercely tight as he could make them, he pushed Mercury on harder, faster, racing away from Moira, from Preston, from everything he had cared about in the last week. It was time to start over, to move forward, to press on, all by going back.

Life would go on as it had gone on before.

However that had been.

Chapter Eighteen

Three days later, Nathan found himself in a place he had never in a million years expected he would be. He had ridden hard from Preston, stopping only for sleep and brief meals. He left before sunrise and rested long after the sun had set. If he could have raced ahead of his thoughts, he would have. But they were quick, his thoughts, and kept pace with him rather handily. They were his only companions, and received their share of his wrath.

Nights were the worst of all. He could not control his mind as he slept. While he used to envy those who dreamed, now he wished for his dreamless sleeps. He yearned for the nothingness he once knew.

The day after he had left Preston, he had known his course. He would not return to his estate and tenants yet, that would be far too much solitude for his current state of mind and being. There was one more thing he had yet to accomplish before he could fully move forward.

Dirty, tired, miserable as he was, he stood at the front door of a fine looking London town home, number twenty-one Russell Square, to be exact, and though he was determined to not leave the city until he had accomplished the task before him, he balked at it.

Of all horrid things, this was the chief of them. He had suffered too much already, why put himself through more pain? There was too much, it had been too long, it would be better left alone.

But he could not turn away. Moira had told him he had to do this, that it was imperative. And he was helpless to resist anything that Moira had instructed him to do.

He swallowed painfully and knocked on the door. He had to wait only a brief moment before a man appeared, balding and shuffling, but sturdy enough.

"Can I help you, sir?" he asked importantly, as if he were trying to be imperious. He was not succeeding.

Nathan tried not to smile. "The Earl of Beverton to see…"

"Nathan?"

The butler turned in surprise and Nathan looked past him to find the master of the house standing there, looking as if he had seen a strange apparition.

"Hello, Spencer," Nathan managed, his eyes starting to sting a little. His younger brother, once his closest friend. He had not seen him in over six years. He was fully a man now, tall and strapping and so much older than he remembered.

"It's all right, Fisher," Spencer said weakly, laying a hand on the butler's shoulder. "This is my brother. I'll take it from here."

"Very good, sir," he replied with a bow. He turned back to Nathan, and bowed to him as well. "My lord." Then he shuffled out of sight to places unknown within the house.

Spencer stared at Nathan for a long moment, his eyes wide.

"You said you hoped I would know how it feels to lose the woman I love," Nathan said, his voice breaking in spite of his attempts to prevent it. "Now I have, and I understand."

In an instant, his brother stepped forward and threw his arms around him, in plain view of anybody that might have been passing in the streets. "I didn't mean it, Nate. I never meant any of it. I'm sorry."

Nathan clamped his arms around his brother and held him close, allowing the burning in his eyes turn into tears, and letting the tears fall. "I'm sorry, too, Spencer. I'm so sorry."

It was a long moment before they released each other, and neither had dry eyes when they did. "Well, are you going to let me in, or do you want to keep standing out here crying like a couple of girls and let the neighbors comment?" Nathan asked with a laugh, wiping at his eyes.

Spencer grinned and stepped back. "I hate my neighbors, but I would rather they think me a hermit than an emotional nonnykins."

Nathan clapped him on the back and entered the simple, but well-furnished house, and followed when Spencer waved him on down the hall and into his study. Spencer shut the doors behind them and gestured to a pair of rather comfortable-looking arm chairs.

"Now, I know we have much to catch up on," Spencer said with a fond smile as he took his own seat, "and Lord knows, I am desperate to hear about your new title, my lord Earl."

Nathan snorted and rolled his eyes, but said nothing.

His brother turned serious, his dark eyes boring into Nathan's with more intensity than Nathan ever remembered seeing in them. "But I want to know about your words to me out there just now."

"My apology?" Nathan asked, knowing that was not it at all.

Spencer only flicked a smile. "You have lost the woman you love."

"Yes."

It was a brief, painful response that seemed ripped from his chest, but he would not comment further. He had just spent the past three days trying to put it from thought. Opening the wound when it was still so fresh would only expose it to infection.

"Nathan," Spencer prodded gently, leaning forward, his elbows on his knees. "An infection must be let out or it will kill you."

"Infection," he muttered with a scornful laugh, choosing to ignore that his brother's words had echoed his thoughts in a bizarrely similar fashion. "That may be the word for it, yes."

"So let it out."

Nathan looked up at his brother, whom he had not anticipated to be the least bit pleased to see him only a few minutes ago. He hardly knew this man before him anymore, how could he share his pain with him now?

"All I know is that you need to fix that relationship." Moira's voice echoed in his mind and he struggled to push it out. She was so

blasted obstinate, even in his thoughts. "*You would be surprised at what sort of miracles can take place when one only has the courage to take a first step in the right direction.*"

He smiled a touch at the memory of her words, but he felt it shake even as it formed. As usual, as much as he hated to admit it, even to himself, Moira had been right. He needed to mend this relationship with his brother, and this would be a fine first step. Besides, wasn't that what a brother was for?

In a low voice devoid of emotion, Nathan told Spencer everything. He started from the first day he had seen her and the only interruption was Spencer's crying "Wait, *those* Dennisons?" and then at Nathan's reply of, "Yes, *those* Dennisons," a muffled expletive and a wave to continue. He did so, finishing with his determination to come here. "I am afraid it was more because she had insisted upon it than for anything else," he admitted, feeling only slightly ashamed for that.

"I don't blame you," Spencer murmured, leaning back in his chair, looking rather blown about by the story. "I hardly gave you reason to seek me out. She actually told you to come see me?"

"Not in so many words, but her intent was clear. She makes no secret of her opinions." He swallowed down a lump in his throat and glanced to the window.

"Well, in spite of your obvious pain, which I am truly sorry for," Spencer said in a consoling tone that Nathan could only nod in response to, "I'm very glad you met her. And that her opinions were so very direct."

"So am I," he murmured, his eyes dropping to his boots. Despite everything, he could not, and would not, ever regret any of it.

"I wrote to you, you know," Spencer quietly told him.

That brought Nathan's head up with a jerk. "You did?"

Spencer nodded with a hint of a smile. "Quite a few letters, actually."

"I never received anything," he whispered, wishing he had known that. How much of the distance between them could have been prevented by his reading one letter from him?

"I never sent them," Spencer replied with a shrug that was a poor attempt at carelessness. "They still sit in that desk drawer over there." His smile faded and for the first time, he actually looked as uncomfortable as Nathan felt. "I didn't know how to make amends for the mess we were in, and a letter seemed a poor excuse for a first step, but the thought of coming to you personally was terrifying."

Nathan fought another difficult swallow. "I'm sorry you felt that way." He shook his head, clearing his throat. "Can we talk about something pleasant?" he begged with a laugh.

"Please," Spencer agreed, grinning. "As a matter of fact, there is something of great importance that I have been wanting to discuss with you for some weeks now, but as our situation was, I didn't..."

"I'm here now," Nathan said with a firm wave of his hand. "What is past is past. Discuss it now."

Spencer nodded and sat forward, obviously excited. "Well, I know I told you I would never love anyone as I loved Anna, but I was an idiot."

"Could have told you that myself."

That earned him a glower he was more than familiar with from days past. "Regardless," his brother said, choosing to ignore the comment verbally, "I have found that, in spite of my doubts..."

"Many of them, no doubt."

"...I have done so."

"You have?" Nathan asked, all teasing and sarcasm gone.

Spencer nodded, barely restraining his grin. "I have. And I love her far more than I ever dreamed I would be able to."

Nathan sat back heavily, his astonishment all-consuming. And the sudden twinge of pain and jealousy in his chest burned fiercely, and brought with it a measure of guilt.

"I know my timing is deplorable," Spencer said apologetically, "but it's all that I can think about."

"I know what you mean," Nathan replied in a low voice, offering a humorless smile. "But just because I am thwarted in my situation doesn't mean that we should ignore the joy of yours." He reached out a hand and clapped his brother on the shoulder, his smile turning genuine. "Now, tell me about this lady love of yours, and when am I to wish you joy?"

"I don't know about the when," Spencer laughed. "I have yet to speak of marriage to her at all. But her name is Caroline Templeton and we met at a ball."

"Oh, how very English of you," Nathan drawled, feeling his humor return.

"She spilled her punch all over me."

Nathan's brows shot up and his smile grew. "That is not very English. How did that come about?"

"She was most enthusiastically defending a maid who had unintentionally slighted and offended Lady Greversham that evening."

He could hardly believe what he was hearing. "To whom was she defending this maid?"

Spencer grinned. "Lady Greversham."

Nathan exploded with laughter. "I think I am going to like Miss Templeton very much indeed!"

"I hope you do. I want to introduce you at once. I want your approval before I speak to her father about it." Spencer looked so keen and earnest that Nathan was touched.

"You don't need to do that, Spencer. I trust your judgment."

His brother smiled. "Thank you, but I want your approval first all the same. You are an earl, after all."

Nathan waved his hand impatiently. "Title and wealth mean very little as far as romantic matters go. If you like her, that's good enough for me."

"So you don't care that her fortune is considered by most to be a rather pitiful sum for a family of the *ton*? That society sees them as lowly despite their respectability?"

"Not a bit," he said with a shake of his head. "In fact, I think I like her better for it." And he honestly did. Her fire and strength of character would be good for his brother, and he thought Moira would like her considerably. Which was the best indication of good taste he knew of. "When shall I meet her?"

"Oh, perhaps tomorrow, we can call over there," Spencer said without much concern, sitting back. "We need to spend some time together, don't you think?"

"Yes, I do," Nathan agreed instantly, feeling a touch of warmth spread into his chest again. "But I don't think it will take us forever. We have never been very good with words. Invite Miss Templeton and her family to dinner this evening."

"Really?" Now the excitement in his voice was plainly evident and Nathan grinned, nodding.

"Really. The sooner we can get her into this family, the better. We have a desperate need for feminine influence."

The Templetons, as it turned out, were just the sort of people that Nathan would want to bind his family to. The parents were respectful and proper, but with enough wit and good humor to keep them from stiffness. Their two daughters inherited those traits, Caroline being the obvious beauty, and her younger sister Gemma being far more outspoken. Caroline's tale of intentionally spilling punch on Spencer in order to meet him spoke of a surprisingly conniving mind, and Gemma's detailed description of everyone's reactions to the events added a colorful and cheery quality that was no less amusing in the skill of the telling. There was obvious affection among the entire family, and it took Nathan only moments to approve of all of them.

He made the point very clear to Spencer and at an appropriate moment, his brother begged a private word with Mr. Templeton, and thereafter with the eldest Templeton daughter. The rest of the family dashed to a nearby window, at Nathan's instruction, and the engagement proceeded perfectly, to the satisfaction of all.

Nathan could not help but to smile as he took in the entire table, now regrouped. The majority of his day had been spent with Spencer, and they were already closer than they had been as children. Caroline would make him a fine wife, and it was evident that she cared little about the superiority of the *ton*. She was prone to smiling and had more than enough wit to keep Spencer on his toes.

Spencer needed such a woman.

And Nathan doubted Spencer, God bless him, would ever

know just how fortunate he was. Fate was not always so kind.

He cleared his throat as congratulations began to dwindle and he grinned at his brother and his new fiancée. "Well, now that all that is settled, how about some dessert?" He waved at a maid with a tray.

They all settled and Caroline flashed Spencer an evil grin. "Don't worry about me," she said in a bright voice. "I've already had mine."

A series of groans went up from most of the table, along with an additional "Bad form!" coming from a thoroughly disgusted Gemma, who also felt it necessary to mimic gagging, much to her mother's dismay. Spencer, on the other hand, seemed genuinely pleased by Caroline's words, in spite of his now rather flushed cheeks, and Nathan had the sneaking suspicion that they were holding hands under the table. Yes, indeed, Caroline was going to be good for Spencer.

Nathan smiled and helped himself to more of the pudding, thinking he was rather going to enjoy having an actual family again.

The rest of the night was filled with laughter and cheer as wedding plans were discussed and a date a month hence settled upon, and the entire company ended the evening with nothing but pleasant thoughts in their minds.

Well, most of them did, anyway.

Chapter Nineteen

After almost a full week in Preston, Moira was no closer to getting married than she had been before. They didn't even speak on the subject. Her visits with Charles were amusing, and terribly so. But there was something missing from it, something she could not define. She was certain Charles was feeling it too, though he was not commenting on it. But something was not right.

She had been spending quite a bit of time with Gwen, as Charles seemed to be always working. Gwen assured her that it was typical of the Allenford men to throw themselves into their work when there was something on their minds. Still Moira was unsettled and could not place a finger on it.

But what was most troubling to her was the fact that, as much as she admired Charles, she was in no hurry to be married to him either.

He had told his family about their attachment, which was received with great excitement and enthusiasm, and he had even confessed that his brother had offered to assist them in procuring a house of their own, if they needed it, so thrilled was he by their engagement. Moira had nearly told him about her fortune then, but still she hesitated. It was not something she wanted to toss about like some ribbon-strewn baton at a fair. It would change the whole course of things for them.

"You are positively drowning in thoughts," Gwen's voice said from somewhere next to her, sounding wry, but concerned.

She shook herself out of her reverie and forced a smile. "I'm a bit prone to pondering of late, I fear."

"On what?"

Moira shrugged and picked up little William, who had been tugging at her dress. "Oh, this and that. A bit of everything, really."

"A bit of everything does not cause frowns like that on anyone's face, Moira," Gwen said in a scolding tone that she suspected was used on William quite often.

She met her eyes and bit her lip, shrugging again, embarrassed that tears began to prickle at the corners of her eyes.

"Oh, Moira, what is it?" Gwen asked in a softer voice.

"I don't know," she whispered, holding the baby close as he sat contentedly in her lap. "I cannot even put a name to the feeling, but I just…"

"Is it Charles?" Gwen interrupted gently. "I can tell he has been distracted of late, but I know that he loves you very much."

"I know he does. I know." And she did. He may not have said it, but she knew that he loved her. She could see it in his eyes, and could feel it when he held her hand in his. "But he is not… that is to say, we're not who we used to be."

"Do you still love him?"

"Yes, I do. He is the dearest friend in the world, and I'm dreadfully fond of him, but…" She trailed off and fumbled in her mind for the best way to say this without giving Gwen the wrong impression.

"But there is a 'but'," Gwen said finally, her voice still as gentle as ever, not the faintest hint of scorn in it.

Moira nodded, relieved that someone, at least, could see the problem. "I don't even know what, really, and…"

"I do."

Moira stopped instantly and looked up at Gwen in shock, her heart freezing in her chest. She could not possibly…

"That man you came with. Nathan, was it?"

Moira's throat went dry and she could not even manage to

swallow properly.

Gwen smiled, her eyes kind and soft. "You were not merely friends, were you?"

"I-I… I love Charles," Moira stammered.

The smile deepened and became a touch more amused. "That was never in question."

Moira looked away, embarrassed and flustered beyond reckoning.

"Moira, do you have feelings for Nathan?"

She hesitated only a moment, then nodded.

"Love?"

Again, she nodded.

"How does he feel?"

"I don't know. I know he cares for me, but I don't know about the rest." She looked back to Gwen. "But I do love Charles."

"Yes, so you've said," Gwen said, reaching a hand out and placing it on Moira's knee, "but I wonder what kind of love it is."

Moira could not have answered if she wanted to. To hear aloud what she had been wondering in her heart for days was more confusing than anything she had ever known. She loved the man Charles had been, and she loved the man he was now. But the feelings were so different that she hardly knew what they were.

"I don't know what to do," Moira whispered. "I love Charles, but how can I possibly consider marrying him when I haven't told him I have feelings for Nathan? And Nathan is… he…"

"He has gone, hasn't he?"

She nodded, swallowing with some difficulty. "He left the day after we arrived. I have no way of knowing where he went, or of anything else. He… he did not seem keen to continue our acquaintance."

"No, I can imagine not," Gwen murmured, sounding oddly amused. "Well, I think the first thing that you need to do is to talk with Charles."

"I know, but I am so afraid," she confessed, looking down at the little boy in her lap and letting him examine her fingers. "How can I tell him that I have developed feelings for someone else? He has been working for us for all this time, and I have…"

"Oh, just talk with him, Moira," Gwen insisted, patting her knee. "Charles has not been the most dedicated fiancé, having not written you in all this time. He deserves at least half of the blame. And he is the most reasonable of men, I am sure he will understand."

"I wish I had your confidence."

Gwen laughed and shooed her out the door. She took her bonnet, scowling at it as she did so, but any way that she could make herself look more proper would certainly help her cause.

She walked down the road towards the town with her hands behind her back, head bowed. How was she going to approach the subject? How could she possibly tell Charles all that she needed to without hurting him? They could still marry, she supposed, but would he still wish to?

She was so distracted that she failed notice the man walking in front of her, and they collided, apologizing profusely as they tried to avoid falling. Then they looked at each other.

"Charles!"

"Moira!"

They stared at each other for only a moment, and then, at the same time, said, "We need to talk."

They must have looked comically identical, for she saw his eyebrows shoot up as hers did so. Then they laughed, albeit awkwardly.

"Perhaps we should talk," Moira said with a smile.

Charles nodded and took her hand. "Perhaps we should."

They walked to a small park and sat down on a bench, but had yet to speak again. Charles looked anxious, rubbing his hands together and sitting on the very edge of the bench. Moira's anxiety was entirely internal, and she wondered faintly if there was any way that the butterflies currently residing in her stomach would be migrating throughout the rest of her.

"I think I ought to speak first," Charles said finally, his words rushed.

Well, if he really thought so, then she was more than content to let him do so. The more time she had to consider her own words the better. "If you would like, you may."

"You know I love you, Moira," he began, taking her hand in his, and rubbing it softly. "You were the brightest part of my youth, the only thing I had to keep me going. I will always love you for that."

She smiled, but said nothing, feeling as though her heart was quivering in her chest.

He inhaled softly, then let it out in one rough exhalation. "I told you that the reason I headed for Preston was because I received word that Peter might still be alive. I found him and started working with him, determined to make a living for us. I didn't write you about that because I thought, at the time, it was something to keep to myself until I knew how it would end. It was a ridiculous excuse for not writing, but there it is."

Moira knew all of this, but sensed there was something else that Charles was working up to, and she was in no state of mind to rush him.

"But there is another reason why I didn't write to you. Why I haven't spoken of marriage since you've been here." He took a deep breath, and it sounded very much like he was bracing for some sort of impact. "I met someone. About a year and a half ago. Her name is Maggie, and she works down by the merchant office for her parents, who run an inn. She also does some of the mending and occasional stitch work for one of the seamstresses in town. We met when she nearly dropped a bit of laundry as I was walking by. I just happened to walk by every day I could around the same time, and…"

"Charles," Moira interrupted with a gentle hand on his arm. "Have you… have you fallen in love with Maggie?"

He met her eyes, and she was stunned to see fear and apprehension in his normally so steady gaze. "Yes," he said in a low voice, his hold on her hand clenching. "Yes, I have. She may be just a scullery maid at the inn, and a seamstress's helper, but she is the most wonderful, patient, kind, delightful woman in the entire world, and unequal match or not, I want to marry her." The light in his eyes died a little and he sighed. "I wish I could, but I cannot. I have enough to live comfortably, but taking her away from her family and their business would put them in a terrible lurch, and no wife of mine will work in an inn. So… tell me what you think."

Moira couldn't even remember how to breathe, let alone how to form a concise thought. But she licked her lips and tried. "So… you don't want to marry me anymore?"

"Did I forget to say that?" he asked, looking surprised. "Good heavens, I sounded like a miserable cad if that is the case." He shifted on the bench and took both of her hands in his now. "I love you, Moira. At one point, that love was romantic, but since then, it has become… well, don't hate me for this, but now I think of you as a sister. So no, I do not want to marry you anymore."

All of the breath vanished from Moira's lungs as she digested his words. She probably ought to feel a little upset about this, but all she felt at the moment was relief. She wanted to laugh out loud, but that hardly seemed appropriate.

"I'm so sorry, Moira," Charles said, sounding anguished. "I couldn't write to you, knowing that I was falling in love with Maggie. I didn't know what to say, or how to tell you, and you were all alone, and I could never take away the promise that I had made, knowing what alternatives awaited you if I abandoned you like that, and I cannot…"

Moira stopped him with a hand to his mouth, allowing herself to smile. "Charles, do let me speak, please."

He nodded once, still looking worried.

"I'm not upset with you," she assured him, smiling for effect. "I'm relieved, actually. You see, I love you, I do, but you are quite right, it has become more of a brother and sisterly affection now." She shrugged, feeling lighter than she had in ages. "I did not want to break my promise to you, knowing you were working so hard for our future. But as much as I care for you, and always will, I don't want to marry you either."

"Are you serious, Moira?" Charles asked, his eyes still as anxious as before, but with a light of hope in them.

She nodded, determined to be serious. "I would not lie or joke about something like this, Charles. I mean it."

"It would have been a wonderful marriage, you know, you and me," Charles said, still looking at her closely.

"Yes, it would have. We would have been very happy." She

shrugged and allowed herself to grin. "But as it is, I think it would be best if we remain only close friends."

Charles' grin matched her own and suddenly he was laughing, and Moira gave in to her own, and it was quite some time before they were calm again.

"Oh, you have no idea how long I've been in agony over this," Charles said on a sigh, still holding one of her hands in his.

"I think I have some idea," she assured him, smiling. "I want to meet Maggie, very much."

"You do?" he asked with obvious surprise. "I would have thought…"

"Oh, please," she scoffed with a roll of her eyes. "We are friends, Charles, one time the very best of friends. I want to meet the woman you love."

"You don't care that she's a…" He trailed off, looking uncertain.

"Not a bit, and you shouldn't think it is such a major obstacle if you don't want others to think so," she quipped, rapping him on the knee. "So, when can I meet her?"

He jumped up and offered her his arm. "How about right now?"

Moira laughed at his eagerness. "Well, all right then, if you insist," she drawled, standing and taking his arm.

In rather short order, Moira met the girl that had captured Charles' heart, and she approved of her at once. Maggie was sweet, shy, and adored Charles with the innocent sort of abandon good girls always seemed to achieve. And Moira thought up a rather ingenious plan to remove all obstacles to their future. More than that, she interfered and insisted they become engaged despite circumstances, and Charles, being a rather intelligent fellow, took care of the matter at once.

After seeing to a new wedding gown for Maggie, Moira left the new couple to their own devices, and slowly wandered Preston alone, heart and mind rather far away indeed.

Later that evening, Moira and Charles broke the news to Peter and Gwen, who were surprised by the sudden change, but not unhappy. They were quick to ask to be officially introduced to Maggie, which made Charles exceedingly pleased. It took some discussion, but eventually, they agreed that they would not help Charles financially, understanding his desire to provide for his family himself. They couldn't offer help to Maggie's family, for it was too much of a burden for even them to assist in.

Moira, for her part, could do so, as part of the plan she had devised earlier. She could be an anonymous donor of some considerable amount to the Younge's inn and family. She would never confess to Charles that she had done so, and there was no reason for him to ever think of her when it was done. She had no intention of revealing just how extensive her fortune was, now all knew she had inherited a little. What would be the point of it? He cared little for fortune, and only wanted happiness.

She would gladly have traded the two as well.

Now she stood in the front room of the Allenford's home, her thoughts awhirl. Not engaged any more. It seemed so strange to think that she was a free woman. She had not been able to claim that in her life. She and Charles had always planned on marrying.

Had she ever loved him with the passion that she seemed to for Nathan? It seemed horrible to admit, but she did not think so. The Charles from memory was so attentive, so charming and handsome, and the Charles in reality was still all of that, but it didn't stir her imagination as it once had. He didn't make her heart flit about like a caged bird. She didn't feel feverish when he smiled at her. Never once had she had trouble breathing in his presence.

Not that those things were all that mattered, but she could not deny that those sensations, when combined with the deeper, more profound emotions, made for a far more pleasant experience.

Her thoughts turned to Nathan and she sighed. If only she was aware of his feelings. She was free to marry whomever she chose now, and she would choose him faster than a heart could beat, if she knew he would have her.

But she didn't know.

There were times when it seemed possible, but then the

moments were gone so quickly, and he was back to being either her friend, or some cold stranger she didn't know. How could she possibly throw herself at a man without knowing his feelings?

Was she a fool for thinking it? Or was she a fool for remaining?

"So," came a soft voice from the hall behind her. "You are a single woman again."

She smiled and turned to face Gwen, who came up beside her. "I am, and it's the strangest feeling in the world."

"What will you do?" Gwen asked, watching her with interest.

"I don't know," Moira admitted. "I was just thinking about that."

"Will you go after Nathan?"

She smiled sadly. "No, I don't think so. I love him, but I cannot be assured of his feelings. We didn't part well, and I dare not hope that… Well, regardless, I need some time to think about things. Rushing off into another man's arms would only look desperate. A woman does not throw herself at a man, no matter how in love she is."

Gwen started to protest, but Moira shook her head, silencing her. "Please, Gwen. I'm trying to regain some balance in my life. If I am meant to be with Nathan, then a way will open up, but I have no intention of making a fool out of myself for a man who may have already forgotten me."

Without waiting for a response, Moira walked out of the room, ignoring the way Gwen stared at her as she collected her things, and further ignoring the protesting of her heart. She really would love to run back to Nathan, to tell him that her hand was now as free for his taking as her heart had been. But how could she without knowing how she would be received? Looming over them the entire time they had known each other had been her engagement.

How could he love a woman who loved someone else, even if her feelings had changed? It was as if she were an indecisive bird, flitting from one man to the other, and perhaps another, should one so well suited yet come along.

She knew herself better than that. There would never be another she could love as intensely as she did him. Had things been different, perhaps he could have loved her as well.

As she entered the boarding house, Mrs. Farrow trotted over excitedly, waving a card. "Miss Dennison, you have received a notice from Madame Guilford's! They want you to come in for your fittings!"

"My fittings?" Moira asked in confusion as she took the card and read over it. "I don't understand, I haven't requested anything."

"You will be so pleased with Madame Guilford's work," Mrs. Farrow gushed, having either ignored or simply not heard Moira's words. "She has the most excellent taste. She is French, you know, and fell in love with an Englishman who brought her over. He is quite dead now, but she has kept the shop going, and gets all of the finest fabric and patterns, and och! Miss Dennison, you will positively expire with joy at her work!"

"I'm sure I shall," Moira murmured, still looking at the card. "Thank you, Mrs. Farrow."

Mrs. Farrow headed back to the other patrons, still fluttering about Madame Guilford, and Moira ascended the stairs to her room. This was quite an odd mistake, but she would certainly correct it in the morning.

After looking around a bit, of course.

Chapter Twenty

Moira entered the rather elaborate-looking establishment known as Madame Guilford's, and the sound of a bell over her head signaled to a girl sticking pins into a skirt on a manikin that she had arrived. The girl pushed some hair out of her face and smiled pleasantly. "Can I help you, ma'am?"

"Yes," she said, reaching into her reticule and pulling out the card. "I am Miss Dennison, and I fear there has been some mist…"

The girl shrieked a sort of gasping squeal and turned around, running towards the back of the shop. "Madame! Miss Dennison is here!"

Moira had no idea what prompted that reaction, but the next was even more disturbing as another three girls came racing towards the front as if to get a look at her, and they were followed, at a much more leisurely pace by a tall, rather thin woman with a few wrinkles and very dark hair, which was pulled back into a tight bun at the base of her neck. All of the women were smiling as if Moira were a heavenly gift they had been blessed to receive.

"Miss Dennison," the tall woman said in a pleasant voice, the French accent still heavily present. "It is such an honor to have you in our establishment. I am Madame Angelique Guilford. Welcome."

"The pleasure is all mine, to be sure," she responded, still very wary of the sheer number of eyes fixed so intently on her. "As I was saying, Madame, I am afraid there has been some mistake. I received a card to come in for a fitting, but I have not as yet ordered anything from you. I would be happy to do so, but I hardly…"

A collection of giggles stopped her again, and Madame shushed her girls firmly. "Forgive the girls, Miss Dennison, they are overly excited to begin working with you. Now, if you would please step over here, we will begin measuring you."

"But I have just told you…" Moira began protesting as two of the girls rushed behind her and began pushing her, taking her bonnet and coat off in the process.

"Never you mind, Miss Dennison, it has all been taken care of. We are to prepare your trousseau for your wedding, and the payment is already received," Madame called as she followed her girls and Moira.

"I'm not getting married," Moira tried as the girls began to measure her.

Madame shrugged. "That is your concern, not mine. I have already been well paid to set you up with a full wardrobe, plus a few additional things, so that is what we will do. What you use it for is your choice. *Mes filles, le tissu, s'il vous plait!*"

In an instant, the three younger girls vanished and came back with yards and yards of the most exquisite fabric Moira had ever laid eyes on. Bolt after bolt was brought out and Madame gave swift responses, all the while the one remaining girl pinned and cut and measured alongside Madame with such precise skill and speed that Moira had a hard time believing that only two were doing it.

Before she knew it, they had piled, measured, and cut material for what had to be twenty gowns, and now the assembling began, and Moira found herself stuck with more pins than she thought existed in the world, and more were coming.

"You said all of this is paid for already?" she asked the girl currently working on the hem of the deep midnight blue gown she was now being fitted for.

The girl looked up at her and grinned. "Oh, yes, ma'am! The gentleman was most insistent, and generous. He requested we send a card to you about week hence, and paid for all of the finest we could offer. Madame had to send off to France for this very material, which was a color the gentleman himself selected."

"Gentleman? What gentleman?" Moira asked, fingering the material carefully, which was the most delicate and beautiful she had ever seen or felt.

"Marguerite, hush!" hissed Madame, who reentered the room right at that moment.

Moira looked at her in surprise, and Madame looked only slightly embarrassed. "*Pardonnez-moi*, Miss Dennison, but we were also paid not to say anything," she said, emphasizing the last words very firmly as she cast a warning glance at the girl. She looked back to Moira and smiled fondly. "It is really no matter, my dear. Just let the gift be a gift, eh?"

Moira thought about it for only the briefest of moments, then said, musing aloud, "I don't know any gentleman well enough, or one wealthy enough, for that matter, to be receiving a gift such as this from him. I wonder who it could be."

"Oh, but you must know him, Miss Dennison!" one of the younger girls cried out, then clapped her hands over her mouth in horror as Madame spun around to look at her.

"Sophie, s*e taire*!"

"Who, Madame?" Moira begged, no longer contriving to get the girls in trouble. "I will not ask any more questions, but I cannot be so ungrateful as to accept something so generous from someone I do not know."

Madame looked at her, obviously suffering an internal torment at her earnest words. Finally, she heaved a sigh. "You must swear that I never told you."

"I swear," she replied immediately.

Madame looked around as if to be sure no one was listening, then leaned in. "It was the Earl of Beverton."

All four of the other girls sighed and giggled, only to be silenced by Madame's rather intimidating glare.

Moira's brow furrowed and she shifted on the stool, much to the frustration of Marguerite, who was still pinning. "I don't know the Earl of Beverton. I have never even met the man."

"Well, he certainly knows you!" cried one of the girls from the back, who ducked her head back down instantly.

"Yes, he loves you!" chimed another.

Madame hissed rather like a cat, and the three younger girls scurried away, looking half-terrified, half-amused.

"He loves me?" Moira asked, completely lost now. "How can a man I have never met love me?"

A heavy sigh came tumbling out of Madame as she approached Moira and began adjusting the bodice herself. "I do not know, Miss Dennison. Perhaps it is a man you do know, but do not know well. Perhaps he merely fell in love with you from a distance. My girls should not have spoken so."

"So he does not love me?" she asked with a laugh, feeling suddenly rather amused by the whole affair.

Madame Guilford met her eyes, and Moira sobered at the serious light in them. "I have never seen a man so in love, Miss Dennison, in all of my years. And I am French."

Part of Moira, a very small part, wanted to laugh out loud at the woman. It was impossible. And yet… "But how?" she asked quietly.

"I do not know, my dear. Love is funny that way. Now, this dress is almost done here, but we have more to do, and then there are the undergarments, the gloves, the slippers, the boots…"

"Boots?" Moira interrupted, curious.

"Oh, yes. We have specific requirements to give you at least three pairs of boots, and very sturdy ones at that. Now, after the boots, we must do hats and bonnets."

"I would rather ignore the bonnets," Moira grumbled, wincing as Marguerite accidentally pricked her.

"We have strict orders to give you bonnets, but ones that have an open front, so you can see better. Very elegant choice, my dear," Madame said approvingly. She rattled off a few more things, but Moira wasn't listening anymore.

Three pairs of boots, very sturdy. Bonnets with open fronts to see better. Someone knew her tastes very well, indeed.

Someone who loved her.

The Earl of Beverton? Who the devil was he and how could he possibly love her when she had no idea who he was?

Piled down with more boxes and bags than she thought possible for one person to carry, Moira made her way back to the boarding house, her head still spinning. Fifteen dresses, ten sets of undergarments and stockings, seven nightgowns, three coats, four spencers, four pelisses, three cloaks, two wraps, six pairs of gloves, four pairs of slippers, three pairs of boots, two hats, and three bonnets.

The sheer volume was enough to make the sturdiest of people dizzy. Aside from the one they had stripped from a manikin and made to fit her, the dresses were not done yet, but they would be in two days, Madame promised. So in reality, she was only carrying one dress… and every other accessory she had been given.

Madame had requisitioned a lad from the cobbler's shop next door to help her, as they were the ones providing the boots, and the boy was struggling every bit as much as Moira, but he was eager and willing enough. That was probably due to the fact that he assumed there would be a tip in this for him, and he was right.

They reached the boarding house eventually, and once everything had been deposited onto the floor, since she had no idea where else they were supposed to go, she paid the boy a half a crown, which delighted him so much he asked if she had any other boxes for him to carry. Amused, she told him that, if he wanted, he could help her with the rest of the dresses in two days' time. He nodded vigorously and rushed back off to the cobbler's, grinning the whole way.

Moira looked about her and felt absolutely bewildered. Who in their right mind would pay for a woman to receive so much? Whoever this Earl of Beverton was, he was remarkably generous, and terribly wealthy, to boot. If this was his way of trying to court her, he was not going to succeed. She was not to be swayed in this manner.

Well, perhaps a little, but it was hardly appropriate.

Madame had said it was to be for her wedding trousseau. So the Earl of Beverton had known she was to be married, and still he bought her all of this for love?

She shook her head, unable to make sense of the whole affair. Nobody would buy a woman all of this if he knew she was about to be married. It would be a fruitless gesture, however generous, for she couldn't give him anything in return.

She wondered about the earl. Who was he? Did he know her family? Perhaps he was an old friend of her parents, and had somehow heard of her being of age and being engaged, and wanted to be sure she had the proper garments befitting her parents' daughter.

But why then would Madame and the girls say he loved her? If the earl was an older man, it was entirely possible that he could have been a godfather to her. She had no memory of any godparents, so perhaps that was it.

She shook her head and sank onto the bed. No, even if that were true, her engagement was not known anywhere. Even in Gillam, people were not aware of the attachment. That had been their secret, only to be revealed when they would marry.

She could hardly accept the attentions and gifts of a man who might have been in love with her when she didn't even know him, which obviously meant that he didn't know her, and therefore, *could* not love her.

She groaned in frustration and lay back on the bed with a sigh. The dresses were lovely. Indeed, she had never seen anything like them. The fabrics, the colors, the designs… she would be far more richly dressed than she ever imaged anyone being. And everything suited her so well, which was a very pleasant surprise. Such care had been taken for her clothing, such detail. Everything thought of and planned out. Who could possibly know her well enough to care so much?

She wished Nathan were here. He would find great delight in the whole affair. She could imagine his face laughing at her as she was stuck with pins and draped in fabric, a living, breathing manikin who was not permitted to speak anything beyond "thank you" or "*oui*". No choice in the matter at all. Nathan would have loved it.

He was also terribly clever. He could have helped her solve the mystery of who this Earl of Beverton was, to be buying her such things. Together, they would have figured it out and she would have been able to return the favor somehow to the earl.

Of course, Nathan would have thought she was deserving of

every bit of attention she received.

He was sweet that way.

Tears sprang into her eyes and she curled up into a ball. She missed Nathan fiercely. Now that Charles and Maggie were to be married, she had no one in whom to confide.

She missed Nathan's smile and his laugh. She missed the way he could cheer her up in an instant. She even missed the way he had the power to make her doubt everything she had ever known and set her heart aflame, as disconcerting as the habit was.

Again, she felt the urge to run after him, to throw convention entirely aside and accept the life of mediocrity she was used to. Life with him would be anything but mediocre, regardless of their fortune or situation. It would be heaven on earth, even if they lived in a hovel with pigs.

Well, maybe not the pigs. Nathan would never live with pigs.

She laughed to herself, tears still rolling down her face. Oh, she missed him. She was so much better with him than she was without him.

But he was not here.

And her words to Gwen had been quite right: A woman did not throw herself at a man, no matter how in love with him she was.

Especially if she had no idea of his returning the sentiment. A rebuttal would have been too much to bear.

So she would wait. And hope. And wait some more.

And someday, it would not hurt so much.

Chapter Twenty One

"Wait, *those* Dennisons?"

Nathan rolled his eyes, tempted to throw the remnants of his drink in Colin's face. "Yes, *those* Dennisons."

A rather colorful amount of expletives came from the group, and Nathan waited, not so very patiently, for them to finish.

"If I had known that then, I would have gone with her myself," Duncan said with a laugh.

"She didn't ask for you," Nathan growled, clenching his glass tightly.

"And for good reason," Geoff crowed with a loud laugh, slapping Duncan on the back. "You'd have taken her all the way round to Eastbourne and Brighton before realizing that you should have turned north!"

More good-natured laughter came from the group, Nathan excluded. Why had he decided that he ought to tell his friends everything? He was strongly tempted to shove off from the table and go back to his empty house and attempt to play the role of benevolent earl to his tenants, rather than sit here and relive his time with Moira with the jackals he had for friends.

After resolving everything with Spencer and swearing to return in two weeks so the brothers could spend more time together before the wedding, Nathan had decided it was long past time to return to Hampshire and Beverton House, assuming it was still standing. Given the state of his friends at the moment, he was astonished that it was not burned to the ground or worse.

They had been delighted to see him, but more delighted at the prospect of the story he had to share with them. He had been shuffled off to The Horse and Rider and had a drink shoved into his hand before he had said more than five words all together. He had been rather plagued with questions, until Derek had shut them all up and asked Nathan to start from the beginning. He had gotten no further than Moira's revelation of her fortune before Colin had interrupted him with his inane babble, and now he dearly wished he had stayed away longer.

"Gents," Derek said with a loud banging on the table, effectively shushing them all again. "I think Nathan would rather get on with the story, if you have quite finished with your squabbling."

"Well, well," Colin said in a grumbling tone as he scooted his chair back in, "Derek is playing Mother Hen? Rather awkward, isn't it?"

"He has turned a bit sensitive lately," Geoff mused aloud, attempting to appear rather concerned about the notion.

"Shut up, the lot of you," Derek muttered with a roll of his eyes, looking back to Nathan. "Go on, Nate. What happened then?"

Nathan shot him a grateful look, and continued with his story for a time. Of course, he had not gotten very much further before he was again interrupted.

"So, you just kept asking each other questions?" Duncan asked, looking bewildered.

"Yes," Nathan said with a sigh, realizing that there was no way he would be able to get through the story quickly and resigning himself to having to talk. "It provided some very useful and pleasant conversation. You should try sometime."

Duncan laughed and toasted Nathan as the others snickered.

"I personally would like you to go back to the breeches part," Colin said with a wry grin. "I can only imagine what a sight that was."

"And your imagination is where that is going to stay," Geoff broke in quickly, seeing the murderous look Nathan was gathering. "I have no desire to break up a brawl in this fine establishment, so that will be the end of that line of query. Nathan, she utterly refused to let you be a gentleman?"

"At first, yes," Nathan said, allowing his anger to abate and smiling at the memory. "She was determined to be as independent as she had been in the past. Only after several pleadings on my part did she relent even the slightest."

"Can't imagine that went over well with you," Derek said in an amused tone. "Mr. Perfect Gentleman, and all that."

He chuckled. "No, not at all. Eventually, it became a sort of game, when it was not infuriating." He continued on, and attempted to convey his emotional state as it had progressed, and he suddenly found that his friends were no longer straining to interrupt. They sat attentive, no questions or teasing in their eyes, but more of a stunned silence. He appreciated the opportunity to share a little of what he had felt with them, and prayed they would somehow understand.

When he finally reached the end of his tale, he sat back, exhausted. Each telling of the story came easier, but it still expended the same amount of energy from him. When he heard nothing from his companions, he looked up at them, and found them all watching him with a mixture of confusion, amusement, shock, and disbelief on their faces.

"Well?" he asked quietly, when no one said anything. "Have you anything to say about what I've just told you?"

"I don't know that there are words," Duncan said slowly, shaking his head, his eyes wide. "I can't even make sense of it. I mean, we all knew she was perfect for you when she walked in, but I, for one, never even…" He trailed off, as if losing track of his thoughts.

"So," Geoff began, looking more troubled than anything else, "you fell in love with a woman who employed you to find another man, fought with you the entire trip, and turned your whole world upside down, knowing the entire time that you were never going to have her?"

"It's not as though he asked for it," Derek said in defense

before Nathan got any further than opening his mouth. "Nathan is the victim in this. She practically abducted his heart and set his life on fire in the process. He had no defenses against such an attack." He shook his head and sat back. "Hard to ignore something like that."

"Why would he want to?" Colin murmured, though he appeared the most dazed of the group.

"I couldn't," Nathan said, finally breaking in. "If only you all could meet her, and could come to know her the way that I have, you would love her as well. You would understand."

"We don't need to understand."

Nathan turned to Colin in surprise, wondering what was going on in that head of his. "What do you mean?"

Colin looked a little surprised that he had actually spoken, but he seemed to choose his next words with a great deal of care. "It's not for us to understand how or why you love her. We don't need explanation or reasoning or a defense. Love is not about logic or sense or what any of us would have done had we been in your place. It's your life and your heart. If you have come to love her, in spite of everything that was stacked against you, against all the odds, and all of your attempts not to…" He shrugged and sat back. "That's enough for me. Good for you."

Nathan offered a smile, though now he felt more tossed about than any of them had been by his story. He had expected shock and mockery, but hardly understanding. He knew very well how ridiculous the whole thing sounded, and he had lived it, but if Colin, of all people, was siding with him, and could on some deep, previously unheard of level of his soul, comprehend a bit of what he was trying to say, then surely it was not as insane as it seemed in his mind.

But then, it was Colin. One could never be too sure about these things.

"Well said," Geoff murmured in approval, nodding with the rest of the group. "If any of us deserve to be so happily tossed about by a woman, it's you, Nathan."

Nathan found himself getting rather choked up by that, and could only nod his thanks.

"Hang on a minute," Derek said, leaning forward and peering at the group intently. "Did Colin just say something deep and profound then?"

Grins appeared on every face, including the man in question. "No, no, you must have heard wrong," Duncan said, waving his hand. "Colin doesn't have any deep and profound parts to him."

"Unless he is completely foxed out of his mind," Geoff brought up with a finger. "I have heard him say some quite intuitive things when under the influence of a good vintage. In fact, I think I have some of them written down back at home…"

"I will pay you any sum you can name to shut up about it," Colin announced, still smiling.

"Are you sure? I can count very high."

"Only if his shoes are off," Duncan snorted to Nathan.

"And if someone helps him," Derek added with a nod.

"Excuse me, weren't we talking about Colin?" Geoff protested as more laughter rang out.

"I can't help that I'm the favorite," Colin said apologetically. "Everybody loves me. Women, men, babies, animals…"

"Clara Maxfield," Derek broke in absently, sending the rest off into peals of laughter.

"Not funny!" Colin cried out, his cheeks flaming.

Nathan sighed to himself as he listened to his friends pounce on the new and all-too inviting topic of the Colin-crazed Clara Maxfield. It felt good to be sitting here around a table, drink in hand, laughing and making jokes with his friends. The topic didn't matter, nor had it ever. What mattered was that they were laughing.

These were men that knew him. They had seen him through everything in his life, and they would see him through this. They would keep him from being too serious, from dwelling on painful memories too much.

They would help him find his new state of normal.

He took a deep breath, wondered briefly when it would not hurt to do so, and joined in the teasing, much to Colin's dismay.

Moira smiled happily as she walked down the streets of Preston back to the boarding house she was starting to think of as home. She had just witnessed the rather rushed, but quite proper, wedding of one Charles Allenford to Miss Maggie Younge.

She had been surprised when Charles had called on her at the boarding house that morning to inform her of the wedding that was to take place no less than three hours hence. She had been shocked, appropriately apprehensive about the haste, as the engagement had only been a mere five days in length, and then, after being consoled on that score, had exploded into a terrifying sort of feminine high dudgeon about what she was to wear, sending Charles flying out of the room for his sanity's sake.

After he had gone, she had sat and worried. It had been just as long since she had sent her letter off to Uncle George about the funds for Maggie's family, and still she had heard nothing, which made her anxious. She wanted to make sure no one would suffer because of the marriage, but it appeared they were going to go ahead without any sort of resolution to that problem.

Thankfully, Maggie had already started her new line of work as a seamstress assistant, so that would bring in a little bit of extra income for her family. Moira had visited the shop to congratulate her and had come away with a beautifully embroidered handkerchief, which Maggie forbade her to pay for, and a lovely, very warm shawl, which Moira had refused to take change for. Maggie was in her element at the shop, and so happy that one would have thought it was her dream to be there.

But she had been delighted by the honor of being asked to attend such a small and intimate ceremony as they were having. She had never been to a real wedding; she had only pretended at them with her dolls when Aunt Miriam was not looking. She had always thought that the first wedding she would see would be her own, with Charles.

Well, at least half of that was true.

Still, she was very happy for them, and she had always intended on coming to Preston for a wedding. It had been a lovely, and very short, service, which was all she could have hoped for. The lovely part had been watching Maggie and Charles together, and practically feeling just how much they loved each other. The short part had been additionally wonderful, as Maggie's quite extensive family was not conducive to remaining still for much longer than fifteen minutes, and that was only after Moira had bribed the youngest with the promise of sweets afterwards.

But it was done now, and the couple was delighted, so everyone else was as well. All was as it should be.

Almost.

She sighed a little at the too-familiar ache, and shook her head. It was far too happy an occasion to dampen with thoughts of Nathan. She could do that tomorrow.

She had no doubts she would.

"Miss Dennison!"

She looked up at hearing her name called and saw Mrs. Farrow waving at her from the boarding house, standing next to a man in livery Moira did not know, and only then did she see the coach standing out in front.

"Miss Dennison, I'm so pleased you have come at this moment," Mrs. Farrow gushed, wringing her hands a bit. "This man here has been looking for you. He says he is your coachman."

Moira's brows shot up and she turned to the man, who bowed to her. "Mr. Jackson, at your service, Miss Dennison. And whatever you may think, I am to be your coachman for however long you and your husband have need."

"Husband?" she asked in abject confusion. "I haven't got a husband, Mr. Jackson. Nor do I have any need for a coach, or a coachman, if you will forgive me."

He chuckled good-naturedly. "I'll forgive you, Miss Dennison. But, if you will in turn forgive me, that makes no difference. I've been well paid to take you and your husband wherever you would like to go."

What exactly was going on here? There were far too many questions to ask, and her mouth worked to try and ask them all at once. Gradually, she managed, "Say that again?"

He smiled and she was somehow able to notice that he had quite a good set of teeth on him, for a coachman. "I have been well paid to take Miss Dennison, as was, and her husband wherever they have need of going, or wherever they would wish to go."

"Wherever? How far exactly is wherever?"

He squinted up at the sky, as if a map were written in it. "As far as the land will take us anywhere, I suppose. Don't travel very well over water, now do I?" He laughed at his own joke, paying no mind to the fact that she was not laughing at all.

"How well paid?" she asked suspiciously.

Mr. Jackson gave Moira a very serious look, in spite of his smile. "Miss Dennison, I could take you all the way around England, Scotland, and Wales, and back again twice over, if you wanted."

That was rather well paid indeed. She swallowed back more questions, and went with just one more: "Who?"

"I beg your pardon?" Mr. Jackson asked, leaning a bit closer.

"Who paid you to take me and my imagined husband all the way to France and back again, if we so desired?" she asked in a very clear, more than slightly agitated voice.

"Ah, that I cannot say, Miss," Mr. Jackson said with a sigh. "He also paid me very well not to say."

Of course, he did. "If I paid you more, would you tell me?" she asked in a hard tone, getting quite fed up enough with these anonymous games.

He shrugged. "Perhaps, but it would take a pretty penny to top his offer."

"If I guessed the identity," she tried, her mind whirling, "would you tell me if I was right or wrong?"

"I might," he said slowly, his eyes amused. "But I might not."

Throat suddenly dry, Moira swallowed again. "The-the Earl of Beverton?" she asked, not sure if she was hoping for a positive or negative response.

Mr. Jackson looked away. "Could be," he replied evasively with another shrug, but his smile told her she was correct.

"Why does he think he can do this?" Moira muttered, stomping her foot a little, knowing as she did so how childish an action it was. "I don't even know him."

"He knows you, Miss," Mr. Jackson assured her, still smiling.

"Yes, so I've been told," she sighed as she rubbed her brow.

"He's in love with me, am I correct?"

"Well, that I don't know, Miss," Mr. Jackson admitted, scratching the back of his neck. "My wife says I don't know anything about romance or that sort, but she is of the opinion that no man extends himself in such a way unless he is either very much in love or completely daft as a loon." He shrugged again, which seemed to be his trademark. "I've never been able to tell much difference between the two."

Moira glowered at the man, who chuckled. "Thank you for that, Mr. Jackson." She sighed, still very much troubled indeed. "I haven't got a husband," she said again, mostly to herself.

"As I said, that makes no difference to me. I can still take you wherever you want to go, and can bring my wife for a chaperone for you."

"Well, I have no need of you right now, Mr. Jackson, but I…"

"Moira!"

She whirled at the sound of her name, and saw, to her great astonishment, Uncle George walking towards her at a rapid pace. She allowed him to take her briefly in his arms, but looked up at him in confusion.

"Uncle George? What in heaven's…?"

"I came to inquire about the reward money," he said, overriding her. "You wanted to anonymously donate some funds to this Younge family, which I applaud you for, but you have yet to withdraw the funds for the reward you requested. The moment I received your note, I came straight up to see to the matter."

"What do you mean, the funds were never withdrawn?" she asked slowly, an odd choking sensation starting in her stomach, of all places. "I spoke with the bank manager, and he…"

"I do not know, child, but the funds are still there." His furry brows snapped together and his eyes were troubled. "This is worrisome."

"No, this is suspicious," Moira said, a glower forming on her own face.

Without a word to him, she turned and marched to the bank, where the manager was found in his office, and seemed rather wary at her appearance.

"M-Miss Dennison," he stammered, trying to bow and get up from his chair at the same time. "To what do I owe the pleasure?"

"Why have the funds for the reward not been released yet?" she demanded, throwing all pretense of politeness aside. "When I came here, you assured me that the moment my friend came in to retrieve it, the money would be his and available for his use."

"Yes, but he did not come in!" the bank manager protested, very nearly quaking under the combined indignation of Moira and Uncle George, who was not a small man by any measure.

Moira rocked back, stunned. Did not come in? How could Nathan not have come in and collected the reward they had agreed on? But then, they had not precisely agreed on anything. Never once had he asked about the money he would receive. He had never said a word on the subject. Ever.

She bit down on her lip hard, her heart swelling.

"What do you mean he did not come in?" George asked, not convinced of anything yet.

"No man came in for the reward, sir," the manager insisted.

"Well," George said after a moment, sounding relieved, "that would change things. Perhaps we could just donate the funds you requested for the reward to this family, Moira. It would be prudent, as they are already available."

"Fine," Moira replied with a wave of her hand, her mind still feeling as though it were working backwards. "That would be wonderful. See to that, would you, George?" Not waiting for him to reply, she stepped forward, engaging the trembling manager again. "Are you sure he did not come in?" she asked, needing to be certain it was not some misunderstanding. "Perhaps you didn't see him, but someone else did. He is very tall, rather muscularly built, dark hair, dark eyes..." Remarkably handsome, caring, amusing, polite, respectful, stubborn... The list continued on and on in her mind.

The manager thought for a moment, then shook his head firmly. "No, Miss. The only man matching that description I have seen of late was the Earl of Beverton, when he came to secure an order for a rather expensive pianoforte."

Moira stiffened and all of the breath rushed out of her in one swift swoop. "Beverton?" she managed, her words halting and tremulous.

He nodded. "Yes, Miss. He was just passing through almost two weeks ago, and merely requested we take care of purchasing and sending the instrument, along with his personal note, to…" He broke off, as if suddenly realizing that his clients, particularly the wealthy and powerful ones, expected privacy in their dealings.

"To whom?" she asked through tight lips, her mind whirling.

He wrung his hands, grimacing. "Oh, I really…"

"Tell me."

"The Squire Cutler and family, Miss Dennison," the bank manager confessed, looking as though he would like to put his hands up as a defense. "They are just outside of the town borders."

A shuddering gasp escaped Moira as her world began to slide very drastically into a realm she had never even imagined could exist. The boots… the bonnets… Squire Cutler… Her knees trembled and she gripped the manager's desk tightly for support, her knuckles white. "Let me see the order," she insisted, her entire body starting to tremble.

"Moira, dear, are you all right?" George asked, taking her arm and looking at her with concern. "You look white as a sheet!"

"The order, George, please," she begged, feeling somehow both weak and emboldened at the same time.

"Get her the order, man!" George barked, sending the manager racing to his papers. It took him only a moment, and then he was back before them again, holding it out for them to see.

Moira's eyes raced nearly as fast as her heart as she scanned the document and everything in her entire world froze as she caught sight of the signature of the Earl of Beverton.

Nathaniel Hammond.

She stared at it for what could have been days as far as she knew. The name seemed to leap from the page and burned itself into her mind. Nathaniel Hammond… the man *she* loved… was the Earl of Beverton. The same earl of Beverton who had bought her an entire wardrobe because she was to be married, who had sent her a coach for whatever she and her supposed husband might have need, who was sending a new and expensive pianoforte to the good squire and his family, the man who thought himself so in love with her that everybody who saw him knew it.

He loved her. It had to be, it was the only explanation… but he had never said a word about it. She had hoped, and wished, and sometimes had thought… but then it was never certain…

Well, it was fairly certain now, she supposed.

Eventually, she realized that people were talking to her, and that her breathing had turned from a somewhat normal state into a series of rather loud, dangerously shallow gasps and her quaking body began to be seized by a fire of sorts. She felt at once unable to move and yearning to fly.

Nathan *loved* her!

"He… he loves me," she managed to get out, only able to blink.

"What was that, dear?" George asked, leaning close, worry creasing his brow.

"He loves me," she said again, her heart threatening to choke her.

Poor George could only shake his head in confusion. "Who does?"

She laughed breathlessly and clapped a hand to her mouth as tears welled. "He loves me!" She kissed George soundly on the cheek, then sprinted for the door to the bank.

"Moira!" he called, following her at a run.

She could hardly believe it. All this time, not only had Nathan been a rich earl, but he had been in love with her. She had one purpose now, one thing she was determined to do regardless of what anybody else thought or said or did. She was not going to wait any longer. She had waited quite long enough.

"Moira?"

She jerked slightly as Gwen touched her arm, having somehow managed to sneak up on her. "Oh, Gwen. Hello."

"Moira, what are you doing?" Gwen asked, looking worried and trying to match Moira's frantic attempt at walking gracefully while running at the same time.

"I am going to the boarding house, and then I'm leaving," she said bluntly, picking up her pace even more. "Mr. Jackson!" she called out, seeing him standing there still. "I have need of you and your wife after all! At this very moment, if you can bear to!"

"Of course, Miss Dennison, right away!" he replied with a grin, touching his hat. He vanished inside the inn, no doubt to retrieve his wife.

"Mrs. Farrow, I need everything from my rooms brought down at once," she ordered to the kind woman, who rushed off. "Quickly!"

"Moira, what is this?" Gwen asked as Moira paced around anxiously in the taproom, watching as no less than six lads brought her things out to the coach. She had never been so grateful to have been slow to unpack in her entire life.

"I'm leaving, Gwen," she said again, unable to decide if she wanted to laugh or cry or shout or some combination of all of the above. "Now. I'm going to Hampshire."

"What?"

Moira didn't have time to give her all the details, as she saw Mrs. Farrow coming towards her with a valise and a parcel of food. She took it from her and thanked her hastily, then walked very quickly to the waiting coach, and the two Jacksons nearby, who were all smiles. She waved Mr. Jackson up to his seat, and Mrs. Jackson, biting back a grin, climbed inside the coach to wait for her.

"Moira, what are you going to do?" Gwen asked as she followed.

"I'm going to find Nathan, throw myself on his person, and beg him at the top of my lungs to love me," Moira announced as she handed her things to Mrs. Jackson, then tossed her bonnet in the carriage as well. "And then I plan on beating him quite severely for lying to me. And *then* I plan on kissing him until I'm incapable of thought." She grinned wildly at the last. The thought made her quiver even more with anticipation.

Gwen looked bewildered, but stepped back from the carriage all the same. "But I thought you said a woman never throws herself at a man, no matter how in love with him she is!"

"Oh, bother with what I said, Gwen!" Moira huffed as she hauled herself into the carriage. "Everything I told you is a load of rubbish if the man in question loves you in return! Go!" she called up to Mr. Jackson, who instantly snapped the reins and they barreled off at such speeds that no less than four people had to dive out of the way, and Gwen was left standing at the boarding house, slightly dust covered, but grinning from ear to ear.

Chapter Twenty Two

Sleep was impossible. She had tried every day of her trip to manage it, but all that she had succeeded in doing was sink herself into a sort of dreamless dozing that varied somewhere between the conscious and unconscious, and was more exhausting than being awake. Her mind must have been overworked indeed, for not even her nightmares could find her.

Eating was tolerable, but only just. Mrs. Jackson had insisted on meals, but much further than that, Moira could not bear. She was far too agitated and far too nervous to do much more than what was absolutely necessary.

Mostly she thought of Nathan. Of their time together. Of the signs she had missed.

He had backed away from those moments they had shared, where they had been so close to something intangible, because of her engagement, and he was, above all else, a man of honor. He cared for and respected her enough to honor the existing commitment she had made, regardless of how it might hurt him.

She rather wished he had been a bit less than honorable in that regard.

What surprised her was how he had managed to allow her to lead them and make all sorts of demands when he was not only a gentleman, but an earl. The very fact that he had come along with her was shocking in and of itself, but to allow her such liberties…

Why in the world didn't he tell her off more than he had? She certainly deserved it, and he couldn't have loved her from the beginning as he did at the end. What had made him come along? Why had he endured her endless torrent of absurd demands and questions and stories? Surely a peer of the realm, and an egregiously wealthy one at that, had better things to do with his time.

"*Perhaps I liked that you told me off before I had said four words,*" his voice echoed in her mind. "*Perhaps I liked that you could shut up my friends so effectively just by standing there. Perhaps I thought your story was touching and wanted to help. Perhaps I am really a gentleman and could not allow a lady to travel alone. Perhaps you fascinated me and I wanted to know more. Perhaps I wanted to tell you to shove off, but I just couldn't do it.*"

She clamped her lips together and fought back a sob. Had he loved her then? Could he have imagined the battle that had been waging in her heart, with each wound growing deeper and deeper the nearer to Preston they traveled?

All those times he had been watching her, all of those times he told her she was beautiful, all of those when it felt as though they actually were married, instead of pretending at it, all rushed through her mind. When had it started to become more of what she desired instead of only a role to be played?

It would have been impossible to determine a place or a time or a moment. It was all of them together, every moment with him.

What would she say when she saw him again? What would *he* say? She grinned as she imagined it. No matter what he thought of her, she highly doubted that he could imagine that she would come chasing after him in the very coach he had hired for her.

No, she had reached heights, or depths, as the case may have been, that even she herself could not have predicted ever attaining.

Love was funny that way.

The coach started to slow and her heart jumped to her throat. Suddenly, every single part of her body was tingling with anticipation, and she very nearly shouted at Jackson to stop the coach so she could run from here, but she resisted. She could run at Nathan later, and she had no doubt she would. For now, she needed to at least pretend to be calm. She didn't want the poor man to think her completely demented when she needed to convince him she loved him and only him.

Mrs. Jackson must have sensed her discomfort, for she patted her knee and offered a smile.

Moira tried to return it, but found herself unable to do so.

The coach came to a halt and she heard Jackson jump down, then the door was opened. "Beverton House, Miss Dennison."

She swallowed and allowed him to help her out, then looked up at the house before her. It was, without a doubt, the most majestic house she had ever seen. The windows were tall and stately, the entry grand and elegant, and the overall effect the imposing edifice had on the eyes and the mind was really quite stirring. It was a glorious masterpiece of a building, though it was a good deal older in appearance than she had expected it to be. It was in need of repair, which she could see was in process, but it was warm and welcoming nonetheless. And the grounds were absolutely breathtaking. The house sat amongst some of the finest hills and valleys and beauty of nature that Moira had ever seen.

Though she was delighted to have arrived, she hesitated, unbearably ill at ease. "Wait here for me, will you, Jackson?" she asked in a small voice.

"Of course, Miss Dennison," he said with a bow.

She nodded, then walked the last few meters to the stairs that led to what had to be the largest door she had ever seen. It could very well have been a drawbridge, for all she knew. How appropriate, for she was suddenly feeling as though a dragon and a moat of lava would make her more comfortable.

Taking a deep breath, she stepped forward and rapped the knocker on the door, then shuffled backwards quickly and waited.

She shifted around anxiously, glancing behind her at the Jacksons, who smiled cheerfully at her. With a loud creek, the door opened, and a middle aged butler with a pleasant face and a very full head of graying hair appeared.

"Yes?" he asked with a kind smile. "Can I help you?"

"I am Miss Moira Dennison," she said, feeling slightly more encouraged by his gentle manner. "I was hoping to speak with the earl, if he is at home."

His eyes twinkled just a touch, though his expression never altered. "Are you acquainted with the earl, Miss Dennison?"

She nodded, though she would rather have laughed out loud. "Yes, I am. We are… that is to say… he and I…"

The butler flicked a smile at her. "It is none of my business at any rate, Miss Dennison. I am Rosemont, the butler, and I run the household here at Beverton House. The earl is, unfortunately, out on business at the moment, but we do expect him in the near future. Would you like to come in and wait for him?"

Wait? Moira would rather do anything in the world but wait any longer. She sighed in frustration and looked up at the sky, then around at the grounds, and finally back to him. "No, thank you, Rosemont. I should rather go for a walk. It has been a rather tiresome ride in that coach, and I feel the need to stretch my legs, if I may."

He nodded, his smile having been retracted, but not from his eyes. "Of course, Miss Dennison. If you walk directly down that path there," he said, leaning out a bit and pointing, "you will find some very pretty trails leading to the village. The earl has been taking quite a good deal of care to assist his tenants with repairs and the like, and he walks this way very often."

A fond smile formed on her lips as she imagined him doing so. Of course, he did. It was so like him. What a fine earl he must make. She turned back to the butler, who was now watching her. "Your master is quite the best of men, is he not, Rosemont?"

"Quite, Miss Dennison."

She smiled at him and his frank reply. "I think I like you very much, Rosemont."

"Thank you, Miss Dennison."

She turned and walked back down the stairs and began on the path Rosemont had indicated, removing her bonnet and holding it by the ribbons as she walked, swinging it absently. She took a deep, cleansing breath of the fresh air, and exulted in the peace it brought to her mind and heart. If she had it her way, this would soon be her home, and she, too, could go walking down these paths and revel in the glory of nature as it presented itself in this piece of the world.

There were simply too many hours in the day.

Nathan rode Galahad hard through the countryside, heading back towards the village from a neighboring estate, where he had been conferring with other landowners in the area about ways to improve their farming estates. It was a necessary meeting, but it took far too long, and he had little enough to say about the subject. He cared about his tenants and those who worked his lands, but he did not want to spend an entire day with a bunch of puffed up, spoiled men who didn't even know their tenants, let alone really care what they could do to improve the way things were done. The only man of sense among the group was the Viscount Blackmoor, and he was not a particularly loquacious man. Nathan had met the man's eyes more than once, and knew immediately he felt the same about the situation.

He had escaped the moment he could, thinking that surely it was nearly dark, but it had not been. It was only mid-afternoon. He shouldn't have been surprised. With only his friends for company and working with his tenants for distraction, each day back in Hampshire had been as long as a month. His nights were equally as painful, and far less pleasantly spent. Days had distractions. Nights had memories.

He urged Galahad on faster, growling in the back of his throat as he attempted to shove away the alluring image of Moira as it flitted into his mind. He would never be able to move on if he was going to sabotage himself in this matter. He needed to stop, needed to push her out of thought and feeling, if he ever wanted to regain clarity of self again.

But he didn't want to let her go.

He saw his friends up ahead, working with some of the tenants to repair another cottage and chop wood for a widow who lived in it. Manual labor, that would drive this madness from his mind.

"Well, if it isn't his mighty earlship!" Geoff called out as he approached, setting his saw aside and wiping his brow with a rolled sleeve.

"How did the meeting go?" Duncan asked, sitting on the ground next to the bucket of water they used for drinking.

Nathan only rolled his eyes and dismounted, yanking at his cravat.

"I know that look," Derek said with a laugh as he came over, carrying a rail on his shoulder with one of the older sons of the Widow Martin, whose house they were fixing. "Nathan needs an axe and some wood and a good deal of space."

Nathan tossed his cravat aside, stripped off his coat and his waistcoat, and took the axe Colin handed him, rolling his sleeves as he did so. "I didn't know my expressions were so eloquent, Derek," he grunted, as he headed for the pile of logs waiting to be cut.

"They're not. But you forget that I know landowners, and know the inanity of large groups of them." Derek grinned. "Wasn't Blackmoor there?"

"Of course, but…"

"But getting that man to speak is rather like asking a pig to quack," Colin overrode, his brows snapping together in a rather un-Colin-like manner.

"You know him?" Geoff asked, standing and shouldering his saw again.

"Vaguely, but Kit does, and likes him very much." Colin shrugged, and the cloudy expression passed. "My twin has impeccable taste in people."

"Are you going to stand around talking about Blackmoor, or are you going to work?" Nathan muttered as he began splitting logs.

Colin grinned. "Says the man who spent an entire week on a whirlwind romantic trip, then got his brother engaged in London, and has hardly done anything remotely resembling work in weeks."

Nathan stopped and glared at him, but Colin only laughed and held up his hands in surrender. "I will just go see if Widow Martin wants me to clear out her chicken coop, then," he said, backing away.

"Wise notion, Mr. Gerrard," Nathan growled. Then he turned to the youngest son of Mrs. Martin. "Tommy, would you take Galahad back to my stables, please? And have Parker show you the new foals while you are there."

The boy nodded and raced off, practically dragging the horse along behind him.

Nathan almost smiled, but went back to his logs instead as his friends scattered with the rest of the men to various parts of the yard. Some climbed on the roof to patch it, some worked a two-man saw, and some mended the pens for the animals. All were suddenly busy and talkative and laughing with each other, but they blessedly left Nathan alone.

At the moment, he didn't want to see or speak with anyone, let alone pretend that all was well with him.

It could not have been more wrong.

The warm sun of the day beat down upon him mercilessly as he worked, splitting log after log, until there was quite a decent sized stack of wood next to him. But he kept going, loving the feeling of power from something so raw and primitive as physical exertion. He swung his axe again, releasing the slightest hum of pride as the log split cleanly.

He grabbed another, wiping at his perspiring brow with his sleeve. His shirt was starting to dampen in various places, and he enjoyed the sensation. It was proof of his strength and hard work, and it felt good. The fine linen of his dress shirt was not ideal for this, but he didn't care. It was just a testament as to the type of earl he was; one who dressed as nobility, but would rather split logs instead.

He would have given anything to be a common man, to marry whomever he chose whenever he chose without having to answer to anybody. He swung the axe again, grunting in annoyance as it split the log unevenly. He shoved the smaller piece aside and adjusted the log again.

Moira and her husband were no doubt enjoying their new life as married persons. He hoped the git was treating her like the queen she was. He hoped she was happy with her life. He hoped he never had to see her again. That wasn't true; he hoped he never had to see her with *him* again.

The axe swung down again as a barbaric cry was torn from his throat, and the log split so powerfully that both parts shot from the block off into opposite directions.

Nathan sighed with irritation at himself and set the axe down, then retrieved the stray pieces of wood. He needed to at least attempt to be calm and contained. Raging about something he had no control over was hardly going to help the situation at all.

He set the logs in the pile, and took up one more. He prepared to swing the axe, but halted as a sudden, all-too familiar scent drifted by. He closed his eyes and groaned. Why was she forever invading his senses? He was trying to move on, damn her! "Get out, woman," he growled, hefting the axe again.

He swung the axe down with another savage cry and grunted in satisfaction at the precise splitting. He did another four pieces with equal force and precision, then set the axe aside, chest heaving a bit, now perspiring more than ever. He picked up the pieces and set them into the pile, then examined his work for a moment, hands on his hips. It was a fine afternoon's work, but he wanted to do more. He needed more. He wiped his sleeve over his brow again and turned to pick up the axe another time.

But as he turned, a sight met his eyes that, even in his wildest daydreams and most desperate nightmares, he could not have conjured up.

Moira stood there, her new grey coat that he had picked out fastened over the blue dress he had seen in Madame Guilford's shop, the one he had instantly known would match her eyes. They suited her far better than even he had ever imagined. Her bonnet was in hand, leaving that beautiful hair of hers uncovered and, as always, threatening to tumble completely out of its holdings.

Her expression was one of shock, interest, hurt, and dare he say hope? Her eyes, wide and amazed, were trained on him, but they darted to varying bits of his person, taking in the entire, disheveled state of him. He couldn't breathe as she stared at him, and his tongue felt as though it was swollen to three times its size.

Gradually, he realized that there was no sound about them at all. The men that had previously been so apt to chatter and laugh as they worked were now unnaturally silent. Part of his mind, a very small part, wanted to turn and see their expressions. But while she was here, staring at him like that, he would look nowhere else.

He could not.

Moira was having trouble catching her breath at the sight of Nathan, and not just because he was perspiring in a maddeningly attractive way or because his hair was slightly mused or because his cravat and waistcoat and jacket were off and his sleeves rolled, which was suddenly her favorite way to see him. No, the real trouble was nothing more or less than the fact that he was there. Just him.

Her heart thudded quite precariously in her chest and she fought for the strength to even swallow. Now that she was here before him, her mind utterly fled at any and all attempt at conversation. Her strongest instinct was to fly at him, just as he was, and have him hold her close until her heart and breath returned to their normal functions. But his eyes, so dark and intense, held her back. In them she saw pain, confusion, need, anger… and yet, amidst all of that, passion was still there.

It was prudent to wait for a bit, she decided. After all, she did have some questions she needed answered before she lost her mind to him entirely, and she did have a reputation of wit to uphold.

A slender man nearby suddenly broke from his frozen state of bewilderment and turned to the other men behind him. "All right, you hens, get back to the coop with you. Focus on egg laying or weaving a basket out of straw, or something. There is nothing to see here." He quickly gestured them all off, looking back at her and Nathan so many times she thought he would be dizzy. But he and three others walked a good distance up the hill back to Beverton House, though they obviously would rather have stayed to witness whatever was going to happen.

"Colin?" she asked with a tilt of her head towards them, knowing that had to be the leader.

"Who else?" Nathan replied without much emotion.

What a dreadful beginning this was. "So," she began, folding her arms. "You are a rich earl."

"I am."

She pressed her lips into a thin line, eyes narrowing slightly. "Is there anything else you didn't tell me?"

"No," he said with a brief shake of his head. "Everything else was the truth, I swear."

"There is nothing else?"

"No," he repeated. Then he winced a touch. "Well… Derek is a marquess."

"Ah," she said with a nod, glancing back up the hill where the men had disappeared. "That does explain a lot."

She turned back and saw Nathan was about to return to chopping wood. "Where is your husband?" he asked with no small amount of derision as he set a log on the block.

"That is an excellent question," she said with an approving nod, wanting to break out into a grin at his blatant envy and bitterness.

"Is it?" His voice held absolutely no interest as he swung the axe down again, splitting the wood cleanly and kicking the pieces aside.

"Yes, it is," Moira replied, knowing he would absolutely hate what she was about to do, but determined to do it anyway. "You see, after the wedding in which Charles married the woman he loved, a carriage arrived, and the driver informed me that he had been paid to take me and my husband wherever we want to go. It was quite startling, to be sure, considering the fact that the only person that had recently obtained a husband that I knew was Maggie, who is now Mrs. Allenford, and I didn't have a husband at all."

Nathan froze in his preparation to cut another piece of wood, but didn't look at her.

"And so I told the driver that I appreciated the offer," she continued, as if nothing had happened, "but as I did not have a husband, it would not be possible for him to take me and my husband wherever we wished to go. On account of my not having a husband, do you see?"

Nathan straightened slowly, looking at her now, his expression carefully composed, though his eyes were rampant with curiosity.

"But then I thought," she went on, "perhaps it would be possible to get a husband, since I did not have one, and so I asked the driver if he would mind taking just me for a little side trip, to see if I could get a husband. Since I do not have one. He was so good, he agreed, and brought me here, and said he would be happy to wait for however long it took for me to get a husband. Since I do not have one." She very carefully emphasized the last words, and at last allowed a smile to begin to form on her lips.

Nathan's chest heaved with his now rapid breaths, and she knew that if she didn't finish quickly, she never would be able to.

"So I will ask you again, Nathaniel Hammond; is there anything else you did not tell me?"

"Yes," he rasped, dropping the axe to the ground and starting slowly towards her. "I love you."

She swallowed back a sudden wash of tears and released a small laugh of relief as she smiled fully at him. "Then will you marry me, Lord Beverton? Because I love you quite madly. And I have come all this way in that blasted carriage just so I could tell you…"

He cut her off instantly with a hard kiss, taking her face in his hands. "Yes," he whispered, stroking her cheek, and kissing her again. "Yes."

She laughed and threw her arms around him, kissing him back with everything she had in her, with all of the love, hurt, and longing she had held in her heart for so long. Then she pushed back and looked up at him seriously. "You don't mind that I asked you? It's not very ladylike, I know, but…"

"I don't mind," he chuckled with a shake of his head, stroking her cheek once more. "I don't mind at all. Now will you do me a favor, Moira?"

"Of course, Nathan. Anything you wish."

"Stop talking. I want to kiss you."

She rolled her eyes. "So demanding."

"Get used to it," he murmured as he kissed her.

She hummed with delight at his kiss, and found herself gripping at his shirt and pulling him closer. Then, while she could still remember she wanted to, she punched him in the arm.

"Ack! What was that for?" he yelped in indignation.

"You lied to me!" she cried, wishing she felt more furious than she actually did, and knowing she probably ought to.

"I did no such thing," he said very patiently. "I merely withheld certain information."

"Semantics!"

"Moira..."

"Don't 'Moira' me!" she protested, shoving at his rather strong chest. "Have you any idea how tormented I've been?"

"A little, yes," he said quickly, taking her face in his hands once more and forcing her to look at him. "Moira, I will gladly pay penance the rest of my life to you for not being entirely truthful, but please, for the love of all that is good and holy, don't make me do so now."

He pressed his lips to hers once more, managing to silence her rather pleasantly. His fingers dug into her hair, sending it tumbling down her back. Moira felt herself falling just as freely into him, and her growing desire brought forth a moan from the back of her throat. Before she would be entirely insensible, she broke away, determined to have the last word, even as her hands gripped the back of Nathan's shirt.

"Don't think that you can forever get out of trouble by kissing me, Nathan. It won't work." She was quite certain her words would have more force if they were not quite so breathless, but that couldn't be helped at this moment.

"Oh, I know it will not work all of the time," he said as he brushed his lips along her jaw. "But I think I can say with some confidence that it will work most of the time."

He kissed her again, and it occurred to her that he was probably right, but she would never tell him so. It was only a moment more of being so deliciously assaulted by him that she knew for a fact he absolutely was right. She didn't interrupt any further as she reveled in being in his arms, of being here with him, of being home.

"Praise the Lord, there's going to be a wedding!" a rather boisterous voice crowed from somewhere in the distance.

Nathan groaned and broke from Moira's lips, resting his forehead against hers. "I think I need to shoot Colin, my love."

"Oh, don't do that," she scolded, toying with the hair at the nape of his neck. "Poor, dead Colin would make a terrible mess of things."

"It might be worth it." He glanced over, and then shut his eyes quickly again. "They're coming down here, you know."

"Excellent," she said brightly. "I have long wanted to meet them."

"You will have to be strong, Moira."

She gave him an odd look. "When have I been anything but? You don't think I can be run off by your friends when I have handled you so triumphantly, do you?"

He kissed her quite thoroughly, then pulled back, grinning at the dazed expression on her face. He released her, but kept a firm hold on one hand. "No, I don't. That's what worries me. I'm more concerned for them than I am for you."

She grinned rather proudly. "You do know me well, don't you?"

He nodded. "That I do, and I love you all the more for it."

She winked rather boldly at him, which sent a delightfully visible thrill coursing throughout his frame. "I love you, too, Nathan, and every day with you is all I will ever need again."

She would like to have him kiss her again, and spend quite a long time doing it, too, but his friends were upon them, so she had to settle for him tightly squeezing her hand, with the barest hint of his thumb rubbing against her in a promise of later.

And the further promise of forever.

Epilogue

"And another thing. There will be no quarrelling about who is the Queen's favorite. The Queen loves all of her subjects equally, and that is all she will say on the matter."

The loyal subjects said nothing under the power of the Queen's piercing blue eyes, which was to be expected, as they were dolls.

The Queen nodded firmly in approval at their reactions, her dark tresses bouncing as she did so. "That will be all. Now, the Queen would like to have some tea and cake, but only three of you may accompany her. Which of you shall attend?"

Without waiting for volunteers, she picked up the nearest three and walked over to the desk nearby. She carefully sat all three facing the great chair behind it, then climbed up into the chair herself. Once situated, she nodded again. "Thank you for coming to tea. The Queen will take her tea on her throne, because the Queen can do whatever she wants."

A sudden war cry of sorts was heard, and a dark haired urchin flew into the room through the open doors to the terrace. "Long live King Richard!" he roared, aiming his bow and arrow at the Queen, who shrieked in horror.

"Robbie!" She stood in her throne and put her hands on her hips. "Do you mind? I am *trying* to have tea with my royal subjects!"

"Robin of the Hood does not answer to any Queen!" he cried, still aiming his arrow at her. "Swear loyalty to King Richard, or be struck with my dastardly arrow!"

"Don't be stupid, Robert," she sniffed, climbing off of the chair and adjusting her crown. "The Queen is *married* to King Richard."

"Is not!" he cried, dropping his bow and arrow, his face indignant. "King Richard would *never* marry my sister!"

"I am *not* your sister," she said with a stomp of her foot. "I am the Queen Lizzie."

"Well, then, Queen Lizzie," he sneered, his dark eyes rolling dramatically, "give me all your gold so I can rob you and give it to the poor."

The Queen huffed in frustration. "But I don't *have*..."

Whatever she had been about to say died in her throat as a terrible roaring came from just outside the room, and the two froze, turning towards the closed door to the rest of the house with identically horror-struck expressions. With a crash, the door burst open and a ferocious growling filled the room, and suddenly the Queen was swooped up into the clutches of a vicious beast.

"Papa-monster!" the creature roared, maintaining quite the grip on the flailing queen.

"Robin Hood! Save me," she squealed, trying to beat the monster back.

"I'm coming, Your Majesty!" he hollered, pulling out his bow once again.

Arrow after arrow shot rapidly from the mighty outlaw, and pierced the thick hide of the creature, who groaned and moaned in agony, as he sank slowly to the ground. Sensing her rescue was nigh at hand, the Queen shimmied herself loose from its hold, and together, she and Robin of the Hood beat upon it with their fists and arrows until the creature thumped the floor once more, silent and still at last.

They cheered and danced about in victory.

Until...

"What in heaven's name is going on in here?"

Three suddenly anxious pairs of eyes turned to the new voice, their owners completely still and frozen. The little girl's wide eyes fixed upon the identical ones of her mother, and then, pointing at the fallen creature, very rapidly said, "Papa-monster kidnapped the Queen and Robin of the Hood saved her and they killed the monster dead."

Her mother's eyes twinkled merrily and she tried not to smile. "Oh, well, if that's all." She sighed as she looked at the monster in question, now not so very dead and grinning without reservation. "If you have quite finished," she said with only a touch of scolding, "then perhaps you would like to get your things and go on out to the coach? I don't think Uncle Spencer and Aunt Caroline would like us to arrive after they have gone to bed. Lizzie, Robbie, come on."

The children scampered out of the room cheering even more loudly than before.

Moira looked down at her husband, and finally shook her head. "You are the worst of the lot, you know."

He shrugged, still grinning, and got to his feet. "I just try to keep you on your toes, my lady."

She rolled her eyes, adjusted the weight of their youngest child, a girl so identical to her mother it was disconcerting, and snorted. "Don't 'my lady' me, your mighty earlship. I had to keep on my toes long before those two came along."

"Yes, yes, I'm quite the handful, I know," he sighed, kissing her soundly, then giving an equally sound kiss to the plump cheek of his daughter, who giggled at his actions.

"Yes, you are, and I think I should scold you most severely," Moira said, still trying to sound firm. "How do you think a trip to Spencer and Caroline's is going to go with those two so wound up?"

"Down, Mama," the little girl insisted, pushing away from her, eying the fallen bow with interest.

Moira sighed and set her down, watching as she toddled over and picked it up, studying it intently. "Wonderful," she groaned. "Now even Charlotte will be roped into their games, and not as another queen."

"Charlotte can be one of Robin's merry band if she wants," Nathan said soothingly, pulling her into his arms. "Robbie would love having someone to follow him around, and it would hardly hurt you to join in once in a while, you know."

"I do," she assured him. "Who do think plays with them when you are off being the mighty earl?"

"Why don't you play when I'm here?" he asked with a mock pout.

"Because I can't compete with Papa-monster," she said, smiling at last.

"You're right. You're far better." He kissed her gently, lingering, taking her face in his hands.

"You're still in trouble, you know," she whispered as he pulled away.

"After six years of marriage and three children, you still expect me to believe that I cannot kiss my way out of trouble?" he chuckled softly, his lips dancing lightly over her cheeks and down her neck.

"Four," she corrected with a satisfied smirk. "And no, you cannot."

Nathan froze and reared back, looking at her in disbelief. "What?"

"You cannot kiss your way…"

"Moira."

She laughed merrily and planted a quick kiss on his unmoving lips. "Four. Honestly, Nathan, one would think you could count your own children. And we may be able to catch up to Spencer and Caroline now, what with little Nathan being so…"

He clamped a hand over her mouth and gave her a look. "Explain four," he growled, having learned long ago that the best way to shut his wife up was a physical impediment.

She quirked her brows, and he removed his hand. "Come winter," she said with a grin, "there will be four, not three."

"Are you sure?"

"I'm sure."

With a whoop, he picked her up and swung her around, kissing her and laughing all the while.

"I take it this news pleases you?" Moira laughed once she was returned to the ground.

"It pleases me," he said, kissing her gently yet again. "I love you."

She smiled up at him. "I love you." Then, hearing the boisterous noises of her children, she sighed. "We never have time to ourselves anymore, do we?"

"We have tonight," he murmured, quirking his brows and flashing a would-be wicked grin.

Shaking her head, she snorted at the blatant suggestion, kissed him once, and stepped away. "We have to go, or we will never get there before nightfall."

"Don't worry," he said, patting her cheek. "Spencer and I grew up at Fairington. Even if we're late, I know all the secret ways in."

"Why does that not surprise me?" Moira muttered.

Little Charlotte, having seen something she thought she would enjoy far more than her brother's bow, came back towards her parents. "Me, Papa. Swing me," she demanded, holding her arms up for him.

He laughed and picked her up, carrying her out to the carriage where the servants and the other two rather anxious children waited. "I'll swing you, poppet. I'll swing you all the way to the carriage, and all the way to Uncle Spencer's, and all the way to London, and…"

Moira shook her head and smiled to herself, unconsciously resting a hand on her not-yet-swollen abdomen. Though all four of those people drove her to distraction, and this new little one would as well, she would not have traded anything in the world for the life she led. Had she ever imagined that her life could be this wonderful?

No, perhaps not. But it made no difference.

Some things in life were so glorious they simply could not be imagined.

"Mama!" her children screamed in unison, no doubt urged on by their father. "Time to go!"

"Coming!" she called, with a laugh, shaking herself from her reverie and walking out to the carriage where her family waited for her, and then they were off on yet another adventure, one of many before and many still to come.

Coming Soon

Married to the Marquess

"For better or for worse...
the very worst."

by

Rebecca Connolly

CPSIA information can be obtained
at www.ICGtesting.com
Printed in the USA
BVOW01s0226151216
470760BV00008B/70/P